Toddler-Hunting
& Other Stories

KŌNO TAEKO

Toddler-Hunting
& Other Stories

TRANSLATED BY LUCY NORTH

With an additional translation by Lucy Lower

A NEW DIRECTIONS BOOK

Translator's Note: Ted Fowler and Jay Rubin offered unstinting encouragement and assistance at different stages of this project. My sincere thanks also to Howard Hibbett; and to Kobayashi Fukuko, Yori Oda, and Ken Sasaki.

Publisher's Note: Grateful acknowledgment is made to the Japan Foundation for the grant which assisted the publication of this title.

The decoration displayed on the title, half-title, and chapter title pages is the Kōno family crest.

Manufactured in the United States of America
New Directions Books are printed on acid-free paper
First published clothbound by New Directions in 1996
Published simultaneously in Canada by Penguin Books Canada Limited

Library of Congress Cataloging-in-Publication Data

Kōno, Taeko, 1926–
    [Selections. 1996. English]
    Toddler-hunting & other stories / Kōno Taeko ; translated by Lucy North, with an additional translation by Lucy Lower.
        p. cm.
    Contents: Toddler-hunting (Yōji-gari) — Snow (Yuki) — Theater (Gekijō) — Crabs (Kani) — Night journey (Yoru o yuku) — Ants swarm (Ari takaru) — Full tide (Michi-shio) — Final moments (Saigo no toki) — Conjurer (Majutsushi) — Bone meat (Hone no niku).
    ISBN 0–8112–1305–6 (cloth : alk. paper)
    1. Kōno, Taeko, 1926-   —Translations into English. I. North, Lucy. II. Lower, Lucy. III. Title.
PL855.O44A25 1996   95-47600
895.6'35—dc20   CIP

Celebrating 60 years of publishing for James Laughlin
by New Directions Publishing Corporation
80 Eighth Avenue, New York 10011

Contents

Night Journey (YORU O YUKU, 1963)

WHEN THE NIGHT GAME ENDED, HER HUSBAND reached over to switch off the TV. The cheering crowds shrank down to a spot on the screen, and vanished.

"Hey, what's taking them so long?" Murao asked, recrossing his legs and looking up at the clock. They'd told the Saekis to come after dinner, but it was nine-thirty and their guests were now long overdue.

"Well they can't have forgotten," Fukuko replied. "But maybe they won't come now that it's this late."

Murao grunted, looking grouchy for a moment, but then his expression changed: "Shall we go barge in on them?" he suggested. "They're bound to be home."

"Shall we?" Fukuko didn't hesitate. "Let's go for a walk, and just drop by. If they're out, they're out."

It was a Saturday night, so they could stay up as late as they wanted. Murao declared he would go as he was, in his yukata. Fukuko didn't change out of hers either, and only put on a different sash.

Turning her key in the front door, Fukuko paused: "Did I lock the kitchen door?"

Murao walked around, and tugged the glass door.

"It's locked."

Fukuko drew the key out, and tucked it under her sash.

The night was unusually clear for the muggy season, moist and cool, and the stars were out. The evening train heading to the city was almost totally deserted. As Fukuko and Murao sat down comfortably on two of the empty seats, a fresh breeze poured in through the open windows—and everything, even the compartment's milky lights, seemed shiny with a strange sort of excitement.

Fukuko had had no idea that a summer evening train ride could be such a pleasant experience. They and the Saekis were always visiting—it only took half an hour. The Saeki couple lived at the end of the railway line, four tram stops away. But this was the first time she and Murao had set out in the evening just to drop by. The Saekis mostly came to them, since they had a car. They would visit the Saekis on their way back from a trip into the city, or else arranged to meet up at the couple's apartment at the end of a workday. But sitting there, enjoying that pleasant night train, Fukuko was surprised that they'd never thought to take it before. It was strange, she realized, considering what good terms they were all on.

Fukuko had known Mrs. Saeki, or Utako, since they'd been little girls. Their families were neighbors, so once they had become friends, they spent all their time together. Utako was older than Fukuko, but only by two years.

When Fukuko started kindergarten, Utako was already in elementary school. Fukuko's kindergarten, however, was the same one where Utako had been just before. Fukuko had gone to the same elementary school, too, and though she didn't try to follow in her friend's footsteps on purpose, she ended up going to Utako's secondary school and women's college as well. The war was in its final stages by the time Fukuko entered college, and students were being mobilized by class to work in factories, so she hardly ever saw anyone from different grades. When the students did return to college at the end of the war, the seniors were forced to graduate six months early, in September. Utako, however, joined the graduate studies program and continued to commute to college with Fukuko the following fall.

Fukuko didn't copy her friend to the point of becoming a research student. She didn't have any particular ambition, and when she graduated, she took a job as an ordinary clerk in a company. Utako, however, remained in college for years, becoming a research associate, then a lecturer, and now an assistant professor.

As a girl Utako had been an exceptionally good swimmer. She had spent so much time in her secondary school pool that she was never home until after six o'clock, even when she was studying for exams—her scores were outstanding, anyway. Fukuko had been taken aback by Utako's preparations for the women's college she herself was planning to enter a couple of years down the line. Utako came from an academic family. Her mother was unremarkable, an ordinary housewife, but her father was a university physics professor, and her two older sisters also studied science, and later became doctors of physics and medicine. Fukuko had assumed Utako would at least try to get into a prestigious teacher-training college or medical school. Utako, however, said she would be "bored to death" in those places.

Perhaps her older sisters' bluestocking manner had put Utako off: even now as a college professor, she hadn't the slightest trace of the stuffy scholar. Utako was the youngest of an academically inclined family, that was all—it was only natural for her to accumulate degrees. To Utako, hers was just another job.

Back in school, Fukuko could remember Utako helping her in all sorts of ways. She had learned to swim, for example, because of her friend. One day during Fukuko's first year at secondary school, Utako had come over and made her practice swimming strokes, standing on the tatami. "You'll soon get the knack of the sidestroke," she'd said, and followed up with two lessons in the school pool. Fukuko, who had been incapable of anything more than floating face-down in the water and a few struggling strokes, suddenly found herself able to swim the length of the pool and back—and the next year, she qualified for the school long-distance race. Utako had invited her to go camping (otherwise Fukuko, then a new student, would have been too shy to go). She had helped Fukuko with her algebra homework when she had all but given up on getting it done by fall, coolly drawing up equations in the wink of an eye and practically providing the solutions. She'd even brought Fukuko the application form for college. When Fukuko was preparing for exams, Utako gave her advice on possible essay subjects: for the past few years, she said, the topic always had to do with the war.

"The dean marks the papers," she told Fukuko. "He really likes it if you say things like, 'Women are the lubricating oil of wartime society.' Make sure you work that in somewhere."

On the day of the exam, when Fukuko read the essay title, "The Role of Women in War," she had quickly settled down to write.

Even so, despite all these favors, Fukuko had never felt weighed down by a debt—Utako never put on any airs. Fukuko was an eldest child; Utako was the youngest in her family; Fukuko never thought a gifted older girl was looking after her. She thought of Utako as a friend her own age—an extremely close friend.

In secondary school, the days they could spend at each other's houses had necessarily become fewer, but in the afternoon, they would wait for each other at the station and walk home together. If that was their only time together for more than a month, Fukuko would start to feel that she simply had to have a proper talk with Utako, who seemed to feel the same way. Fukuko remembered them meeting during exercise drills on Saturday mornings. "Can I come over this afternoon?" one or other would say. "Can you come visit tomorrow?"

During the last part of the war they'd been assigned to different factories, which had put an end to their meetings. But afterwards, they'd made a point of getting together every other month, even when they'd grown up and left home.

Soon after Utako became a research associate, she met a young professor, one of her father's former students. They became engaged. Six months later, eleven days before the wedding, Utako called off the marriage. She never said why she decided to do this, even though they'd always confided everything, and up until then she'd told Fukuko all about that relationship. Utako had then remained unattached for a long time.

Meanwhile, Fukuko resigned from her job and married Murao, a colleague two years her senior. They had taken their time deciding to get engaged, and Murao had delayed the wedding to wait for his younger sister to find a spouse, and again when his father died. By the time they were finally married, Fukuko was almost thirty. She had told Murao about Utako, of course, and Utako about Murao, but she hadn't managed to introduce them. Murao was not a sociable man, and the opportunity never arose.

When Utako finally paid them a visit, though, Murao could not stop staring at her.

"She looks so young!" he exclaimed, as soon as she left. "You'd never guess she's my age. She looks twenty-three or twenty-four!"

Utako was pleasantly slim and petite, not even of medium build. Her oval face, without an ounce of spare flesh on it, still looked as young and lovely as a girl's, and the expression in her eyes was so innocent it was hard to believe she had been observing the world for thirty years. She looked the picture of supple fitness, though she apparently no longer swam very much. Her manner, too, was modest and unassuming. She never spoke of her sisters (one was married, and both had gained high academic positions) in a denigrating or critical way, but with simple and genuine admiration. That evening, she had left early, saying she still had to buy a book for one of her sisters: "If it gets too late, the store'll be closed and it'll be my fault that her work's not done."

"Your friend may be bright," Murao remarked afterwards, "but she's odd, isn't she? Even for somebody who seems so young."

Of course, this did not mean Murao disliked her. Utako was fond of drinking, that was all, and whenever she got slightly inebriated, she would get up from the table and dance for them. She would twirl around the room, humming a tune, raising her arms in sharp, graceful movements. And she had done this on their very first evening together.

"I'd like to go to one of your lectures sometime," Murao had said, as he watched her admiringly. "To see the look on your face when you teach."

"Out of the question. . . ." Utako dismissed the idea with a wave of her hand.

"I can't understand why such an attractive woman isn't married," Murao came to wonder out loud, often, to Fukuko.

After Utako canceled her wedding, Fukuko had learned nothing more from her about it, nor about any other men she might have gotten to know. Fukuko once tried to broach the subject of the broken engagement, but all Utako said was: "He hasn't married yet, either." Of course, through other channels Fukuko had heard that two or three men had since made Utako offers of marriage. Apparently, however, they'd all been turned down. Since Utako never referred to these matters, even with her, and had canceled her engagement eleven days before her wedding, Fukuko supposed the reason for her reluctance to get married had to be personal and awkward—something that had left quite a scar.

When they were little, they'd affectionately called each other "Utako-chan" and "Fukuko-chan." As adults, however, they'd become slightly more formal, with "Utako-san" and "Fukuko-san." Murao, however, called her "Uta-chan" whenever talking about her in private, and Fukuko naturally began to do the same thing. When Murao started using this form of address directly to Utako, Fukuko again followed suit. Utako, however, continued to use the somewhat more distant appellation.

Every so often, Utako stayed the night at their house. If she were due to give a lecture the next morning, Murao would urge her to hurry along with him, and the two of them would leave together—looking for all the world like a pair of lovers, Fukuko would remark to herself as she happily watched them from the doorway. She informed them that this was what she thought, and made sure Murao knew that she took pleasure in the notion: "When you want an affair, have it with Uta-chan, please, then we'll all live together."

"Hm, not a bad idea," he had replied.

But then, one afternoon, about three years later, Utako came to tell Fukuko that she was engaged.

"Actually," she added, embarrassed, "it's somebody you know."

Not Murao, surely? Fukuko wondered for an instant.

"Somebody you know very well," Utako continued. Smiling broadly, she announced that her fiancé was Saeki: "Don't you think that's funny?"

Fukuko had once, some years before, employed Saeki as an English tutor for her sister, when she was preparing for her high-school entrance exams. At that time he was a freshman at the university, her sister was fifteen, and she herself must have been about twenty-five.

Fukuko had at first attempted to tutor her sister herself, but Toshiko had done nothing but complain, accusing her first of incompetence and then of teaching her nonsense. All they'd done was quarrel. Fukuko had suspected that she probably wasn't teaching her sister correctly. She had gotten her teaching certificate on graduation, but that had been at the end of the war when there were hardly any classes to take, so she'd found tutoring a strain.

"All right!" she'd told her sister: "Your next teacher won't make mistakes, but he won't stand your whining either!" And she went straight to the university, asked for names of any students needing part-time work, and arranged the tutor: that's how she ended up hiring Saeki.

In the late autumn of that same year, Fukuko was on her way back from work and nearly home when she saw Saeki walking along a little way ahead of her.

"I really appreciate your helping my sister," she said, catching up with him.

"Not at all," Saeki replied, and after a few more steps, he added: "There is a matter I would like to discuss with you."

"Oh?"

"If you don't mind, I'd like to talk to you after her lesson. In the living room, perhaps."

"I see." They had reached the house. He probably wanted to broach some uncomfortable topic, Fukuko thought, her sister's exams, or perhaps her lazy study habits. Fukuko had employed him, and he no doubt thought she'd be easier to talk to than her parents.

"Well, see you in a little while, then," she said, opening the gate.

They sat, facing each other in the living room, three hours later.

"Well, actually," Saeki began, "it's about some letters I've been receiving." Undoing a gold button halfway down the front of his jacket, he drew out three, already opened, small blank envelopes: "Please read these." He pushed them across the table to her, and buttoning up his jacket, sat with bowed head.

"Well, all right."

Fukuko picked up one envelope and took out and unfolded a letter. At the top of the unlined page, she saw the words, "To my beloved," written clumsily. Its next line began: "Oh, Teacher, I think you're being so mean. . . ."

"What?" Fukuko said, frowning. "So Toshiko—"

Saeki looked up, and snatching the letter back, turned it over to show her the name of the sender—a name Fukuko did not recognize.

"Who is this?"

"She's my other student," Saeki replied, "in her second year at high school. What should I do? Please read the other two."

Fukuko had never seen a love letter in her life so she had nothing to compare these with, but all three began with the same words, "To my beloved," and seemed appallingly over-written. Petulant and complaining, they accused Teacher of being too mean to even acknowledge his student's feelings, though he knew she was writing him letters.

"She's really fallen for me, hasn't she?" Saeki asked.

"It looks like that way."

"What should I do?"

As far as he was concerned, he said, he had two options: either inform the girl's parents and have them talk to her, or else give up the job as her tutor. But he was worried that the girl might do something drastic. That was why he wanted Fukuko's advice. She had a sister. She had been a girl this age herself. She was equipped to predict the emotional reactions of adolescent girls.

What a genuinely sincere person, Fukuko couldn't help thinking. If they'd been sent to her, she would have treated these letters like a joke, hooting with her friends over them. But here was this man, taking them seriously, bowing his head, and having her read them so she could tell him what to do. Well, her sister was quite safe with somebody like this.

In a state of relief that the letters had nothing to do with her sister, she found herself wanting to play to the hilt her role as Saeki's counselor. Delivering as tough-minded an opinion as possible, she declared that whatever his course of action, nobody could prevent the girl from having such feelings—and, for that matter, the only sure way of preventing her from doing something drastic would be for him to return her feelings. But then, was it *his* responsibility, if a girl decided to get obsessed with him, and make trouble for herself?

"Well," she concluded, self-importantly: "I'd stop teaching her, if I were you. Unless you actually have some interest . . ."

In the end, Saeki did give up being the girl's tutor, though his decision was probably based on more than just her advice. His student didn't do anything drastic. It wasn't until several years later that Fukuko told her younger sister about the incident. She did inform her parents, however. She told Utako, too, creating considerable amusement.

Utako gave Fukuko a quick update on Saeki's career—after graduating, he had taken a job at an English-language newspaper. Utako had met him at a conference just six months before, and she hadn't realized at first that he was the Saeki of Fukuko's story. It was only after dating him for several months that she had made the connection.

When Utako said her engagement was "funny," Fukuko thought, she meant that it was a funny coincidence, but she might also be referring to Saeki's age. Saeki was much younger than Utako—he was even considerably younger than Fukuko, who was two years younger than her friend. Utako was quite open about it: she was six years older than Saeki. But Utako looked at least six years younger than she really was, and anyway, Fukuko thought, what mattered was how well a couple got on together.

"Why not bring him next time?" Fukuko said. Once she'd made the invitation, it struck her that Saeki was no longer the student she'd been picturing.

"What's he like now?" she wanted to know.

"Oh, very nice," Utako answered, somewhat disappointingly.

Saeki did, in fact, come with Utako to pay one visit during their engagement. When the love-letter episode came up, he said to Fukuko, "I'm so glad I asked for your advice." It was the kind of thing one is obliged to say, of course, but he seemed to mean it, and Fukuko felt embarrassed and didn't know how to reply. He had lost none of his sincerity. But he was a man now, and quite the adult.

"Didn't I tell you?" Fukuko said to Murao afterwards. "They're well suited, aren't they?"

Murao grunted. "Uta-chan looks at least six years younger than she is, and Saeki looks about right for his age. When you see them together, though, she still looks a little older than him. Strange, isn't it, for somebody who's always referring to herself as the baby of her family to turn and tell her husband so firmly, 'Well, dear, time to go.' It suits her, though, doesn't it! And her manner is so gentle. Their marriage should go well."

"Too bad for you, hmm?"

"That's true." Murao grinned.

Whenever Fukuko came across something particularly fresh or delicious, her first thought was to ask the Saekis over for dinner. Her hospitality toward Utako, of course, was nothing new, but now Murao, too, whenever he particularly liked a place they'd gone, would often remark, "I wish the other two were here. Let's ask them next time." This sociability on his part had started after Utako's marriage. It was easier, perhaps, to double date. So, occasionally they'd go out places as a foursome.

"Utako tells me she prefers coming here to seeing her own family," Saeki announced one day, while they were visiting.

"Well, I hope so!" Fukuko replied.

Utako's mother had died a few years before, and a sister had married and moved away. The only ones left at home were her father, the professor, now retired, her other sister, and a middle-aged housekeeper.

"And what about you?" Fukuko asked Saeki.

"I feel exactly the same way!" he said, laughing.

Fukuko laughed too, imagining her friends' faces at tense family visits. Murao and Utako joined in, and then, as they all laughed, it dawned on Fukuko that they weren't really laughing about Utako's family at all, but rather about a certain complicity—an understanding that they had come to about relations between the four of them.

The Saekis lived four or five blocks away from the tram stop. Fukuko and Murao walked off the main road up a small street, and as they turned at the second intersection, they saw an empty plot of land with a notice board painted in white letters: "For sale: twenty-five *tsubo.*" The Saekis often parked their car here, although illegally, and sure enough, Fukuko and Murao saw among the four or five cars their small buff-colored vehicle, parked at a slight angle, with its dark windscreen toward them.

"They're home all right," Murao remarked.

"What on earth can they be doing?" Fukuko exclaimed, and her voice was excited too.

Turning a corner a couple of streets farther on, they came face to face with a two-story building, opposite an art gallery, consisting of twenty apartments, all with identical doors and windows. The Saekis' apartment was on the second floor, the second one along. The kitchen window, however, was dark.

"They'll be in the front room," Fukuko said, going up the iron stairs. The Saekis had been renting this small one-bedroom apartment for three years now, and Fukuko and Murao knew which rooms the couple were likely to use at different times of day. But Fukuko only mentioned the front room to try to dispel her disappointment at not immediately seeing that they would be met with lights and good cheer. The Saekis weren't home, she realized. The darkness behind the frosted window pierced her to the bone.

"Anybody home? It's us." Murao rattled the door knob. But the door didn't budge. "Hey, Saeki!" he called out loudly, knocking.

"Looks like nobody's home," he said to her. "The car is there. But if they were anywhere around . . ."

If they were anywhere around, true, they would have left the lights on as they always did when they walked Murao and Fukuko to the bus stop at the end of a visit.

"Well, they must be out," Fukuko said. She tried tugging the sliding glass window, but it wouldn't budge, either. She yearned to hear the light snap on inside, and to hear Utako call "Coming!" in that direct, clear way she had. . . .

The door of the next apartment opened, and a young woman with wet hair stepped out.

"They're not home," she said. "Mrs. Saeki set off in a car with a foreigner around five o'clock."

The woman didn't know if Mr. Saeki was going to meet her somewhere, or if he was off on his own. But either way, they probably wouldn't return till late. "Can I take a message?" she asked.

"No, that's all right," Murao replied. "We were just out for a walk, and dropped by on the off-chance."

They thanked the woman, and went down the stairs.

"Would you like to walk a little?" Murao suggested, when they reached the road.

"What time is it?"

Murao paused, holding out his wrist so the light from the street lamp fell on his watch.

"Not even 10:30."

They turned, and kept walking, still heading away from the main road. At the end of the street, a small grove of trees which they always saw from a distance when they walked from the tram stop to the Saekis' loomed into view. Fukuko had been convinced it housed a shrine to the fox god Inari, but they saw when they drew near that there were only several tall trees.

Now they had to choose to turn right or left. To the right lay a narrow street of scraggy houses with here and there a public bath or eating-place mixed in. The road to the left looked more promising for a walk. They could see some residences, not too large, but still impressive enough with their traditional wooden gates.

"I'm amazed these weren't burnt in the air raids," Fukuko remarked. Even in the dim light, she could see that some of the gates and fences predated the war.

"You're right," said Murao. The silent road was free of pedestrians, and no cars sped along; it was probably just as deserted during the day.

"It's so quiet," Fukuko remarked, when suddenly, there in front of them, a tiny point of white light made an arc in the air, and vanished. Then, farther on down the road, one more arc was traced in the darkness.

"Oh! A firefly!"

Fukuko felt she'd come across something the very existence of which she had forgotten for a very long time. She saw the light glimmer again, two or three feet away, at the foot of the fence, like a tiny beacon.

"I'm going to catch it," Fukuko announced and crossed the road.

"Leave it," Murao said.

She ignored him, bending down by the fence.

"I said leave it, damn it!" Murao ordered.

"You're in a sour mood," she replied, but let her hands fall, and crossed back to him. Murao didn't reply. As they started walking again, he took her right hand, caressed it for a while, and then, holding out her index finger, he put it in his mouth and bit down, hard.

"What do you think you're doing?" Fukuko spoke lightly, but flinched with pain. The firefly flew up over her head, and vanished.

Nearly two months before, Utako had visited Fukuko early in the afternoon. Fukuko had suggested that Utako telephone Saeki and get him to come over too, after work, and she would call Murao. This was the way the two women often arranged their get-togethers.

Utako had danced for them that evening, too. They could

only tell she was tipsy from the fact that she performed—her speech remained clear even when she was quite drunk. If she got at all unsteady on her feet, she was far gone. That evening, they all watched as she stood up and danced for them three times, her movements becoming more and more languid and tottering.

"Hey," Saeki pretended to instruct her. "Now you're doing an Indonesian dance. Get a grip."

"No, those hand gestures . . . they're exquisite," Murao said, though he was laughing, too. "We ought to catch this on film. Don't you think she's better than she was?"

"Sssh. Don't speak." Utako said, twirling about. She started humming imaginatively, and danced on, lost in her own pleasure.

An hour or so later, Fukuko had brought out tumblers of ice water for everybody, and Saeki had made his suggestion.

"I wonder whether I should leave from here tomorrow?" he remarked, staring at his empty glass as he turned it around in his hands.

"Yes, why don't you?" Murao said.

"Neither of you should drive," Fukuko agreed.

"Oh, we're not that bad," Utako said, "but it might be a nice change."

The Saekis had stayed the night once before. A few months after their marriage, they'd had a fight, and Utako had run away to Fukuko and Murao. Saeki had soon followed in the car. That night, Utako, normally so placid, seemed genuinely offended about something. She refused to say a word to her husband all evening. Only when it was so late that Fukuko invited them to stay over did she deign to acknowledge him.

"I came here so I wouldn't have to see your face," she snapped. "Can't you do me a favor and leave?"

"Well, maybe I should go," said Saeki, looking defeated. From the start he had obviously been at a loss, embarrassed by his role as the young husband humoring his older wife.

"There's no need for that," Murao interceded. "Your charming wife left the car expressly so you could follow her."

In the end, they'd both stayed.

Only one other time had they all slept under the same roof—when they'd taken a trip to Nasu the summer before, and stayed in a hotel.

And now, gazing at Saeki, Fukuko registered that he had made the suggestion himself that he wanted to stay over. So casually, so intimately, but also so indirectly, dropping those words into the conversation, he hadn't addressed anybody in particular, hadn't even looked anyone in the eye. . . .

"Hey! Hey!" Murao brought her back to her senses: she realized Utako had started to clear away the glasses on the table.

"Let's not bother to actually wash up," Utako was saying. "I'll help tomorrow morning. I don't have to leave."

Fukuko hadn't had nearly as much to drink as Utako, but washing up was now the furthest thing from her mind.

Once the glasses and plates had been taken to the kitchen, the car pulled up into the driveway as far as it would go, and the front door locked, nothing remained but for them to settle down and relax. Murao brought out some more wine, and they were caught up in talk—it was almost two o'clock by the time they realized they should go to bed.

"I'll set the alarm so we don't oversleep," Fukuko said. Saeki was just returning from the bathroom, so she pointed to the clock on the shelf, asking, "Could you get that down? Thank you." Taking it from him, she sat down and hunched over it in her lap.

Saeki turned back to the shelf to look at an ornamental plate.

"Watch out," Utako warned: "He'll break something."

"What's this?"

"Oh, that's too big, and crude," Fukuko said, her eyes on the little alarm hand she was moving around on the clock. "Someone we know who's a potter gave it to us a while ago."

"No, not the plate," Saeki said: "This."

She looked up. Saeki had lifted the plate from its stand, and was peering into the space behind it.

Fukuko blushed: "Oh don't."

"Oh, I see," he continued, "it's a candlestick, isn't it? Where did you find it?"

"It was in the antiques section of T— department store," Murao answered, who had found it and brought it home.

"Let me have a better look," Saeki said, putting the plate back on its stand, and moving them to the side. He brought the candlestick, together with a candle he found beside it, over to the table, and sat down.

The candlestick was a small bronze one, fashioned in the shape of an aboriginal man, who stood with his chest thrown out, offering up the decapitated head of a woman.

"The candle goes here, I suppose," Saeki said, fitting it into a hole in the woman's head. "Do you ever light it?"

"Ask Fukuko," Murao said. "She'll tell you."

Fukuko liked physical pain during sex, and Murao willingly complied, but occasionally, when they were doing certain things, they couldn't reach full satisfaction without a special light in the room. The archaic candlestick and the mysterious effect produced by the deep, dark candle-light would bring their excitement to fever pitch. Her eye on the trembling flame and the flickering dark shapes it brought to life on the walls, Fukuko would feel lifted out of the present, as if she were participating in an orgy of pain and pleasure—all the pain and pleasure experienced by women, highborn and low-, since ancient times. But the next morning she'd quickly tidy away the now everyday household objects devoid of magic. She used to store them in the closet, but since acquiring the plate, she'd started hiding them behind that.

Saeki, following Murao's lead, said, "Tell me, Fukuko, do you ever light the candle? You light it and watch it, don't you? Let me try it."

He struck a match, and a flame rose from the candle in the

woman's head: "Look at that." Saeki held the woman's head in his fingers. "She's got her eyes closed, poor thing," he said, stroking the woman's eyelids with his thumb. "You do go in for some strange things, Fukuko."

"Stop it." She blew out the flame, embarrassed, but also highly aroused. "Please put it away."

"As you wish." Saeki obeyed.

"What a *nice* man!" Fukuko said. How nice that he was so obedient, was what she meant; she found herself thinking of when he had been in her employ as the tutor. But she also meant how nice that he seemed to be able to enjoy his wife so much more when in their company.

"What a nice man!" she repeated and then, all at once, the significance of the words seemed to grow greater and greater. She began to feel as if something had gone to her head: "Yes, you're nice. I like you, Mr. Saeki," she gushed. "I really do."

"Careful now," Murao said. "This one didn't even drink, but she's losing all self-control."

"That's right!" Fukuko replied. "But you're always saying you like Uta-chan."

"That's true. I'm very fond of her."

"Well, what are we going to do about it?" Utako responded.

"We should do something to express our gratitude to each other," Saeki said.

Fukuko was feeling even more elated by the time she got into bed. "We're in a fix, the four of us," she called through the sliding doors. "What'll we do?"

"We're ready," Saeki called back.

"Just say the word," Murao replied, poking Fukuko in the shoulder.

"What about you, Uta-chan?" she asked.

"I will if you will."

Fukuko nudged Murao and he pushed her back. They prodded each other, and Fukuko knew very well that all she had to do was step in to the other room and say, "Well, here I am. Go on, Uta-chan, he's waiting." But her body wouldn't obey her, and a few moments later, the opportunity had passed. The men were calling each other cowards. "Pretty funny!" Fukuko called out to Utako, who agreed, "Yes, wasn't it!"

They all said good night, and that was that.

Then, last week, they had visited the Saekis and the episode had come up in conversation. Each had teased the other three for being too cowardly to see it through to the end. But just as Fukuko and Murao were leaving, Saeki had remarked: "It's only nine o'clock—are you running away?"

"No, no," Murao replied. "I have to leave early tomorrow. I'm seeing someone off at Haneda." This was the truth.

"Sounds suspiciously like an excuse," Saeki teased.

"I don't need excuses," Murao answered. "I'm not a coward like you."

"All right. Should we make a date?"

"Yes," Murao had replied. "You come to our house. You shouldn't drink too much this time, and don't come too early."

They had half-jokingly agreed upon a date, which was supposed to have been tonight.

The sound of running water met their ears, as the road started to slope down. The houses on the left petered out, giving way to a low railing that ran alongside a canal. They came to a bridge, and crossing it, they walked on, now following the course of a meandering stream.

The water grew louder and they saw another bridge. Splashing underneath it, the level of the water dropped away sharply, falling in a rushing cascade. On the opposite bank a giant mercury lamp shone cool and white, lighting up some of the small shrubs and trees growing along the foot of the bridge and a large wooden gate.

"That must be the back entrance of that restaurant," Murao said, his face caught in the light falling over to their side of the stream. The restaurant was noted for its magnificent gardens.

The realization dawned on Fukuko: "Oh, so the fireflies came from here." They walked on, catching glimpses on the other side of traditional buildings through the trees.

They came to another bridge.

"What's that?" Fukuko pointed beyond the stream, looking up at a steep bluff with a single large building like a hotel on top.

"I wonder," Murao said.

At the foot of the bluff were dim yellow lights, like those on a playground, and crossing the stream, they discovered exactly that. Trees and bushes covered the stream bank and the sides of the cliff, but in between them was a long stretch of ground with two slides and a double swing. Fukuko had an urge to try them just when Murao called her over.

"Looks like we can get up this way!" He went to the foot of the cliff where some round stones marked a path leading up through the trees.

But when the two of them started up the path, they found the stones, zigzagging around thickets and bushes, were arranged as a maze. Every time they came to a bend they faced a choice of two or three paths forking off in different directions. Though they'd choose the one that most looked as though it would go up the bluff, before long they would find the path winding down, then up for a while, then down all the way, so they had to retrace their steps and start again.

Finally, the tall building was directly above them. They couldn't be too far from the top, but then they had to double back several times.

"I need to rest," Fukuko said, out of breath, as they went around a bend.

"We're almost there!" Murao called. He went right, left, then straight ahead, and reached the top. Then he turned around and stood with both hands tucked in his sash, gazing out. "Come and take a look!" he called, and making one last effort, Fukuko scrambled up and joined him.

"Oh, this was worth the climb!" she cried, when she turned around.

Directly below lay the dark playground and the stream, and beyond these, stretching out to the hills on the other side of the plain, were lines of countless twinkling street lights. There wasn't a single neon sign, but they could see a few yellow lights, the same size as the white ones, scattered in, each and every one shining stunningly: it was a beautiful night scene.

Over to their right an illuminated clock showed 11:20, and they heard the far-off sound of a tram, probably the last one for the night.

"It's too late to catch that home," Fukuko remarked.

Murao grunted.

"If we don't hurry," she added, "the trains won't be running."

"Who cares," Murao said. "We can always take a cab." He looked behind him at the building. "Or stay the night here. Or sleep outside—it'll be nice and cool."

Silent now, Fukuko leaned up against the railing, gazing out at the lights.

Next they found themselves on a narrow dirt path behind the tall building, which was encircled by a fence. At the end of the track stood two neat little houses, beyond which they could see a wider road.

They headed that way, and turning right on the paved road, they found themselves facing the front of the building they'd just been standing behind.

"Well, it's only an apartment block!" said Murao.

They turned left—home lay in that direction, whether or not they caught a cab. After a few minutes, houses came into view which were even more stately than the ones they had glimpsed by the stream. The sound of their geta rang out clearly on the pavement, but everything else was absolutely hushed and still.

As they crossed the next intersection, they saw that the opposite left-hand corner was illuminated as brightly as a stage set. They stopped in their tracks to gaze at what stood there: a modern two-storey house, still under construction. A powerful light was fixed to one of the lower eaves to prevent the theft of the various stacked-up building supplies.

"What a nice house!" Murao said and crossed the road.

The roof sloped up and down over various wings of the house. The second-floor windows were gaping holes, but the doors on the first-floor balcony were fitted with sheer panes, each with "g-l-a-s-s" scrawled a little too energetically in white paint across it.

Murao leant forward to peer inside, then beckoned to her.

"Come on," he said, "it'll be useful, for future reference. One day, I'll build us a house like this."

Fukuko crossed the road, stepped up onto the balcony, and picked her way to him through the building materials. She put her face against a section of the window free of white paint and looked inside. With the balcony lit, she had no difficulty seeing into the room, even with the reflections. The size of the room was perhaps twelve tatami mats.

"The stairs look like imitation stone," said Murao.

She could see them, narrow, with banisters, going up toward the left along the opposite wall. There were two doors, half-open: one below the staircase, and one in the right-hand wall, but it was too dark to tell what lay beyond them. To the left was a fireplace made of the same stone as the stairs, a gas point sticking out at one corner. The lamp hanging from the ceiling was still wrapped in paper, and the floor, perhaps yet to be laid with finished planks of wood or varnished, was covered with muddy shoe prints.

Nobody had ever lived in this half-finished house, Fukuko realized: such places have their own peculiar atmosphere, different from that of an old abandoned house. An abandoned house would be creepy and cold, too frightening to enter. But this one almost seemed to taunt her with its own strange vitality. There was nothing hateful about it, but she felt an urge to scrawl graffiti on the broad doorframe of bare wood, or throw a wooden clog through an empty second-floor window.

"Let's go," Murao said.

"All right." Fukuko gazed at the dazzling balcony: "What a waste of electricity, but it's probably worth it."

They returned to the road, which some railway tracks cut across just two blocks farther on.

"Let's catch a cab up there," Murao said. He'd seen cars on the main road ahead, going along full speed now in the absence of trams. When they gained the road, however, hardly any taxis were to be seen in the heavy stream of traffic. The few that did come along were occupied. One cab approached with a red vacant sign, and they stood on the edge of the pavement waving, but it went right by.

"It's because of our yukata," Murao said, after more empty cabs had passed. "They must think we're only going a short way."

"How far is the station?"

"About a mile and half."

"Well, we'll get a cab there."

"Can you walk that far?"

"I think so—we can still try to wave one down on the way."

Walking along the main road, here and there they saw red lanterns under the eaves of drinking establishments, and stand-up neon signs on the street, but all the stores were closed.

"It'll take a good thirty minutes." Murao looked at his watch. "We'll get there about half past."

"Half past one?"

"Half past twelve. It isn't even midnight yet."

"I bet those two haven't even got home," Fukuko mused.

But what if the Saekis had come over to their place tonight? What, she wondered, would they all have been doing now?

Calling each other "cowards" again? How shocked Utako would have been, holding out her arms to embrace Murao, only to have him grab them to pin her down. With that lithe, supple body, one yank and her wrists would be crossed at the base of her spine and bound firmly. And how would Saeki have reacted when she, Fukuko, asked him for the same? Would he refuse, embarrassed? What would he do when she begged him? The more details Fukuko put into her fantasy, the more desire she felt for the man walking like a shadow, almost invisible but ever present, at her side.

"That's the third bus stop we've passed," she heard Murao remark.

His words returned her to the streaming traffic, the honking cars, the rows of shuttered shops, and the sound of their own wooden clogs on the road.

Up ahead, suspended over the middle of the road, she saw a blinking orange traffic light. Behind it loomed a stately Buddhist temple gate. The temple was a famous one, though Fukuko had never visited it. Three tram routes intersected there.

"Good timing!" she said. "Shall we rest at the temple? We'll be able to get a drink of water."

"But the gate'll be shut."

When they drew near, however, it was wide open and they headed up a long gravel path.

"A splendid place," Fukuko remarked, looking up as they passed under the wooden gate.

They emerged in the spacious pitch-dark temple grounds. Only three or four wooden buildings had any lights on, apparently offices and storehouses. To their right lay an unlit massive concrete building like an assembly hall and directly in front of them rose the sweeping black roof of the main sanctuary.

The stars had disappeared, but the cloud cover reflected the pink glow of the city, so in fact the night was brighter. Or perhaps their eyes had grown accustomed to the dark—they could discern vague outlines in the grounds.

They advanced up a stone path around a corner of the main temple building.

"There's no water, is there," Murao said. "Buddhist temples don't have places to wash your mouth and hands before praying. Only Shinto shrines have the dragon waterspout and a row of metal ladles."

"Yes, but this is such a grand temple, there must be water somewhere."

They walked on for a while. From the corner of the main hall, the temple's rear gate came into view, and a few yards away was a round wooden pavilion. Beside that stood a small post with a faucet.

"Didn't I tell you?" Fukuko hurried forward to have a drink. "There's even a little place to sit," she said, as he took his turn. Looking inside the pavilion, however, she saw the seat was covered with dust. Even after wiping her handkerchief over it, she couldn't bring herself to sit down.

They decided to try to exit on the opposite side of the temple. As they walked over, a light in the far corner appeared—it came from a small house.

"That must be where the gravekeeper lives," Murao said.

He had seen the cemetery to the right beyond the hedge.

"I've heard the graves here are really old," she replied, "I think one belongs to a noble lady from Tokugawa times, or somebody."

When they got nearer, they found a gap in the hedge. Through it, they saw the dark rows of gravestones stretching away into the night.

"I think the famous graves are deeper in," Fukuko said. "If it's not too far, let's have a look at the noble woman's."

"It's so dark," Murao grumbled, "we won't be able to see a damn thing."

But they were already heading toward the entrance. As they went in, Fukuko felt her blood run cold—something white lay across the path. But it was only a notice board that had fallen over. GRAVEYARDS AT NIGHT ARE DANGEROUS, she read, by the faint light of the house. DO NOT ENTER.

Fukuko realized that she'd been in a particular mood for some time now, a mood that would keep her walking beside Murao into the night, walking on and on until they became the perpetrators—or the victims—of some unpredictable crime.

Full Tide (MICHI–SHIO, 1964)

THE CHILDREN HAD GOTTEN THEIR MOTHER TO help them change into travel outfits: their hats on, they were all ready to go. But their mother was now busy getting herself dressed, and told them as she tied on her sash: "Now, all of you go and say goodbye to Grandma Hotta."

A merchant family, they had always lived in the section of the city that was traditionally home to the wholesale trade. From now on, however, they were going to live in a new place in the suburbs, away from the family business. For a long time the girl had been hearing from her parents how nice it would be to live in their own house, on the city outskirts where the air was clean. And now, finally, it was happening: it was summer, and the girl was just ten years old.

The house they were moving to had been built on a plot of land an hour away from their business—her father intended to commute every day. With her younger sister, she would switch schools, and her brother, who wasn't in school yet, would start kindergarten in their new neighborhood in the spring.

A few days before, after attending her primary school's final assembly and closing ceremony before summer vacation, the girl had felt strange as she walked out the gate and realized that she wouldn't be back next fall. But she didn't feel too sad—the family shop would stay where it was. She was bound to come this way occasionally. Her friends seemed to take that for granted. "When will we see you again?" they asked when she said goodbye. "Can you come visit over the holidays?"

She was, in fact, longing to start her new life in the suburbs. She'd already visited the area a few times with her family—it was right on the sea, with mountains close by, and in between the sea and the mountains was a river with sandbars and beautiful grassy banks lined with rows of pine trees. At the foot of the mountains was a park with a slide said to be the highest in Japan. "Just one more time," the girl remembered begging her parents, as they tried to persuade her to leave. She had scampered back to the slide which rose steeply above her in the late-afternoon spring sunshine—and, thinking back on it, the girl felt a fresh stab of nostalgia. The strap of her rubber swimming cap smelled of the sea, and she recalled her mounting excitement as she walked along the grassy bank, smelled the salt air, and listened to the pounding of the surf get louder and louder.

But the girl had not seen her new house yet.

"What's it like?" she couldn't help asking her parents. Apparently, it wasn't creaky and dark like their old house—and it was only a stone's throw from the sea.

"You'll be able to go to the beach in your swimsuit and robe!" her father told her.

The girl's eyes opened wide: "Really?"

It didn't matter one bit that they would leave the streets where the girl had lived all her life. She felt a little anxious about going to a new school in the fall, but that was still more than a month away. Her whole heart had been longing for the day of their departure and the idea that they would have to go say goodbye to Grandma Hotta hadn't even crossed her mind.

But when her mother told them to go, the girl stood up immediately, took off the hat she had been trying on in front of the mirror to see if the elastic strap belonged in front of her ears or behind them, and flung it aside.

"Remember to tell Grandma that you'll write. And that

you'll come back and visit from time to time," her mother added, glancing at her back in the mirror, her hands busy with the knot of her sash. "And don't forget to say, 'We hope that you stay well!'"

The girl nodded obediently, and beckoned her brother and sister.

"Go through the front today," their mother called.

Grandma Hotta was an old lady who lived all alone, just three doors down the street from them. She had suffered a series of terrible misfortunes, the girl had heard. She and her husband had once run a wholesale paper business, but had gone bankrupt, soon after which her husband and her only child, a daughter, had died. Now she lived at the end of a small alleyway, in a tiny place, consisting of the kitchen and one two-mat room of her former residence. The rest had been sold off and made into the accounting office of a copper-ware dealer. Despite her poverty, however, the neighbors still acknowledged the old lady's previous status as the wife of a prosperous shopkeeper: they called her "O-ie," "O-ie-san," or, in the local dialect, "O-e-han."* In the girl's family, too, the grown-ups always referred to the old lady as "Hotta no O-e-han."

It was possible to enter the old lady's house from the back of their own. At the end of the garden, by the little cottage where the children often played, was a wooden warehouse built up against the family storehouse: at its far end was a sliding door, and opening that, they would find themselves right inside Grandma Hotta's house. The door was usually kept closed and locked, however, with a bolt on the old lady's side.

That day, the girl escorted her brother and sister out to the street, where trucks, carts, and bicycles were busily passing, and turned down the little alley to the old lady's front entrance.

---

*The "ie" of "O-ie-san" means "household/family." The name means something like "Mistress," and was traditionally used by the merchant class in Osaka.

They pounded on the heavy wooden door, which had a smaller one set within it, and shouted all together, "Grandma!"

"Yes, yes. I'm coming," they heard her say in the same way she did when they went via the warehouse. They heard her wooden clogs cross the earthen floor, then a pause, and the bolt rattled back.

"We've come to say goodbye," the girl announced as soon as the door opened.

"Really? Thank you, dear. It's very nice of you to remember me."

The old lady looked at the children in their travel clothes. "Are you leaving right away? I suppose you don't have time to come in for a little while. . . ."

The kitchen was spacious, large enough to have catered to the needs of an entire family. Now it served as the old lady's living space and entryway as well. There were two skylights in the ceiling, and directly below them, several detachable planks gleamed darkly, covering a small cellar. A rough mat had been laid alongside these.

O-ie-san stepped back to fetch three cushions stacked neatly at the far end of the mat. She set them on the edge of the raised floor for the children, and settled herself opposite them, in front of the simple unlit charcoal brazier.

"Thank you for coming," she said, formally. She was slight of stature and very pale, and her hair was nearly all white.

"When we get there, I'm going to swim every day!" the girl's sister announced.

"Me too!" her brother said. "Mummy bought me a float!"

Grandma Hotta gave her usual response: she had a habit of opening her eyes, which were very wide to begin with, wider still, so they almost met her eyebrows.

"I see," she nodded.

Now would be a good time to carry out her duty, the girl thought, taking a deep breath.

"But we'll come back and visit you, Grandma!" she said.

"And we'll write you letters. And we hope that you stay well!"

"Thank you, my dear," the old lady replied. She nodded several times, dabbing her eyes with her sleeve.

The girl was only saying what her mother had told her she should, but she realized that Grandma Hotta was genuinely touched. It occurred to her that Grandma Hotta must be terribly lonely, and that she would be even lonelier when they went away. Remembering that she might have left without saying goodbye, the girl felt ashamed.

Her mother always took very good care of poor old O-ie-san. Two years ago, a fierce typhoon had blown up across their part of the country, with gale-force winds and floods. As soon as her mother saw signs of the coming storm, she sent a clerk from the store over to bring O-ie-san back to their house. Their mother took O-ie-san to the theater, and was always visiting her, almost every day. Whenever the old lady wasn't feeling well, her mother would report her health to her father, even though he usually disliked being bothered by anything unrelated to his work.

"She's no longer running a fever," her mother would say. "But she's still a little dizzy. I'll go over after dinner and see how she is."

On summer nights, the children would play with fireworks and sparklers in the back garden. They would go out into the dark with their mother, taking fireworks, matches, and a bucket of water. Glimpsing a pale shape in the gloom, they might suddenly hear O-ie-san's voice say, quietly: "I'm out here enjoying the cool. I hope you don't mind."

"No, not at all," the girl's mother would reply, quickly disappearing into the cottage, and a light would come on, throwing wan rays out the small round window. The girl would see O-ie-san sitting in the small rattan child's chair that she always brought out with her, fanning herself with a round paper fan.

"What a lovely cool breeze," her mother would remark, coming out and sitting on the edge of the veranda.

The children set about lighting their sparklers. Each time she brought a flame to the tip of one, the girl's fingers would tremble slightly. She had to be careful: she could never tell exactly where the first sparks would shoot out. Then the darkness suddenly would be ablaze, and transfixed, she would be in another world. The sparkler would make fiery, spitting sounds, fizzling away before her eyes. In those few seconds, though, she knew the sparkler was living for all it was worth—fiercely, keenly, in a beautiful world of color and light. Even when everything became dark and still once more, the girl would be sure that she still saw something there, glowing and fizzling away.

"This one next," her brother would say.

Sometimes, the girl would be aware of her mother and the old lady gazing at the sparklers, their faces reflecting the light, but they mostly just chatted. The children would light firecrackers, which shot out at unexpected angles with a loud bang. "Oh!" the women would exclaim: "That made me jump!"

Some nights when they went into the garden to play with sparklers, though, O-ie-san wouldn't be out there enjoying the cool night air. Then, their mother would urge them to go and invite her to join them. But no one would want to go alone to fetch her—it was too scary to go all that way through the dark warehouse. Even the girl was afraid, and she was the eldest.

Through the open door of O-ie-san's house, the girl caught sight of her mother walking up the alley.

"Did everybody say goodbye nicely?" she asked, entering the house.

"They're all such good children," O-ie-san said. "Thank you so much for your kindness this morning," she said to their mother. "You're always so very kind. . . ."

So her mother, the girl realized, must have come by herself to see the old lady earlier in the day.

O-ie-san came out to the end of the alley to see them all off.

"Good luck!" she said to the children. "Grow up healthy and strong."

Though the girl was going to switch to a new school once summer vacation was over, that didn't mean she got out of holiday homework. At the closing ceremony, their teacher gave all the girls in her class a copy of *Summer Holiday Companion*. She'd been told that she must be sure to complete all its exercises and hand it in to her teacher at her new school at the beginning of the next term.

After breakfast every morning the girl filled in that day's homework in her study book. Then she went straight out with her brother and sister, accompanied by the maid, to swim in the sea. After that, they all had a snack and took a midday nap, and then the children went out by themselves to play in the parks along the grassy river banks lined by pine trees.

In the old house it had been the rule that their father took his bath first, before anyone else. But after they moved to the new house in the suburbs, he told them to have their baths over and done with before he returned. So every day the children were fresh and clean by 5:30. Sometimes their mother would bring them when she went to meet their father on his way home from work.

Away in the distance, astride the river at its source, the mountain peaks bathed in the warm glow of the setting sun. The evening air around them would be pleasantly cool. Even the rush of the water sounded much less noisy and hurried than during the day. The lights in the windows would have just been turned on, and the houses flashing into view between the pine trees all looked very safe and secure behind their hedges. Far away, they would hear the clang of the railway crossing bell.

One evening, as they all went out together to meet him, the girl's brother and sister headed diagonally across the road, a little in front, and up on to the grassy bank.

"Don't go up there," her mother called. "Stay on the road. That's right."

Then she turned to the girl, who was walking beside her.

"You know," she said, "I often think about all of your futures. Of course, I can't say for sure what kind of husbands you and your sister will marry, or what sort of lives you'll lead, but don't think you're always going to be this happy, dear. We're almost too happy. Life isn't always like this."

The girl didn't know it then, but a time would come in her life when she would recall her mother's words over and over again. That evening, she assumed her mother referred to Grandma Hotta and her terrible misfortunes—it had already been some time since she'd last thought of her.

Several evenings later, a fireworks display was held at the beach. Their parents took them to watch it, and for the first time the children saw real fireworks shooting up high into the sky.

It was a few days after that when swarms of plump moth-like insects with dark brown wings came flying through the garden and along the rows of pine trees. According to her father, the swarms came in even greater numbers to the city—so many that they blotted out the sun. There was a long article about them in the newspaper: the insects were known as "one-stroke skippers."

The girl sent off two postcards to Grandma Hotta. The first one was about the fireworks display, and the second one about the one-stroke skippers. She began to feel a little bored now with the seaside and the river. Addressing the postcards, she found out that Grandma Hotta's given name was Tsuné.

Fall came, and the children had their father take them to the park with the tallest slide in Japan. It was their first visit since moving to their new house. In the summer, he'd told them, the slide would be burning hot, impossible to touch.

On November 3rd, a national holiday, crowds of people started gathering on the shore in the morning. They'd all heard about a naval parade with over a dozen ships. The ships were due to go by at around two o'clock, but just in case, the children urged their mother to take them there a good hour early.

The scheduled hour for the ships' arrival passed, and still nothing appeared on the horizon. In the meantime, the clear blue skies became sullen and gray. A mist seemed to have gathered out at sea. By now, quite a crowd had collected, and a row of stalls selling roasted chestnuts, paper balloons and other festive things had been set up, but with nothing else to entertain them except the heavy waves rolling in and crashing on the shore, the enthusiasm soon dampened. Some people started shivering in the cold sea spray.

It was three o'clock.

"When are the ships coming?" the girl's brother asked.

"Can't we go home?" her sister asked. "We can come back later."

"But what if we miss them?" the girl scolded her. "I'm not going with you." Bored, the children started to quarrel.

"There they are!" somebody shouted. "Now I can see them!"

The girl looked out to sea.

"Where?" she asked. "Where are they?"

"There," her mother pointed to the distance. "Way over to the left. See?" She lifted the girl's brother up in her arms.

All of them stood staring out to the left of the river mouth, where, far away, in the mist joining the low sky with the murky sea, they saw a slightly darker blur.

"*That*'s a warship?" The girl's sister turned back and looked up at her mother.

"Keep your eye on it," her mother said. "It's getting bigger." The blur did seem to be getting longer. But it was just a vague shape slowly extending to the right, not taking on the outline of a warship at all.

The dark gray blur, flat and long like a sash, had reached the midpoint of the bay. Then, suddenly, near the head of the line, far out to sea, a single black silhouette of a ship came a bit more sharply into view. From the shore rose a shout of admiration. But the next minute, like a ghost, it faded back into the gray.

The day had grown quite dark. A dull drone, like an airplane engine, could be heard in the distance. The gray line was still there, but now it stretched from one side of the bay to the other, so they could no longer tell if it was even moving. At one moment, the girl realized no ships were appearing on the left any more. And then it began to rain.

She didn't write O-ie-san about watching the naval parade, nor their visit to the park with the very tall slide. The truth was, her city days were fast fading from her memory. She was preoccupied with the new friends she'd made at her new school. She invited them to her house to play, and was invited to theirs.

Sometimes, back when they'd been living in the city, she would come home from school in the afternoon, and her mother would say, after giving her a snack: "It's *sekki* today." *Sekki* was the last day of the month, the day for settling accounts. That all of the houses in their neighborhood were especially busy with their own affairs meant that she shouldn't go over to her friends' homes, and they couldn't come over to hers.

But in her new neighborhood, nobody seemed to bother with *sekki*. A few of her friends came from families with shops in the city like hers, but most of their fathers worked in an office or a company, so it didn't matter if she visited on the last day of the month. As they played at being grown-ups, she learned new words like "department manager," "company director," "bonus," and "transfer."

At her new school, fathers didn't come on parents' day to observe classes. Only mothers did. She found two of them particularly amazing: one was a lady who wore Western clothes and a hat with a fluffy crimson feather; the other hummed along with the children during their singing class. The girl had never seen such eccentric mothers in her old school.

A year passed. Soon the girl no longer noticed anything

surprising about her new environment. Then, suddenly, yet another change came over her way of life—a change that didn't just affect her and her family, however. It was the beginning of outright war with China.

The army was starting its advance on enemy territory, winning victory after victory. The children were told by their teacher that they should study as hard as they could, so they wouldn't put their soldiers to shame. They should copy the example of the children of Japan's ally, Germany, who were not only robust and healthy, but obedient and industrious too. They were told the same thing again during the opening lecture of summer-school classes.

One evening, playing with sparklers in the garden, the children placed on the ground a spiral-shaped firecracker with something like a candle wick at one end. Holding a match up to this, the girl lit it carefully, and then jumped back. The firework started spitting out blue sparks, somersaulting madly about and bathing the garden in a dazzling white light.

The light turned yellow.

"It's changed color!" her sister cried.

Next it turned red. Her brother put his hands to his ears. The fiery husk leaped into the air, made a terrifically loud bang, and then lay still.

Her sister let her breath out, "That was my favorite."

Just then came a man's voice from the other side of the fence: "Are you the people playing with fireworks?"

"Yes," the girl answered, remembering the loud bang.

"Japan is at war!" the voice shouted, as if he'd been waiting to pounce on her reply. "What'll you do if Japan loses because you've wasted gunpowder on your games? Don't you dare play with fireworks ever again, do you hear? Children who do are not Japanese children! I'll be back to check."

The deep voice was replaced by the sound of wooden clogs on the road, retreating into the night.

The children were crestfallen. Even her brother—who had

been excitedly pointing into the box of fireworks and saying, "This one next!"—was silent.

"What's the matter?" Their mother came out to the edge of the veranda. The children went up to her and explained.

Their father, who was in the sitting-room, commented, "What a jerk!" and went back to reading his newspaper.

"Well, but . . . ," their mother said dubiously. "Are there any fireworks left?" she asked the children. "Or have you used them up?"

"We still have some," the girl replied.

"Well, let's put them away till the war's over. Mommy'll put them in a tin and store them very carefully."

The girl went to fetch the box of fireworks that she'd left on a rock in the garden. Only a few remained, but she could see two fat sticks and a spiral-shaped one her sister had said was her favorite kind. She felt very sad and disappointed as she handed the box over to her mother. The fireworks weren't the source of her sadness: even if she were encouraged to play with them, she knew she would never feel that same joy again.

That summer, the beach fireworks were canceled. When the fall term started, it was clear that the war would already affect the girl's life at school.

Once a week they had a lesson in national ethics: their teacher would lead a party of them to a nearby Shinto shrine and have them pray to the gods for victory in the war. And once a month, during composition class, they were all made to write letters of comfort and encouragement to soldiers at the front.

The girls set about avidly collecting foil—the silver paper, they were told, could be used to manufacture ammunition and military supplies. On the seventh of every month, in commemoration of the declaration of war on China, they would all bring their silver balls of foil in to school to hand them in. It wasn't only the size that counted: the balls had to be packed solid, or they weren't worth anything. The girls could never get enough foil from candy wrappers, so they also looked out for the silver linings of cigarette packs. She and her sister reminded their father over and over to bring home from the shop as many empty packs as he could, and to collect the clerks' too. But often he forgot, and on the night before the seventh, he would find his brand new packs torn open for their spoils and ransacked.

In the fall of that same year, the girl's class made a school trip to the city to view a Great Exhibition on Japan's Holy War. A large relief map showed the enemy territory, with the rising-sun flag sticking out of each place Japan occupied. They saw photographs of soldiers trudging through mud, followed by lines of horses, tanks, and cannon; more photographs taken in the thick of battle; and still more of the army marching in formation and entering a city that had capitulated at last. Grenades and bayonets, weapons of war, were laid out in neat rows for the children to see. Occupying the center of the room was a huge concrete bust of the enemy's supreme commander, his face a grotesque caricature and his head riddled with bullet holes.

A banner went up on the gatepost of a house in the neighborhood to mark a departure to the battlefront. Others soon followed. Every day on her way to school the girl would catch sight of yet another house that had given a family member to the war. Sometimes in the evenings, she heard cheers and shouts coming from two different places in the same neighborhood, celebrations for soldiers going off to fight.

One day at morning assembly her teacher appeared before them in military uniform, his head closely shaven. Her class walked with him all the way to the main train station, and saw him off to war.

In the spring two years later, the girl graduated from her grammar school and started going to girls' secondary school. Her new school was in the city near the family shop. By now the war was in full swing. She and her sister and her brother (who was in grammar school by this time) weren't collecting silver foil anymore. There was no more foil to be had.

The girl, who now wore a wristwatch, began commuting to school by bus and tram, but she still had to wear her primary-school uniform. Finally, in May, the secondary-school uniforms, sailor tops and skirts, were distributed. Though they seemed at first sight like the real thing, the proper navy blue serge, they were actually made of rayon, a cheap synthetic material with a brown tinge, which soon grew fuzzy and developed a nasty shine. Her mother taught her to place the skirt under her mattress every night with layers of newspaper between the sixteen pleats. Sharp in the morning, by midday the pleats would be gone.

All the students in the grades above her wore sailor suits made of proper navy blue wool. The girl felt so envious—of the deep blue of their material, of the way their blouses' collars and cuffs crisply folded back and their skirts' pleats opened and closed like a fan with each step. If only she'd been born a year earlier! Compared to theirs her version was miserable—and some girls in the next grade were her age by traditional count. If she had been born just one month earlier, in March, it would have been all right!

Again and again, the girl bemoaned her fate, weeping, to her parents. After a few weeks, some of her classmates came to school wearing uniforms made of the real material. They were hand-me-downs adjusted to fit, but they looked just like the ones the older girls wore. The girl couldn't help begging her parents to let her have a uniform like these.

Her father at last asked a tailor who was a friend of his whether he would make his daughter a uniform. The man said that he would. Her father had her drop by the family business one day after school, so that he could take her to the tailor to have her measurements taken.

The family had moved to the suburbs three years ago. The girl had been coming into the city to go to school, of course, and she'd also accompanied her mother sometimes on shopping trips. But she hadn't actually visited the family store, and she hadn't visited O-ie-san, either, not even once, since they had all gone to say goodbye.

Seeing her father busy with a customer, the girl told him she'd be over at Grandma Hotta's, and went back out to the street.

"Hey, wait." Her father came out after her. "I'm ready now. Let's go."

"But I want to visit Grandma Hotta."

"We don't have time."

She hurried to collect her satchel, which she'd left inside the store.

The girl could not take her eyes off the cloth that the tailor produced for her school uniform. She looked at it from far away, then peering at it closely, stroked its smooth edge. The more she looked at it, the more difficult it was to tear her eyes away.

"It is a fine piece of cloth," the tailor agreed. "And I'm afraid it's my last." As he occupied himself with taking the girl's measurements over her shabby uniform, he remarked: "I see what you mean. No wonder you hate to wear this."

When they left the tailor's, her father announced that he was taking her out to dinner. The two of them walked to a nearby traditional restaurant. To her surprise, however, when they went into one of the private rooms, somebody was already waiting there: Grandma Hotta.

"Sorry we're late," her father said to the old lady, after greeting her.

O-ie-san brushed this politely aside and turned to the girl, and gazed at her. "Oh, how you've grown. . . ." she said.

The girl found it very strange that her father hadn't said anything about inviting O-ie-san to dinner—and anyway, it had always been her mother who took care of the old lady. Her father hadn't objected, but she had never seen him talk to O-ie-san, let alone do anything kind for her.

But the girl knew better than to question him now.

The waitress placed a brocade scroll of gold and purple in front of her father. The girl wondered what it could be. He took hold of it without any signs of surprise.

"This place is still as nice as ever," O-ie-san remarked to the girl's father.

"What shall we order?" he said, unrolling the menu and studying it.

So O-ie-san must have come to this restaurant before, the girl realized. Quite a while ago, and more than once—when could that have been? Probably before the war began, maybe before she was old enough to go to school—perhaps even been before she was born.

When the dishes came to the table, the girl's father pressed O-ie-san to eat.

"Well then," the old lady said, bowing her head. "I will accompany you, if I may."

"Of course," he said.

"Of course!" echoed the little girl.

"What do you mean?" her father laughed at her. "*You*'re the one accompanying *us.*"

That day, the girl's father, who was fond of saké, didn't drink a drop. The three of them first talked together about how the girl had been since the family moved to the suburbs. Soon, however, she found herself silently listening to the two adults. The names of people she'd never heard of cropped up, and some of them, it seemed, weren't even living any more.

Dinner came to an end, and it was time to say goodbye. They let O-ie-san take the first taxi and waited for a second, but none ever came.

"It doesn't matter," her father said, beckoning to her as he stepped out of the restaurant. "We can walk. We'll go for a stroll."

It was an evening in May, and only a little past eight o'clock, but even so, the streets and shops were almost totally deserted.

"Everything's gotten so dark and gloomy, Father," the girl remarked, carrying her satchel, as she walked with him.

"Hasn't it. Are you surprised?"

"I didn't think it would be this gloomy."

Since the area was once a thriving entertainment district, its lack of excitement was stark. Neon signs were against the law these days, so nothing lit up the night sky in bright colors any more. Very few of the shop windows had lights on. The whole district looked about to fall asleep, as if it were making a futile effort to keep awake only because it was supposed to be a place people spent money and enjoyed themselves. The restaurant owners had all closed up for the night. And everybody out in the dark streets was walking at a strangely brisk pace—not hurrying to reach any destination, the girl realized, but only because the streets were so empty that nobody got in their way. The sight made the girl feel even sadder about all the changes that had taken place.

"We should have telephoned Mother before we left," the girl said, suddenly remembering.

"It's all right," her father replied. "Mother knows we're together. But listen. I don't want you to go telling anyone at home that I invited Grandma Hotta out to dinner today."

"Why not?"

"Just don't."

"Not even Mother?"

"Not even Mother."

"Well, was it a secret from me, as well, really?"

"Don't be silly."

"But you didn't tell me anything before we got there."

"You found out when we arrived. Now listen: today we went to Suéhiro restaurant and had steak, just the two of us. Understand?"

The girl nodded.

They walked along for a while, when she suddenly asked: "But why aren't I allowed to tell them anything about it at home?"

"You really don't understand, do you?" her father said, softly.

Many years later, the girl learned that O-ie-san's daughter had, in fact, killed herself. She had thrown herself into the sea, soon after finding out that Father was engaged to the woman who would become the girl's mother. O-ie-san, who had already lost her husband and all her possessions, was left quite alone in the world. But even though he was the cause of this final blow, O-ie-san loved the girl's father as if he were her own son.

By the time she heard the true story, the girl was nearly thirty years old. The person who told her couldn't say for sure if her mother knew of all that had happened. Of course, by that time, O-ie-san was long since dead. The girl's father, too, had passed away. Only her mother was still alive, but the girl never dared to ask her.

Walking through the deserted streets with her father, though, she still knew nothing.

"You see," her father explained to her. "I wanted to treat Grandma, just once, to something really nice, while she can still appreciate it. Everything is getting so scarce, now, with the war going on. Soon there won't be anything nice to eat. It doesn't matter for us. We'll be able to buy anything we want once Japan has won the war. But that's not the case for Grandma—that's why I thought I'd like to treat her to something special, now, while it's still possible. . . ."

That didn't explain why she should not tell her mother—after all, her mother had always lavished the old lady with kindness.

But all at once, the girl was strangely moved by her father's words.

"All right," she promised, as if she no longer cared about the reason. "I won't tell anybody! Not even Mother!"

Had she been moved by the intensity her father's words seemed to contain? No, more likely it was the intensity of her own feelings about "war."

The girl and her father walked on until they reached a bridge, where they stopped for a while. The river, once full of shimmering reflections from the shining neon night sky, now lay in complete darkness. Only the faint rippling of the water could be heard as the river flowing out to sea rose slowly with the incoming tide.

Toddler-Hunting (YŌJI-GARI, 1961)

HAYASHI AKIKO COULDN'T ABIDE LITTLE GIRLS between three and ten years old—she detested them more than any other kind of human being. If Akiko, like most women, had married and had babies, she might by now have a child just that age. And what, she often wondered, if she'd had a girl? What then?

She knew that men often said they hated children, only to turn into doting fathers once they had their own. But Akiko couldn't picture her own abhorrence ever yielding to maternal love, an emotion she scarcely possessed anyway. Foreign little girls, even at that age, were slightly more bearable, perhaps because their race was more glaring than their gender. If she'd married a foreigner, she might have been able to stand having a daughter of mixed blood, but if not, she was sure that she would have been a horribly cruel mother. She wouldn't have been satisfied just being cold and harsh to her daughter: her loathing would have required more extreme measures.

Akiko's dislike of little girls was of an entirely different order than her disdain for happy, attractive, conceited women her own age, or for young men throwing their weight around, or for smug, complacent old people. It was more like a phobia, the repulsion some people feel when confronted with small creatures like snakes or cats or frogs.

Akiko could not bear to remember that she herself had once been a little girl.

But in fact her childhood had been happier than other periods of her life. She couldn't recall a single hardship; she might have been the most fortunate child who ever lived, a cheerful thing when she was young. But beneath the sunny disposition, in the pit of her stomach, she'd been conscious of an inexplicable constriction. Something loathsome and repellent oppressed all her senses—it was as if she were trapped in a long, narrow tunnel; as if a sticky liquid seeped unseen out of her every pore—as if she were under a curse.

Once, in science class, they'd had a lesson about silkworms, and with a scalpel the teacher had sliced open a cocoon. Akiko took one look at the faintly squirming pupa—a filthy dark thing, slowly binding itself up in thread issuing from its own body—and knew she was seeing the embodiment of the feelings that afflicted her.

And then for some reason Akiko became convinced that other girls her age shared her strange inner discomfort. Grown-ups, however, did not feel this way, and neither did little boys and older girls.

And sure enough, once she got past ten, the queasiness left her. As if she had stepped out of a tunnel into the vast free universe finally she could breathe. It was at this time, however, that she started to feel nauseated by any girl still passing through that stage, and her repulsion grew stronger as the years went by.

The more typical a girl this age, the less Akiko could bear to be near her. The pallid complexion; the rubbery flesh; the bluish shadow at the nape of the neck left by the bobbed haircut; the unnaturally high, insipid way the girl would talk; even the cut and color of her clothes: Akiko saw in all this the filthy closeness she had glimpsed in the pupa. She could hardly bear to look at a little girl, still less touch one. Her horror remained undiminished to the present day.

But little boys, now—Akiko found little boys extremely appealing at that age. She didn't know exactly when her attraction for them first surfaced, but with every passing year she found their company more intoxicating. Lately, her encounters with little boys had been intensely pleasurable.

Sasaki had taken the express to Osaka on business. When Akiko saw him off at the train station, he'd handed her a package, a new shirt. He'd found out it was poorly finished when he got it home, he said. His local tailor had tried to fix it, but Sasaki wanted Akiko to exchange it for him. So she headed for the department store where he had bought it, in Nihombashi.

She ran her errand. It was nearly five o'clock when she left the store for the subway station, hurrying to get ahead of the evening rush. But her pace slowed as she passed a well-known store specializing in children's wear.

It was late in summer, still very hot: heavy afternoon sunlight flooded the pavement. But in the shady showcase window, autumn had already arrived. Pretty little shirts for boys were out on display, pinned up. The clothes leant in various directions, sticking out their sturdy elbows and gesturing with their arms.

One shirt almost seemed to be doing a headstand: its front with its little button-neck opening was folded so its square little chest puffed out. This was probably the only short-sleeved one, to judge by its lack of bulk, but the material looked heavy enough for autumn: it was probably a light woolen weave. Akiko was enchanted by the intensity of its broad red and blue horizontal stripes, and by the soft-looking, neatly folded collar in the same design.

Nothing in the window was tagged, so Akiko tried guessing its price. The shirt probably cost at least fifteen hundred yen. Things she liked tended to be expensive.

Her rapture made her an easy target. A clerk in a white short-sleeved shirt approached.

"For your son, Madam? How old is he?"

Ignoring the question, Akiko asked the price of the shirt.

"One thousand seven hundred yen."

"Just what I guessed!" Akiko said, feeling if anything rather pleased.

"Shall I get it out?" The clerk reached toward the glass panels at the back of the showcase.

"Oh, please don't," Akiko begged, hastily. "It's all right."

At that moment, they were interrupted. To Akiko's relief, the clerk was called to the telephone at back of the store: She knew that once she touched that adorably sweet shirt, she'd never be able to get out of the shop without it.

But before going off to take the call, the clerk quickly took out the shirt and pressed it into her hands: "It doesn't hurt to look."

Akiko stroked the garment tenderly—she could just see a little boy, about four years old, pulling on this cozy, lightweight shirt, his sunburned head popping up through the neck. When the time came, he would definitely want to take it off all by himself. Crossing his chubby arms over his chest, concentrating with all his might, he would just manage to grasp the shirttails. But how difficult to pull it up and extricate himself. Screwing up his face, twisting around and wiggling his little bottom, he would try his hardest. Akiko would glimpse his tight little belly, full to bursting with all the food he stuffed in at every meal. The shirt, though, was not going to come off, however hard he tried.

Drawn by the charm of little boys' clothes, and especially by the scenes to which they gave rise in her mind, Akiko had several times ended up buying something—a pair of reversible shorts with brick-colored cuffs; a deerstalker cap of white terry cloth with a tiny pale maroon check; a miniature pea jacket about a foot and a half high. When she'd purchased something, she would seek out a woman friend with a toddler to dress. Once she'd settled on her prey, she would set out to bestow her gift. It didn't matter that she normally never gave the woman a second thought—sometimes they'd even had a falling out—she would bewilder the recipient or make her cringe in embarrassment.

Indifferent about her own clothing, Akiko was obsessed with garments for little boys—so naturally her taste in these had become extremely refined. The people selected to receive her gifts would be dumbfounded. How could this woman, who wasn't a mother herself, find such wonderfully appropriate clothes? Some thought they could guess the motive behind these fits of generosity: unfulfilled maternal love.

Akiko bought the shirt and left the shop with a box under her arm. In no time at all, she had marked out the recipient of her next gift.

She'd heard that the opera troupe of which she'd once been a member was now performing *Madame Butterfly*, and that the son of one of her old colleagues was playing the part of Madame Butterfly's child. She trained her sights on this little boy.

When Akiko had quit the company, she'd had good reasons. Her prospects weren't improving: she was over thirty; she couldn't be a member of the chorus forever; and besides, a bout of tuberculosis had damaged her health. Rather than having quit, it might be more accurate to say that circumstances had forced her to fade away.

And yet, back when she had graduated from music college, her achievements had been impressive. She had given solo recitals, winning praise from a famous music critic. "Such a feel for the music," he had written in a review, "especially in the last piece, Mozart's 'Longing for Spring.'" The fact was that she'd been on the diva track, but as things turned out, she had landed in the chorus—a source of anguish for Akiko. Even now, she found it difficult to ignore the opera world—though all news of it brought her terrible fits of distress. She'd made no effort to stay in touch with her onetime colleagues.

But that evening—just as Madame Butterfly and Suzuki were singing their lines, *Is poverty upon us? This money is all we have!*—Akiko appeared backstage, astonishing the company.

"I heard Noguchi Masayo's son is performing," she remarked, but her business wasn't with these people. She'd timed her arrival to coincide with the end of the opera, when the child was onstage, and she didn't have to wait long before he appeared.

"I saw an article about it in the newspaper," Akiko said, when Masayo stepped into the dressing room, her little boy in tow. "How exciting! Your son onstage!" She leant down to look at the boy, who was hiding behind his mother.

Masayo had made her debut several years after Akiko, playing roles like Annina, the lady-in-waiting in *La Traviata*, and the gardener's daughter in *Le Nozze di Figaro*. She was a cut above the chorus: when she sang, her photograph appeared in the program. Today, however, she was there to look after her little boy.

"Is this the star himself? And only four years old! Is everything going well?"

"Oh yes. He's a gutsy little guy, really," Masayo replied. "And anyway, he doesn't have to do much. He seems to be managing pretty well."

"Oh, I'm not surprised. You can see it in his face!" Akiko said, her gaze lingering on the boy's soft, plump earlobes and his cheeks, tawny and smooth like little biscuits.

"Do you sing too?" the child inquired.

"Me?" Akiko was slightly taken aback. "No, Auntie doesn't. . . ."

"Yes, what *are* you doing now?" Masayo asked, as if sensing Akiko's discomfort.

What was she doing? Well . . . generally people who are asked such a thing aren't expected to give any impressive reply. Akiko was no exception to the rule. She decided to take the question as referring to how she was making ends meet.

"Oh, I manage with my Italian skills," she replied vaguely.

"Of course, I remember—there aren't many people who speak it as well as you. . . ."

Akiko's Italian was, in fact, splendid. She had shown a remarkable aptitude for the language, now much more than a vehicle for singing opera. In the chorus she'd never had a hope of making a living, and she'd been thrown back on her language skills to survive. She had earned extra money by translating articles for fashion magazines, and tutoring younger company members.

Nowadays, she worked part-time at a compressor factory: she was called in whenever the company had to correspond with Italian clients. The technical language had posed difficulties at first, since no Italian-Japanese dictionary was complete enough. She'd taken the words she couldn't decipher, with their English and German counterparts, to the Engineering Section to ask for help. This was where she'd gotten to know Sasaki, who usually dealt with her queries.

"You've got a good deal," he remarked when they first chatted at length, "not having to work nine to five." But the part-time pay was a pittance. It was impossible to meet expenses with her Italian alone, even with other odd jobs here and there. She'd found extra income as a dictation assistant to one of the translators working on a complete set of opera libretti. This job allowed her to indulge herself by buying little garments for little boys.

But preferring to steer Masayo away from these topics, she cheerfully pressed the parcel into her hands and said: "This is a present to celebrate his debut."

"Oh, my goodness! You didn't need to. . . ."

"That's all right—I wanted to," Akiko said, directing her last words to the boy.

"What is it? What is it?" he asked.

"I wonder now whether I shouldn't have brought a toy," Akiko said. "Won't you try it on?"

Masayo was still hesitant to accept, but Akiko, tearing off the wrapping paper, pulled out her gift.

"Oh, it's a lovely . . ." Masayo was getting more and more uncomfortable. Akiko, however, had already removed the boy's costume and was getting him into the shirt she had chosen.

"What do you think? Isn't it cute?" she asked.

"Oh, yes. And it's a perfect fit."

"What a lucky boy!" a girl who was packing up her costume nearby chimed in.

"Does the little lad have a name?" Akiko asked. "I remember seeing it in the papers, but I . . ."

"Darling, this lady wants to know your name. You can tell her yourself, can't you? And don't forget to say thank you."

"My name is Noguchi Shūichi. Thank you."

Akiko laughed. "Can you get take it off by yourself, Shūichi?"

The child nodded.

"Go on then, show me."

The boy in his comfy red-and-blue shirt shrugged petulantly: "I don't want to."

"You like it, don't you," Masayo said. "Even children know when something's extra special. Will you wear that home, Shūichi?"

The child looked up at his mother and nodded.

Akiko was thrilled: the shirt was a good fit and also a great success with the boy. But she couldn't resist one last shot at getting to watch him try to get himself out of it.

"It's still a little warm for this shirt, you know," she said. "You don't want to sweat, Shū. Let's take it off and have Mommy carry it home. We can wear it as much as we like when the weather gets cooler. What a big boy," she added, before he could object: "Shū can get undressed all by himself."

Akiko unbuttoned the neck of the shirt, and placed her hands on the chubby little arms sticking out of the short sleeves. She crossed his arms, one over the other, savoring their softness and perspiration, and made sure that each hand grasped the hem.

"Now lift your arms up over your head. Got it?"

Just as she'd imagined, the child started to twist and turn about, wiggling his bottom. Akiko backed off to get a better look, but to her chagrin, Masayo decided to lend him a hand. Catching the shirt from behind, she pulled it up, and slipped it off over his head in no time.

"Easy, isn't it?" Akiko said, crossing her own arms. "Like this, then up and over." The child nodded. He copied her, crossing his arms, bringing them up and letting them fall loosely over his bare belly.

"Perfect!" In an excess of joy, Akiko laughed out loud, showing off her soprano voice for the first time in years. "You little darling!"

"I thought you didn't like children, Miss Hayashi," remarked a member of the chorus, standing nearby.

Akiko knew perfectly well what she meant—and Masayo was probably thinking the same thing. Some years ago, when Akiko was still with the company, a woman (now on tour in Europe) had played Madame Butterfly with her own child on stage. Akiko was so blatantly repulsed by that child that it had become something of a scandal. The mother, who had joined the troupe at the same time as Akiko, was the star of the company, and her colleagues had concluded that her loathing sprang from jealousy. "She doesn't have to take it out on a four-year-old!" she'd heard them mutter.

Only Akiko knew the real reason: that the child was a girl.

But tonight Akiko passed it off as a change of heart. "The older you get," she replied, "the more you appreciate children."

On the way home from her transcription job, Akiko bought some things in the shops in front of the station and reached her apartment as dusk fell. Her last purchase, the block of ice, had almost completely soaked its newspaper wrappings, and her fingers were frozen numb. Struggling to hold her shopping, the evening paper, and a postcard from her mailbox, she could barely turn her key in the lock.

As she stepped inside her apartment, she felt something underfoot—a telegram had been pushed under her door, from

Sasaki. He'd been due to visit her place that night, following his morning return. The telegram had been dispatched from the Osaka central post office. He'd had to go on to Hiroshima, Sasaki said, so he'd be delayed two or three days. "In touch soon," the closing words ran.

The delivery time was stamped at 8:30 that morning—she must have just missed it on her way out. Strange, that that had been the requested delivery time. Sasaki had most likely been instructed to go on to Hiroshima by the Tokyo office, or by a superior who'd joined him on the trip. But however the change of plan had been announced, he was bound to have become aware of it some time yesterday between nine and five. Why had he delayed letting her know until 8:30 this morning?

Taking a second look, she saw that he had actually dispatched the telegram last night at 11:37, after which he would have taken the night train to Hiroshima, with an easy morning arrival. It had no doubt simply slipped his mind to send the telegram earlier. He must have been out on the town, and then wanted to avoid giving her a shock in the middle of the night. Akiko tossed the slip of paper aside. To think she had gone to the trouble of buying ice. "In touch soon"—what did he mean? "Forgive me," he should have said!

"Miss Hayashi!" It was her superintendent's voice: "Do you have a delivery from the liquor store?"

Akiko went downstairs where a delivery man was depositing three bottles of beer just inside the entrance. Hovering nearby was the superintendent, an old woman whose rimless eyeglasses gave her an officious air: "You got a telegram, didn't you?"

"Yes."

"Everything all right?"

"Fine," Akiko replied shortly, gathering up the bottles.

Back in her room, Akiko set about stabbing the ice block with a pick used to open milk bottles. Putting some of the ice shards in a glass, she topped them up with beer. She didn't usually drink, and she didn't particularly like the taste, but it was pleasantly chilly, and she downed two glasses one after the other. Remembering the potato chips she'd flung down on her way in, she reached for the bag and tore it open. But after one bite, she stopped. Her heart was racing—a rush of heat came over her. She had to lie down. She remembered the ice: she could wrap some in a towel for her forehead: that would make her feel better. But it was too much trouble to get up. She lay where she was, sprawled out on the floor.

When she opened her eyes, the room was dark. The luminous hands of the clock stood at a little past eight o'clock, and crickets were chirping outside. It was September, and while the days were still hot, there was a nip in the evening air. She had perspired and her clothes felt cold and clammy against her skin, now that it was no longer flushed with drink.

An unmarried woman past thirty losing her temper because a man two years her junior didn't keep his date; who got drunk on the beer she'd bought for him and that was far too strong for her; and who came to her senses in a black room—whoever heard of such a thing! After sneezing several times, Akiko forced a bitter smile.

She stood up, turned on the light, pulled a blanket out of the cupboard, and lay down again. A woman is supposed to weep at a time like this, she thought, not smile.

"It won't be a long drawn-out thing when we break up," Sasaki had once told her. "One day we'll have a fight, and that'll be that."

"Well—you chose the right person, didn't you!" she'd retorted, and was immediately angry at herself. Why did she have to be so disagreeable? This sourness of hers was precisely what made him say such things.

Had Sasaki been pointing out her danger in being such a willful woman? No, that interpretation was too romantic—he'd only meant that he was aware of how little she was committed to him, or, for that matter, to any aspect of her life.

"We both chose the right person," Sasaki had replied. "So we should try our best to get along."

Though they were single and still relatively young, the subject of a future together rarely came up for discussion. They didn't even try living together.

About the sort of marriage he'd want, Sasaki had any number of typical requirements. He would no doubt settle down late in life with a nice little wife able to meet them. Akiko didn't have these qualities, nor did she care to develop them. But she couldn't, on the other hand, tolerate fussy older men, and was bored by ones of high standing in business or society, who would in all likelihood be married anyway.

They understood these things about themselves, and about each other—and were aware of their mutual knowledge. For him, she was a stopgap companion. For her, he filled a superficial role as her partner. And the one thing that kept them together was their compatible sexual tastes.

Akiko remembered the first time she was distinctly attracted to Sasaki was when he'd told her about a night he spent helping a woman in labor. It had happened when he was still a student, right after the war.

"I was getting ready for bed," Sasaki had told her, "when my old landlady rushed into my room, all in a panic: 'The baby's coming! The baby's coming!' 'Well, don't you think you'd better lie down?' I asked. Her belly was out to here, you know. 'Don't be an idiot,' she said to me, very offended: 'You know I'm a widow.' It was the woman on the second floor who was having the baby. Her husband was a drunk of a journalist—he never came home, and he wasn't around that night, either. And the baby was already halfway born, so she couldn't be taken to the hospital—the whole second floor was in an uproar. The old lady told me to heat some water on the first floor, and take it up to them.

"I'd put the water on to boil," Sasaki continued, "when the old woman came to my room again. Now she made me go find a mid-wife. The first person they'd sent out hadn't returned. Well, finding a midwife in the middle of the night isn't easy, you know. I finally spotted an advertisement for one pasted to a telegraph pole, and raced over to the address, only to be told the woman had moved away five years back. By this time I was getting pretty fed up, I can tell you. But I had to do something for the poor woman, and I finally found another old woman. But by the time I brought her back, it was all over. Still, it's good to get the umbilical cord cut by someone who knows what they're doing.

"I headed back to my room, and there at my door was the old woman *again.* Now they needed someone to get rid of the after-birth water, she said. Well, I did what she told me, me and the guy who lived in the next room. She told us to throw it away on some farm patch, as far away as possible, but you weren't going to catch me carrying a tub of water like that any farther than I had to. Sloshing all over the place, scum splashing me right in the mouth. Anywhere will do, we thought—and sluiced it down a drain right there on the corner."

"Was it a boy or a girl?" Akiko had asked.

"The baby? A healthy little boy."

Sasaki's story had had the most unexpected effect on Akiko. Why had she felt so attracted to him? Because of some story about an escapade helping a woman in labor, someone he didn't even know? She couldn't figure it out—was it his freshness, his boyishness? No, it couldn't have been just that. What had drawn her had been the ruthless streak she detected beneath that innocent story of helping a woman in trouble. *That* had gotten to her. And her hunch had proven correct: later, she'd found out that Sasaki possessed just the predilections she liked.

From the way he said, "a healthy little boy," though, Sasaki appeared to also have a paternal streak: how did this fit in?

Akiko remembered the postcard in her mail from Noguchi Masayo. Reaching for it, she started reading: Masayo began with the customary seasonal greetings and some words about the joy at seeing her after so many years.

". . . Last night was closing night," she continued. "Shū-ichi normally wakes up early in the morning, but today he dozed past nine. He must be relieved now that the opera is over—it's funny to think of children feeling that way. He loves the shirt you gave him. He's always telling me he wants to wear it. We can't wait for this hot weather to cool down. . . ."

Akiko wasn't as annoyed as she'd expected. "*Shūichi normally wakes up early in the morning.* . . ." She enjoyed turning the words over in her mind. But, just as she never bought little garments with a particular child in mind, to arrange another encounter with Shûichi to see him wearing her gift was out of the question.

She wondered how Sasaki would react if she told him she wanted a baby. Most likely, he'd pick a fight, storm off, and never return.

Akiko's period was always regular—except for once, when she'd made Sasaki whip her so violently that she couldn't stand up for two days and it came two weeks late. But there was hardly a month when it didn't arrive on time, the bright red blood floating in the white porcelain bowl before being whirled away with the water. When she'd been younger, Akiko had been amazed by her body—by its strangeness. Every month, over and over, it made a little bed inside for a baby, unaware that none would be born, and then took it apart again. And it had seemed to her a grave matter that not one person on this earth was created yet out of her own blood.

But she would always find herself wondering how, after giving birth to the baby, she could get someone else to take care of it—and whether there wasn't some way she could reserve the right to only occasionally oversee its care. She began to greatly envy men, who could avoid parental tasks so easily. All this surely proved how poorly she was endowed with natural maternal urges.

And then, two or three years ago, there had been her bout of pulmonary TB. Her case had been serious, and though her recovery had been surprisingly rapid, she had been told by her doctors that she should never try to have a child—she would never survive. And by now, even had they told her she could have a baby, Akiko no longer wished for one. Aside from the question of how she would arrange it, her physical and emotional stamina had been quite worn down by the disease. And she was so impatient—the thought of being tied down by such a long commitment was insufferable. This, she thought, was probably what kept her in the relationship with Sasaki.

For all these reasons, she had become a woman for whom maternal love was a totally alien emotion—a woman even less able to think of bringing up children. Akiko now felt at ease knowing that having a baby was out of the question for her body—when this fact came to mind, she felt an emotion close to joy.

It was already nine o'clock. She needed to eat, but she stayed sprawled out on the floor. She had recovered her equanimity. The frustration she'd felt began to change into a different sort of excitement. Often, after surges of emotion, a strange fantasy world would descend and take her in its sway. She chose to stay on the floor in the hope of this happening, and already there were signs of it starting.

As the dream world spread out about her, Akiko would plunge herself into it, her pulse beating faster and faster and her skin all moist, and she would reach ecstasy, losing all self-control.

Two figures always appeared in this strange world: a little boy of seven or eight, and a man in his thirties. The details of their personalities and activities varied slightly each time, but the age gap remained constant, as did their relationship as father and child. Their faces were out of focus, but it was important for Akiko to be able to believe that the child, at least, was very very sweet.

The man would be thrashing the boy, and scolding him in so gentle a tone that it was harrowing. The beating would start out as the kind any father might give his son, but gradually it would reach a level of horrifying atrocity. At the very climax of the scene, however, the thought of the impossibility of such things actually happening in the real world would surface in her mind, and Akiko would return abruptly to herself. Her face would be flushed, but she'd know that she was back in reality.

—*You've been a very bad boy, the father starts. I'm going to have to teach you a lesson.*

A crash as the father whacks the boy across the face, almost knocking his head off. The child staggers under the blow, and then gets back on his feet straightaway, trying to bear the pain. But he is unable to resist touching his cheek furtively.

—*Hasn't Daddy warned you time and again not to do that? I suppose it takes more than one lesson to make you understand.*

The father issues an order to someone, and an alligator belt is placed in front of him.

—*Take off your clothes.*

The child does as he is told, and the father begins whipping his buttocks with the belt.

—*How about using our other instrument? The voice is a woman's. The belt is dropped and he picks up a cane.*

More punishment. With every lash of the cane, there are shrieks and agonized cries. The boy is sent sprawling forward, sometimes flat on his face, but he struggles to get up each time, ready to receive the next stroke, a course of action he carries out without being told.

—*Look. Look at the blood. The woman's voice again. There it is, the red fluid trickling down over the child's buttocks, over his thighs. The blood is smeared over the surface of his flesh by yet more thrashes of the cane.*

Another lash, and more blood spurts out from another spot: the two streams trickle down the boy's thigh, as if racing each other. The flow stops halfway down his leg—the blood has already dried.

The scene is, after all, taking place in the full heat of the summer sun.

—Hit me on my back, Daddy, the boy begs.

—I was leaving that till last. There's no hurry.

The father sets down the cane, and taking the boy over to a tin shack, grabs him by the shoulders and forces him against the scorching metal. The child tries to escape, wriggling around and desperately pushing himself away, but to no avail. He is pinned by the heavy body of his father, pressed flat against the searing hot tin. There follows the hiss of roasting flesh.

Pulled away from the wall, the child totters, dazed by pain, but the father hauls him up. Then the father turns the boy around so that the woman can get a good look at the raw flayed flesh on the boy's back, dark red stripes branded into his skin by ridges of hot metal.

There is more to come, but now the boy crumples to the ground when told to stand. More scolding. The father ties the child's hands together and hangs him from the branch of a tree.

—What else should I see to? the man asks.

—You haven't touched his stomach. The woman's voice again, insinuating. The child gets a few lashes on his belly, and suddenly, his stomach splits open. Intestines, an exquisitely colored rope of violet, slither out.

The woman gives the order: the man cuts the cord around the child's hands. The boy drops down from the branch to the ground. Now the man pulls the purple rope until it is tight, and jerks the child's body about as if trying to get a kite to rise into the air. The little body at the end of the purple rope is smashed against the corrugated tin shack repeatedly. Every twitch on the rope brings forth pitiful, horrifying screams.

Akiko saw Sasaki when she went into work at the factory. As they walked down the corridor, he asked: "Feeling better?"

"Doesn't it look like it?"

"You gave me a scare."

"Serves you right—sending telegrams in the middle of the night."

Akiko had spent the previous night with Sasaki, but she hadn't mentioned the telegram.

"But it was delivered the next morning, wasn't it?" he asked.

"Yes, that's what bothers me. What were you doing that you got to the post office so late?"

"Oh, I went to the night baseball game, and . . ."

They were in front of the Accounting Department—Akiko had come in to collect her wages. She disappeared behind the door, leaving him in mid-sentence.

Back at home, Akiko started to clear up. That morning in her hurry to get to work she had left her room just as it was. A few pearls had rolled here and there on the floor.

The night before, Akiko had wanted to add a little variety to their usual routine, and she'd looked round frantically for something to help. Finally, she hit upon a pearl necklace.

"They're not real," she'd said, handing them to him.

"Hmm. Hey, not bad." Sasaki dangled the necklace from his fingertips to tantalize her.

Then, gripping it tightly, he circled around her. Akiko was already so aroused she felt as if every nerve in her body was concentrated in the flesh of her back. When he brought the beads down on her skin, however, the sting and the smart cracking were over as soon as they started. The thread of the necklace snapped and with a dull patter pearls scattered across the floor. Sasaki and Akiko laughed, a little uncertainly.

Two strands of thread, a few pearls still clinging to them, hung from Sasaki's fist. Putting them in the lid of a mosquito-coil box, he began crawling around on his hands and knees, hunting up the others. Akiko watched him with growing vexation: "Just leave them, can't you!" Hearing her own tone of voice, she was disappointed to realize that the mood had left her.

But the next moment, Sasaki caught sight of a vinyl wash-rope hanging in a corner, the type with plastic knobs and metal hooks at either end. As he reached for it and started doubling it up, Akiko was already begging him to use the jagged metal hooks on her—they'd make a clicking sound.

It depended on what they used, but they both enjoyed the sound things made whipped against her skin. The more excited the noises made them, the more they would have to suppress their cries. That night, however, Sasaki had been especially resourceful with that length of rope, and Akiko's screams smothered out the thrashing sound. At first they hadn't realized somebody was knocking on the door.

"What's that?" Sasaki froze in mid-stroke, and by an unfortunate coincidence, a fire-engine siren started wailing through the neighborhood. Akiko's heart gave a leap.

Pulling a shirt over his shoulders, Sasaki put his face round the door.

"I was a little worried." It was the voice of the old superintendent with rimless eye-glasses. "I don't want them to have to carry you out of there dead."

The other tenants of the building were familiar with the goings-on in this room. That night, however, they must have gone a little too far.

"Sorry. We didn't mean to worry you."

"In any case, keep it down, won't you? Remember there are other people living in this building."

"Sorry. Really."

Listening to their voices, Akiko suddenly felt sick. For a moment, she thought she would vomit. She lay down, but already everything before her eyes was black.

"What's wrong?"

"The window . . . ," Akiko said, pushing back the curtain billowing out over her face like a sail in the breeze. "I'm very cold."

The shock thinking that a fire had started: had that sent the blood in her already racing heart into turmoil? A moment before, her body had been a mass of red-hot iron filings leaping around in space. Now she was aware of it cooling down rapidly. She didn't seem to have lost consciousness, though—she could hear Sasaki's voice, at some distance, and herself responding. Or at least, so she had thought. Afterwards, he told her that there had been thirty minutes or so when she'd had no reaction to anything he said, and her pulse had grown steadily weaker.

Akiko brought a hand to her brow and her fingers were stiff with cold. Sasaki released her other wrist, and stood up.

"This is bad." There was the sound of his belt being buckled.

"Where are you going?"

"To get a doctor."

"I'm all right," Akiko said, her eyes closed, and she was beginning to feel a little better. A damp hand-towel had been pushed down between her breasts, she realized, and she was covered by a blanket and quilt.

"I really thought they would have to carry a corpse out of here!" Sasaki said the next morning, recounting the scene to her. "I want you to prepare a testimonial."

"What for?"

"Just so there's something about our sexual habits maybe having certain consequences, and if I do end up killing you, to prove it was an accident."

"All right, don't worry. I'll do it."

It was three in the afternoon when Akiko set out for the public bath. Only seven or eight women were there: a new mother with her baby, some old women with nothing better to do, and young women bathing before going off to work in the evening.

For some reason, perhaps having to do with the design of the bathhouse, clients tended to cluster around the middle of the changing room, while in the bathroom itself they took up places along the outer wall—hardly anyone could be seen elsewhere. Akiko had purposely chosen a time when the place would be empty, and making sure to conceal her cuts with her wash-towel, she picked her way over the tiles, which were covered with dry grains of scrubbing detergent, to an area where there was nobody at all. Opposite the doors was a tub of water so hot that she didn't dare enter it for a while. It was here, in front of the faucet, that Akiko always took up her position. After splashing warm water over herself, she would immerse herself in another bath next to it, where cold water flowed in to modify the temperature.

As she soaked, Akiko would keep an eye on the changing-room, which she could keep in sight because the separating doors had been drawn back. Were there any cute little boys with their mothers? Wasn't even one going to come over and join her?

If she did see a little boy, darkly tanned from the knees down, playing by the edge of the bath with a little boat or a soapbox lid, Akiko couldn't resist giving him one of her special winks. The child never failed to respond. He would float his boat her way on a reconnaissance trip, and she would then make waves, sending it back on a storm, happy to go on playing in the bath forever— rescuing the boat if it sank, and starting up a conversation. Somewhere the mother would be calling her son, but he wouldn't go. Finally, the mother would come and pull him away. One arm gripped by his mother, the other clasping the boat to his chest, the little boy would turn to look back for an instant at Akiko. Then he would head off, his plump little feet smacking the wet tiles. Akiko would get out of the water, a melancholy smile on her lips.

Today, as a result of last night's wild abandon—closer in fact to an act of self-annihilation—Akiko longed more than ever for a little boy to appear. It was a strange attachment that she had to little boys, one which she preferred to keep Sasaki in the dark about.

The bathing area was filling up, but it didn't look as if Akiko's wish would be granted today. Wanting to escape before it got too crowded, she left after a quick scrub without getting into the tub at all.

Akiko walked home, keeping to the shady side of the street. Then, just as she entered an alley, turning the corner by the vegetable shop, she encountered a little boy.

He was about three years old, a toddler she hadn't seen before. Dressed in a grubby athletic jersey and putty-colored pants, he was standing by a stack of cartons and baskets, struggling with a chunk of watermelon.

Akiko got a little closer.

"Good?" she asked, as an opening gambit.

The child nodded without raising his eyes. Wanting a little more of a reaction, she tried again: "Is that good?"

"Really good." He gave a clear answer this time.

Pointing the little forefinger of his right hand like a pistol, he was using it to dig out the seeds. But his finger was poking around a little too eagerly, so all the seeds seemed to dive back deeper inside their holes. It was only a small chunk of watermelon, cut from a larger slice, but the chunk appeared quite unwieldy, his arms were so stubby and his fists so small.

The child was totally absorbed, concentrating on digging out one particular seed. Refusing to go on to others nearer the surface, he held the chunk in one hand, turning it this way and that, vainly trying with his other to hook out that one recalcitrant seed.

Akiko watched as he plunged his finger into the watermelon flesh. The juice spurted out, running down his fingers and all over his wrist, changing to the color of vinegar as it mixed with the sweat and grime collected there from the various escapades of his day.

His concentration momentarily broken, the boy looked up and took in Akiko's presence.

"Difficult, isn't it?" she said.

The child grunted.

Akiko knelt, and put her bath bag on her knee.

"Let Auntie see." She pulled his fingers out of the watermelon. She had wanted to keep the boy's hands in her own, holding the chunk with him, but he gave the fruit up to her, and wiped his dripping fingers on the seat of his pants.

The seed was lodged at the very end of a deep hole.

"Do you want Auntie to get it out?"

The child grunted again, rubbing his fist like a harmonica against his lips. Akiko poked with her little finger, and the seed slipped out.

"Good at it, aren't I?"

"You're a grown-up."

"Well then, leave it to me," Akiko laughed, keeping the fruit. She proceeded to pick out every seed in the chunk (now mauled to an oozing red mass), including the ones that poked their heads out of the loose wet pulp.

"Now," she said, holding it out to him, "Take a bite."

Using both hands, the child brought the watermelon to his mouth, and with each bite, juice gushed over his small soft-looking upper lip. While he worked on swallowing a mouthful, he would pull the chunk of fruit down with a sharp jerk, and hold it in front of him. Two bright red streaks were pointing up like flames from either side of his mouth.

"Hey," Akiko said, unable to resist. "Won't you give me some of that?"

In silence, the child offered up the watermelon. Akiko took hold of it with her hands over his, pulling the boy up to her. She sank her teeth into the fruit, and the mouthful of watermelon was so pulpy and warm, it was like biting into live flesh.

"Good?" the child asked.

Akiko nodded gravely, squeezing as much flavor as she could out of the mouthful of fruit, savoring the tang of the child's sweat, the grime from his fingers, even his saliva, before letting it slide slowly down her throat.

Little boys inhabited such an infinitely wholesome world—Akiko always had the impression that it restored and purified her. Its simplicity was so all-encompassing that anything out of the ordinary about her could pass without notice there. Little boys went along with her in her games—sometimes they almost seemed to egg her on.

Akiko realized that she was still holding the watermelon and the boy's hands up close to her.

"Thank you," she said, letting them go. "That was delicious."

The child stared intently at the watermelon, and before she knew it, he had given it back.

"You have it," he said. "I don't want it anymore."

He probably no longer wanted to eat it now that somebody else's mouth had touched it. He ran off, wiping his fingers on the seat of his trousers. A little way down the street he stopped, turned, and looked back at Akiko, who stood rooted to the spot, not knowing what to do with the unexpected gift in her hands.

Snow (YUKI, 1962)

AT THE END OF THE YEAR, HAYAKO'S MOTHER became ill and suddenly died. Their New Year's vacation had to be postponed, and by the time they decided to set out again it was already late January.

Kisaki told Hayako that traveling would actually be better this way, since there'd be fewer crowds. "Let's go," he said to her. "The trip will do us good, now that all that business is over."

Her mother had lived in Osaka, in Hayako's brother's house. She had moved there along with him and his wife at the time of his company transfer. Perhaps once a year, Hayako would visit them, and usually returned to Tokyo after just four or five days. She'd last been there in the fall. When her mother asked about her next visit, she'd replied, "Oh, I'll come again in the summer," though she suspected she might not make it that soon.

The first telegram informing her that her mother was critically ill had arrived in early December: Hayako had dropped everything and got the first train to Osaka. Her mother had heart disease, she was told, and had had an attack; the doctor said they should expect the worst. But it didn't look to her as if her mother would suffer another attack soon. She spent a few days at her mother's bedside, and then, considering it safe to leave, returned to Tokyo.

Within ten days, however, she received a second telegram

with the same message. Again Hayako went to Osaka, and learned that the night before her mother had had another even more serious heart attack. She had lost all appetite, and mostly lay in a state of drowsiness. But at times she was quite alert, and able to chat with her as if nothing was wrong. The day of Hayako's departure, after about a week's stay, her mother said to her: "Why not get your hair done before you leave? The place Sakiko goes to does a good job." Hayako went to her sister-in-law's salon, and returned to Tokyo certain that her mother would last out the year.

It was a relief to be able to report this to Kisaki, but this time Hayako felt guilty too. "The family is probably overreacting," she said. "I'll telephone next time before going all that way."

"You should go," Kisaki replied. "Don't worry about me. Take all the time you want to look after her. It'll probably be your last chance."

Hayako smiled apologetically. It was her adoptive mother who was dying, a woman Kisaki had, in fact, never met. She found it amusing to see him behaving just like the solicitous husband and son-in-law, even though, legally speaking, he didn't have the right to care one way or the other. So, she thought, perhaps it doesn't matter to a man.

Hayako would always be sent into a panic by her mother's letters—the smallest phrases would make her think: "So she's found out about Kisaki!" Even the last two trips home, Hayako—gazing at her mother's eyelids as she slept, or at her mouth drooped open for a spoonful of food—had been preoccupied: did her mother really still know nothing about him?

Hayako had stayed at home after graduating from school, merely taking a few lessons in flower arranging and the tea ceremony. When her brother married, however, and brought his young wife home to live with them, Hayako decided to take a job in her father's law firm. The company occupied a single room in an old building in Kanda, heated in winter by a kerosene stove. It was staffed by three lawyers, a middle-aged typist who had graduated long ago from M— University's law department, and a younger clerical assistant; the assistants never stayed very long, perhaps because it was hardly the workplace to appeal to a girl with any ambition. Hayako's father gave her the job partly because of his difficulty finding anybody else to take it.

It was at this office that she had met Kisaki, who came by from time to time. He was her age, and had only just joined his company, a firm that manufactured steel. He and Hayako's father shared the same alma mater, and that year both were on the alumni association board, which was why the two men had to meet regularly. Kisaki usually came by at lunchtime, probably the only time he wasn't always busy. He never stayed very long, and he always kept an eye on the clock. Even so, he and Hayako started talking, and eventually they started going out together.

By the time her father died, Hayako had no desire to return to her former life. The job gave her an excuse to spend time away from home, and money to spend on dates with Kisaki. When she asked the new boss of the office, a former colleague and friend of her father, if she could stay on, he had let her. She'd continued to work there until very recently.

The only one in her family she'd told about Kisaki was her brother, Toshio. She had told him four years ago, just before the move, when she realized, seeing him arranging an exchange of houses with a colleague being transferred from his company's Osaka branch, that he intended to take the whole family with him. At first she said simply that she didn't want to leave Tokyo; she would rent a room.

"Oh, all right," he said, immediately. "Well, that's understandable—you have a job. All right. I'll talk to Mother about it."

Her mother, however, had been much more difficult to convince. She was impatient to see Hayako married. If only she'd known Father was going to die so early, she said, she would have insisted he hurry and settle the matter of Hayako's husband. Father always said he would take care of it; that was why she hadn't bothered. Why couldn't Hayako give up her job? she asked. It was out of the question to leave her behind, alone in Tokyo, when she was so overdue for marriage.

"She won't be persuaded," Toshio had said, reporting her objections to Hayako. "I think you'd better come with us." Seeing this sudden change of attitude, Hayako felt she had to tell him the truth: the real reason she wanted to stay was Kisaki.

"Well, if you care so much about him, why don't you get married?" her brother asked, astonished.

"I know it must seem strange," Hayako admitted. "But that's the situation. . . ."

The "situation" was mostly Hayako's making. There was nothing, in fact, to prevent them becoming husband and wife. It was just that, whenever the topic of marriage came up, Hayako got terribly uncomfortable. She could not bear to consider it. Since she seemed to have so many misgivings and was so evasive, to Kisaki himself rarely mentioned it. This silence, however, would start to prey on Hayako's mind, and if it continued too long, she would try, very timidly, to broach the topic. But no sooner had she done so than she would feel compelled to shut it out altogether again, and concentrate instead on the happiness they shared as things were.

Something was blocking her, that much her brother understood. Well, the least he could do, given the circumstances, he said, was help her to be as happy as possible. Yes, he remonstrated with their mother, Hayako was single, but she was earning her own living; she was independent; why shouldn't she stay in Tokyo? In the end, their mother had agreed.

Hayako dreaded her mother finding out that she was living with Kisaki. Not only from fear of her disapproval or the regret of deceiving her at the time of the move, but also because she couldn't bear to witness her mother heap accusations upon herself when she realized that nothing but doubts and vacillation had kept her daughter from marrying.

But surely her mother must know something about her relationship with Kisaki. After moving to Osaka, she hardly ever brought up the subject of marriage, which before had so much concerned her. And her mother had never suggested paying her a visit in Tokyo. Toshio must have told her. Once when he came on a business trip to Tokyo, Toshio had met Kisaki. Waiting till Kisaki was out of earshot, he had said to her: "I'm sure Mother wouldn't mind. Why don't you just get married now?"

Yes, her mother probably hadn't said anything because she was taking a tolerant view of the situation, having been assured by her son about Kisaki, and told that Hayako still needed time. Toshio had told Hayako that he hadn't breathed a word, but surely, she thought with some gratitude, there was room to doubt him.

For a while, no further news came from Osaka. The 30th of December arrived. One more day, Hayako hoped as she went to bed, and Mother really will live into the New Year.

That night, Hayako had a dream about her mother.

In the dream, she was trying to wake up from a deep sleep. "Hayako!" she heard her mother calling: "Get up, Hayako!" But she felt herself drifting off again into a warm, comfortable, pleasurable world. "Hurry, or you'll be late!" she heard, and the door to her room quickly slid open. Hayako peered through her eyelashes over her covers, and saw her mother, looking extraordinarily young in the gloom. The next instant, her mother rushed straight toward her, as if to attack her. Hayako's first impulse was to flinch, as she used to as a child. But instead she defiantly pulled the bedclothes over her head. She was not a child anymore, she told herself; she was a full-grown woman. When there was no reaction, however, she pushed the covers away. Her mother was still there, hovering by her pillow.

"So that's the kind of daughter you are," her mother said, in a low voice. "You're not going to get up. You don't even care that I'm about to die!" She turned to leave.

"Don't go!" Hayako cried, trying to move. "Please! I'll get up!" But her mother was already out in the corridor, framed in the space between the sliding doors. She turned and looked back at Hayako, with the most tender smile. She nodded twice, and faded away.

When Hayako realized that she really was sitting up in bed in the darkness, her blood ran cold. Had she just been dreaming, sitting in that position? That was impossible. Her mother's face, nodding gently and smiling, had been there in the room. The vision had not been a figment of her imagination. Her mother had been there, before her eyes.

Kisaki turned over in bed. "Go back to sleep," he muttered, sleepily.

Hayako pulled herself together. She groped around her pillow, found the switch to the lamp, and turned it on. In the strange glare, she saw that it was just past three o'clock. She turned off the light and eased her cold shoulders under the covers. But it was impossible to go back to sleep.

Before dawn, there was a pounding at the entrance of their building, and a voice announced that a telegram had come for one of the tenants. Hayako prepared herself for the inevitable. She heard the sound of the front door opening, some voices, and then a slam. Footsteps came up the stairs, and along the corridor. They stopped outside their door. A knock, as she had feared.

"It's for you."

"Just a minute!" Switching on the light, she started struggling with the tangle of clothes she'd slipped off that night.

"That's all right, I'll push it under," the voice said. A piece of white paper came rustling under the door.

Hayako opened it up. The message consisted of only two words: MOTHER DEAD.

Kisaki held the note up to his eyes with both hands, squinting in the brightness of the lamp, still lying in bed.

"I see. So she was near the end, after all," he said, after a pause, putting the telegram down. "What time is it?" He twisted his head and looked at the clock.

Less than two hours had passed since the dream. All that time she had struggled alone to control her fear and anxiety. She had once been told that in order to prevent a nightmare from coming true, you have to tell someone about it, but she had been terrified that saying anything about this dream might have the opposite effect, so she'd resisted her first impulse to wake Kisaki up. Waiting for daylight, unable to tear her thoughts from her mother, determined to telephone first thing, she had wept anxious tears. But with the telegram in her hands, the news hardly seemed to affect her at all.

Hayako lit the gas heater. The line of points burst into flame with a bang that seemed terribly loud in the silence of the building. She adjusted it, and tried to speak about practical matters.

"It's New Year's Eve. The trains will be packed."

Despite her fears, Hayako arrived in Osaka rather early that afternoon. At Tokyo station in the early morning, when he had seen the platforms crowded with passengers, Kisaki had told her to board the first rapid train. He knew she could never get a reserved ticket, but she should board anyway, explain to the conductor that she had to get to Osaka for an emergency, and ask for the seat of a passenger who had canceled his reservation. She could travel first-class if necessary. But Hayako had hesitated: what if there were no cancellations? Well, he said, urging her on board, she would just have to ask to transfer at the next stop to a regular express. In the end, she had found herself looking out at him through the thick stormproof glass of the train window.

Kisaki's strategy had been a good one. Hayako had to stand between cars for a while, but when the train left Atami, the conductor came, picked up her suitcase, and told her to follow him. He had assigned her a seat. It was in first class, but she could keep it for the entire trip.

When Hayako reached her brother's house, she found everything remarkably quiet. The commotion that follows a death had subsided, and there were still a few hours to go before the wake. The smell of incense hung in the air.

"Ah, here you are."

"Pity you couldn't be with her at the end."

"Well, come in and . . ."

Hardly acknowledging their greetings, Hayako hurried into her mother's room. When she slid open the door, she saw several people sitting inside: here too, she faced a barrage of greetings. But before she did anything else, Hayako went to look at her mother's face.

Laid out on a pure white bed, covered in a white sheet, her mother gave the impression of being very cold. Sticks of incense had been placed by her pillow. Hayako knelt down by the bed. Her sister-in-law came and knelt on the other side.

"She died very peacefully," her sister-in-law said. "She just slipped away." She touched the white cloth draped over the body.

In the train, Hayako had kept trying to picture what her dead mother would look like. This would have been her sixty-first year. She had never been very robust, but even bedridden in her final illness, she had been quite beautiful and never looked her age. Her hair was still almost totally black; she hadn't needed dentures; and her face was hardly wrinkled. Hayako was sure that her face in death would be just as beautiful. But as for whether it would be peaceful, Hayako couldn't help having her doubts.

Hayako drew back the sheet. Just as she'd thought, her mother's face was beautiful. Her final illness had left no marks of suffering. Yet there was no peace in it. Perfect and unblemished, that was all. How different this dead face was from the image of her living mother in Hayako's mind's eye. The lips, the line of her nose, everything belonged to the mother whom Hayako had known and loved. And yet, at the same time, she realized, they were all utterly alien. Her mother was gone from her forever, it was clear.

"Mother," she murmured, laying a hand on the edge of the cover. "Thank you for looking after me for so long." A sob rose in her throat.

"Oh, don't!" shrieked her sister-in-law.

Everybody leapt to their feet. Hayako herself recoiled. A stream of bright red blood spurted out of the corpse's nose, running down the sides of the mouth onto the neck, and soaking the white cotton sheet.

The elderly housekeeper who had looked after Hayako's mother during her illness came into the room.

"Don't be alarmed," she said. She turned to Hayako. "You were your mother's only daughter, weren't you? But you live so far away. She must have been longing to see you when she died. They say dead people do this as a sign when the ones they most wanted to see come and pay their last respects. This is the third time I've seen it happen now."

The woman took some lint and a bottle of alcohol from a cupboard and started to wipe up the blood, which spread out over the white cotton wads in red blotches, looking frighteningly fresh and alive. Hayako stared in confusion at the bright red stains.

The weather had been fine earlier in the day, with the promise of a lovely Saturday afternoon. But not long after the train left Tokyo Station, the skies started to cloud over. For a while, a few patches of blue remained in the distance, but little by little they vanished altogether from view behind low swathes of dark gray snow clouds.

"It'll be warm in Itô. The weather there will be nice," Kisaki said, from his seat opposite Hayako. He had noticed her looking again and again out the window at the gathering snow clouds.

Hayako resolved not to look out at all. "If it's too warm, I might refuse to come back," she answered, trying to match his mood. "Then what'll you do?"

"I'll leave you there."

"And go home?"

"Yes."

"You won't mind?"

"No. I'll bring this with me," Kisaki joked, patting his jacket over his wallet. Hayako laughed, but she couldn't help stealing another glance out the window.

Hayako was worried that she might get an attack of her usual ailment. It would start with a twinge in her right temple. The twinge always let her know when snow was about to fall. What a relief that the past few winters had been relatively mild! But she knew only too well that only one year had seen no snow at all. And she had already suffered one bout of her illness this winter.

Hayako's well-being was usually unaffected by the weather. She rarely felt queasy during the early spring or the rainy season. On summer days of record-breaking heat, she was fine, surprised at other people's discomfort. On cold winter mornings, she would forget to close the windows after cleaning the house, and sit absorbed in her newspaper. But she could only stand dry cold weather. As soon as it grew damp and snow clouds appeared, Hayako's spirits would flag.

The twinge in her right temple at first occurred every half hour, spreading down her cheek to die out after a few seconds. Inevitably this would be followed by snow, even if only a flurry. At this, the twinge would be protracted into a sharp ache that occurred every few minutes: it felt as if a thick rod of ice were being pushed from the center of her forehead right through her temple. At each renewed attack, she had to hold her breath, using every ounce of strength to endure it.

When the headaches let up, they didn't take long to abate completely. There would be a sudden easing off, both in frequency and intensity, and then they would disappear—but not until at least two days after all traces of the snow had melted away.

Hayako's ailment seemed to be a kind of conditioned reflex to snow. Since her childhood, she had viewed snow with fear and loathing, and even now, the incident that had brought this all on remained a painful memory.

One morning, when she had been quite small, too young even for nursery school, the maid had come into her room to wake her, telling her that there had been a snowfall. When the light was switched on, the shutters were still drawn, but Hayako, normally a lazybones, leapt straight out of bed. She slipped through the hands of the maid, who warned her she would catch cold, out into the corridor. The sight of the snow lying against the glass doors took her breath away.

The length of garden was covered with white hills and hollows, and the snow lay in neat ridges on the tiles atop the garden wall, and even on the finest branches of the trees. It was still falling, whirling and hurrying down, impatient to join the strange, white world being created on the ground. Perhaps no snow had fallen during the few winters that she had known, or perhaps she had not been old enough to feel such an emotion up till then—but Hayako was dazzled by the fantastic scene.

"So much snow!" she cried. "So pretty! Lovely, lovely snow!"

"Who's that?" she heard her mother say from a room two doors away.

"Me!" Hayako shouted at the top of her voice. She heard the door open, and turned to greet her mother, as she came down the corridor. She gasped when she saw her mother's stern expression. By now the maid had caught her, and was trying to dress her where she stood. That must be why mother was angry, Hayako thought, trying to retreat to her room. The scolding that followed, however, was for something else entirely.

"How dare you!" her mother said. "'Pretty, lovely snow' indeed!" She grabbed Hayako's head, and yanked up her chin. "I'll make sure you're never able to say that again!" Hayako was now in tears, trying to squirm free of her grasp, and sobbing, "I'm sorry, I'm sorry!" She had no idea of what she had done wrong. Her mother, pinching the sides of her daughter's mouth, pressed her lips together, very hard. "You still don't understand, do you?" she demanded, trapping Hayako's head under her arm. She pulled open the glass door and flung Hayako into the deep snow beyond the veranda.

"You said you like snow! Well you can stay there," she said, standing over Hayako, gasping for breath. "I forbid you to come back inside!" She went back in and closed the door.

Her father had poked his head out between the doors to his room. Only when her mother swept by and went back inside her room did he emerge.

"Leave her!" her mother ordered. "I put her there because she likes it so much!"

Opening the glass doors to the garden, her father crouched down and beckoned to her. Hayako retreated, shaking her head. She couldn't go back inside; her mother wouldn't allow it.

"It's all right," her father said softly, reaching out for her shoulder. He put a hand under her arm and lifted her out of the snow and into his arms.

"I'm sorry," said the maid. "I'm the one who mentioned snow. Was it wrong?"

Hayako's father was silent. He glanced at Hayako's cold wet feet. "Get a towel," he said. Holding Hayako in his arms, he stepped into her still-illuminated room.

"It's naughty. You mustn't talk about the snow," he chided, as he waited for the maid.

Hayako burst into another flood of tears. "I didn't know I shouldn't talk about it—I didn't," she wanted to plead. "I only did so because I didn't know." But she was too choked for words to come out, which only increased her despair.

She had been so young that the question of why she should not say "snow" did not occur to her. It was the unfairness of the punishment that made her so distraught. Child that she was, she had only needed one cruel scolding like that to ingrain the thought: she must never speak of the snow. Simply mentioning it would merit punishment.

Now the beautiful snow really did seem harmful. She should not celebrate its coming—it should be shunned. Hayako gazed at the tiny flakes falling out of the sky, and imagined that they were the incarnation of some demonic power.

After that, Hayako couldn't remember letting the word "snow" cross her lips. During social occasions, whenever she had to comment on the weather, she would avoid direct mention of snow. "It's started, hasn't it," she would say, or "When this . . . melts, the roads will be awful." Often she would stammer her way to the end of the sentence.

The worst episode of her phobia had occurred while she was still living with her family in Tokyo: Kisaki had suggested one day that they get married since it would soon be his turn to be transferred. The town he mentioned was M— City, in a very cold mountainous part of the country, where his company had a factory.

"But all winter, it'll be—" Hayako started, then found herself unable to finish. Her lips began to quiver, and the trembling became more severe, and finally she was gasping for breath. The mystified expression on Kisaki's face only fed her panic. She covered her mouth with a handkerchief. "I'd die if it got really deep," she managed to say, regaining some composure.

Hayako never recovered from her dread of snow—she still hated any mention of it. And when she did finally learn why her mother punished her that day, her reaction only grew worse. Eventually, headaches, the very malady that had always plagued her mother, made their appearance. Though they shared no blood, this mother and daughter in illness, at least, were related.

But Hayako had never imagined that she might have to live in the snow country.

From morning to night, snow would be falling, for months on end. She would suffer from her headaches continually—the pain, the insomnia, the lack of appetite, the depression. . . . Her body would be consumed. She would die. Either that, or she would lose her mind.

"Are you that affected by the cold?" Kisaki had inquired.

She would have to tell him. But what would happen then? She was overwhelmed by insecurity. No, she couldn't tell him yet. And even as she wondered, she felt the snow's pitiless embrace tighten around her.

The train left Yokohama Station. Fresh air had filtered into the carriage while the train was standing: the windows were clear of all condensation, as if wiped clean. The sky outside seemed more threatening, with baleful icy-looking snow clouds jostling up against one another.

"Are you all right?" Kisaki asked, pointing a finger at his temple.

"Fine," she replied. "P-p-perhaps there won't be any after all."

"You don't think so?" Kisaki looked out at the sky. "Still, I think you'd better avoid this." He knocked the window with the back of his hand, meaning that her head shouldn't be so near it. "Let's change places." He rose from his seat.

Her seat was by the window, it was true, and she would feel the cold, but that wasn't the cause of her malady. And anyway, once the headaches started, precautions were useless.

"It's all right," she said, looking up at him. "Stay where you are."

But the passengers next to them, two older men sitting opposite each other who looked like company colleagues, paused in mid-conversation and shifted their knees, covered with bulky overcoats, as if waiting for her. Hayako squeezed her way around to Kisaki's vacated seat.

Kisaki sat down and lit a cigarette. "What are you laughing about?" he asked her, calmly exhaling smoke.

Hayako did not reply, but simply looked at him in even

greater amusement. She didn't know why it was, but whenever Kisaki took care of her or showed concern for her well-being, he always struck her as very much the little boy.

Six years ago, the talk of his transfer at his company had been dropped. But it was only a question of time, he warned. Every employee had to do a stint at the factory before being promoted to management, and for at least three years. It didn't look as if he would consider getting out of the transfer, still less quit his job.

But, Kisaki had urged her, that did not mean they shouldn't get married, did it? "You can spend the winters in Osaka, with your family," he said. "I'll let you go. I promise."

Again, Hayako had been struck by Kisaki's boyishness. Full-grown a moment before, the disciplined company man was suddenly nowhere to be seen. She knew he was trying his best to show her how considerate and devoted he could be. But to her, his words were empty promises: what faith could she put in them? He was a child, a naive, cruel boy. If she went ahead and married him, she was sure it would not be long before his boyish face turned away from a wife who caused him so much trouble. She longed so much to keep him, but the thought of marriage made her back away in fear. Nothing else in her life had proved reliable: why should she hope for things to be different now? The snow had placed its mark on her. The only existence she could have was like the snow's, forever in danger of melting away.

Long before the snow incident, Hayako had been timid and apprehensive. Ever since she'd been quite small, too small to comprehend how she was treated, she had been indecisive and lacking in confidence.

As a toddler, whenever somebody asked her how old she was, she would stick out the appropriate number of fingers. Adults who asked would always be disconcerted. "Are you really that old already?" they would say. "You're so little!" she would sometimes be told, in obvious astonishment.

It did not take Hayako long to suspect that she must be very small for her age. This was confirmed when, at six, she went to kindergarten and saw that she was indeed much smaller than anybody else. She also learned she was inferior in other ways.

"I went to talk to Teacher today," her mother announced, a few days into the summer holidays. "She says the class is far beyond you."

Hayako had sensed she wasn't as deft as the others, but she still enjoyed her friends.

"Teacher says she can't let you stay in that class. Next term, you're going down to the one below. That's what they call 'failing,' Hayako. Remember that: it's nothing to be proud of. You understand why you're going down a grade, don't you? You can't keep up. Mommy can't stand lazy good-for-nothing children like you!"

Hayako did not feel it was so very bad. What if she did go one grade lower? It would still be kindergarten.

"Next term you must try your best, at games and origami, too. Understand? And I'll be asking Teacher if you're working hard. If you fail any more, Mommy won't let you go to kindergarten at all."

So what? Hayako told herself. She wouldn't care.

But her mother's words made it clear that it was not just her body that was undeveloped compared to the other children, but something about her very being.

Autumn came, and Hayako went back to kindergarten. Since she had dropped down a class, she assumed she would be there for a whole year. The next spring, however, she found herself going to school. She seemed to manage the first year well enough. But in the second year things started to go wrong again: she could not manage the tests. She knew the answers to a few of the questions; but the spaces provided to write on the test sheets were much smaller than the year before. Try as she might, she just could not make her characters fit into the cramped little boxes.

She drew in her chair, pushed it back, and picked up her pencil. Turning it upside down, she stared at its end. She counted its ridges: it was a hexagon. Pressing the hexagon to her cheek, she bent over the exam sheet and sighed. She still hadn't written anything but her name. Failing would mean another scolding at home: she should try to write something. She turned the pencil the right way again. Carefully aiming the sharp point at an easy question, she wrote two or three characters. Then, she realized that she was about to run out of space. Her upper body suddenly felt paralyzed, hot, and in pain. But she knew the answer, she thought, rubbing resentfully at the space on the exam sheet, smudging the print. Before she knew it, the lines were fuzzy, her fingers smeared with lead, and the few characters she had managed to write covered with blotches. What a mess she'd produced—a reflection of her state of mind. This scenario went on until the end of the exam.

Hayako never knew if she had been expelled, but before the start of summer vacation, she was taken away from school. A young man started coming to the house every afternoon to tutor her. The following spring, she went to another school, where she was put in the second grade for the second time. Her classmates were eight and nine years old, and she was ten. She was still the third smallest in the class.

Hayako was well aware that her parents worried terribly about her school performance, and that all in all it was not very good. But she was sure she wasn't incapable or lazy, and it exasperated her that she couldn't keep up with the others.

Little by little, Hayako came to suspect that there was something unnatural about the gap between her age and her development. The older she grew, the more her suspicions grew, until they became a deep anxiety gnawing away at her very being.

Everything became clear later when she learned that she was not her mother's natural daughter. This was a shock, of course, but what really jolted her was her suspicions being proven true.

Hayako managed to pass her classes and graduate, and she

went on to girls' school. It was during her second year there when one winter night, as she went to bed after staying up late to study for an exam, she heard her father return home. A little while later, she heard raised voices from the living room. Suddenly, the voices became very loud. She heard a door fling open, a scuffle, and then from the corridor, her mother screamed, "Don't!"

"This is only to satisfy you!" Her father's angry voice came rushing headlong down the corridor, and he slid open her door.

"Hayako!" he said, his voice calm but trying to catch his breath in the darkness.

"Yes?"

"Get dressed and come to the living room."

She found her mother and father, their faces white with anger, seated on opposite sides of the brazier, waiting for her. Hayako sat down, and looked from one to the other. Her father, who'd had both hands stuck in his sash, took one out and motioned to her.

He then looked at her mother, who was silent. "Well? What's the matter? Can't you start?"

"You're the one who woke Hayako up," her mother said.

"Don't be an idiot! You're the one with something to say! Why don't you get it off your chest?" Then he blurted out: "Hayako. Mother isn't your real mother."

"Now there's no going back," her mother sighed.

Hayako's father had had a mistress. She had given birth to a child. His wife had begged him to part with the woman, and finally he did so, on her condition that he and his wife take the baby into their home.

The family already had a six-year-old boy, Toshio, and a little girl of two. The boy slept with his grandmother, who at that time was still alive and well, but the girl slept with her parents. Now they were to have yet another little baby. Although Hayako's mother had herself insisted on this arrangement, living with the third child came to seem nothing but a burden. There was also a sharp disagreement about how to record the baby in the family register. Hayako's father wanted to register the baby as their own, but after initially consenting, her mother soon started to insist that they first register her as the child of a mistress, and only then officially adopt her.

Late one night, their two-year-old daughter started to cry. Her mother took her on her back to soothe her, walking up and down the corridor outside the bedroom. But the child refused to calm down, howling even more loudly.

"Can't you shut that child up?" her father shouted from his bed.

After a while he dozed off. When he awoke, everything was hushed and still. The baby had probably gone to sleep. A light from the next room seeped in underneath the doors, but when he opened them, nobody was there. And looking round his room, he saw that mother and child hadn't come back to bed.

He got up and went out into the hall: the light was on, and the front door open. There was a snowstorm that night and he caught sight of his wife's silhouette. She was sitting out on the front steps, alone in drifts of snow.

"Where's the child? What have you done with her!" her father shouted, his voice growing sharper as he tried to make his wife stand up. Struggling out of his grasp, she mumbled a denial and sank down on her haunches.

Then her father saw something black peeping out of the snow at her feet. Thrusting her to one side, he hurried to dig it up. His wife fended off his hands. "No, I want to keep her in there," she insisted, scooping up snow to cover it.

Hayako's mother had murdered her own child—in a fit of temporary insanity, it was true, but this didn't change the fact. That her breakdown stemmed from his own infidelity made Hayako's father particularly anxious to hush up the incident.

For the funeral, he asked one of his friends, a doctor, to state in the death certificate that the three-year-old child, born to his mistress, had died of a serious illness. Once that was done, he arranged to have the new baby entered into the family register, in her elder half-sister's space—under the same age, birthday and name.

Her mother had been hospitalized. Hayako had been sent out to a wet-nurse. Six months later, by the time her mother was discharged, the family had moved away from the house in Hongō with its unhappy associations to a new one in Suginami. When Hayako was brought home, she was three years old.

The incident had taken place on December 16th—fourteen years earlier to the very night—and each year, on that day, the couple would make a pilgrimage to the temple, bearing the name tablet of the child who had been buried in the snow. That fourteenth year, however, her father was very busy at work. Her mother set out at the appointed time to the temple, alone, but when she had telephoned him at the office, he'd told her he would go later; meanwhile she was to have sutras read and go home, leaving the name tablet there. When he came home that night, however, he didn't have it with him, so his wife knew he hadn't gone. He had had too much work, he said, but she said this was just an excuse. Finally, she told him: if, for even one day of the year, he could not be bothered about the dead Hayako, why should she care about the living one?

Of course, that night when they told her the story, her parents had probably given Hayako only the barest account. The details she now knew probably came from all the countless retellings. But even then, Hayako had been left in no doubt as to the story's implications.

First her father talked, then her mother. Everything had begun in a fight, but they finally joined forces in telling her how she should take the news. Her mother looked at her: "Do you feel all right?"

Hayako shrugged off the question.

"In that case," she asked, after a while, "I am fourteen, not sixteen?"

"Well, you could say that, yes," her father replied.

"And my birthday isn't the 3rd of July. When was I born?"

"When? Let's see. It was October. It was the twenty-something, wasn't it? I can't recall."

"And my real name?"

Her father fell silent. Finally, he said, "Haven't you had enough?"

"He's right, Hayako," her mother said. "Why bother about that? What's the point? Learning another age, birthday, and name for yourself all over again? You're sixteen years old, you were born on the third of July. Just accept it."

When she saw her mother the next morning, Hayako flushed a deep red. But even more distressing was the moment at school when she had to put her name on her exam—the characters she started to write came out all wrong. She erased them, and tried again. But this time, it came boiling up inside her that how she wrote this name did not matter; it belonged to somebody else anyway; and her second attempt made an even bigger mess.

In the immediate aftermath of the war, for the first few winters there were frequent snowfalls in Tokyo. Hayako had feared and loathed snow for years, ever since being punished for it as a child, but now that she knew the truth, her reaction to it became even more extreme.

Trudging over the snow in her rubber boots, her every step would be met with a piercing squeak. Hayako couldn't help feeling that she and the snow were engaged in mutual torment, that she was crushing thousands of little flakes underfoot, and they, in turn, were squealing out their hatred of her. As the sound started to bother her, her pace faltered, and finally she would come to a complete standstill. Before her and behind her, she could see nothing but a glittering white expanse. The snowflakes under her boots prepared themselves for an attack; a chill passed up through their soles, and the frozen stillness that follows a snowfall would start to gnaw into her shoulders and neck. She felt her whole body begin to change into translucent rock.

At such times Hayako would feel that the person whom her

mother had murdered that night in the snow had been none other than her own self. The self who had survived was only the ghost of the self who'd died. Like a ghost, she was destined to pass through the world, never knowing her own age or birthday. Even when she died, her funeral would be held in somebody else's name.

These thoughts still plagued Hayako as an adult. According to the register, she was two years older than Kisaki, though in fact they were the same age. Older or younger—it made little difference as far as she was concerned: the entry was false; and it would remain so, whether in her father's family register or Kisaki's. No matter that the snowflakes melted after a brief span of time: those few seconds were packed with infinite malice. Even if they did marry, the snow would continue to fall, and cover their union in a blizzard of derision.

Looking at Kisaki—a workman's towel tied around his head for their end-of-the-year cleaning, or on a summer evening, as he relaxed at home in a cotton kimono—Hayako would suddenly be struck by his youthfulness: no other man his age shared it, whether single, engaged, or married. She would feel that the essence of their life together had been revealed, and his hidden depths laid bare.

She dreaded his leaving her to live in the snow country. In the meantime, however, she loved their present life, every day of which was happy, from the bottom of her heart. Yes, she could marry him: she could make him refuse the transfer to the snow country and so give up being promoted at his company. Or she could agree to live with him there, leaving him for the winter months. But whatever she did, Hayako knew that the cruel snow would in time exact its revenge.

The elderly man next to Hayako leant toward her.

"Is that rain falling, or snow?" he asked, removing his glasses and peering through the foggy window.

Hayako glanced outside and blanched.

"Snow, possibly," Kisaki answered for her. "You all right?" he asked her.

"Yes, I am. Really." She felt not the slightest symptom, even though it was certainly snow skimming past the window. "Perhaps it's because of the train's heating system."

"Let's hope so. Let's hope, too, that you can make it to Itô. It's much warmer there. There won't be any snow."

He was trying to rally her spirits—she should try her best not to succumb. But she didn't have much confidence. She'd only made her comment about the heating to reassure him. More likely, her headaches hadn't yet come because she was traveling in the train, keeping one step ahead of the clouds—not enough of them had gathered overhead yet to have any effect.

The train passed through Hiratsuka. Across the black letters of the platform signs the snow swirled down in dense diagonal flurries. Already it was falling so thickly, she thought, watching the station signs go by; she would never hold out as far as Itô. Her headaches would begin any moment. Then, another thought struck her. She turned her face toward the window.

"What's the matter? Has it started?"

Kisaki leant over to peer into her face. She shook her head and bent away from him even more. She was crying.

"Are you in pain?" he asked.

"No, no. I was just thinking about Mother. . . ."

That her headache hadn't started yet, she realized, must have something to do with her mother's death. In the dream Mother had come to say farewell to her; and, according to that woman, she had even sent her a sign from the other world. Hayako could not hold back the tears.

As a child, Hayako had never been conscious of any undue severity from her mother. Perhaps her attention had been absorbed by the inconsistencies posed by her assumed age and true aptitudes, and by her uneasiness and suspicion. Perhaps there was little chance for her to make any comparisons in treatment since her only sibling was a brother four years older.

Nevertheless, she had to admit, her mother had been cruel to her. And she hadn't changed, even after the truth of their relationship had been revealed.

Whenever her mother was upset, she would go two or three days without speaking to Hayako. Even when Hayako begged her for money to go to school, she would be met with silence.

Hayako remembered once arriving home late for dinner and starting to fumble for apologies in the kitchen. "Oh, so it's excuses now, is it?" her mother interrupted, her back turned. "Take your time. Sit down right there, so you can think about what to say." Hayako had to sit on the kitchen floor with an empty stomach until late into the night.

Another time, one summer vacation, Hayako had arranged to go with friends to the seaside the very day her mother decided to clean the house. When she expressed doubts about canceling the trip, her mother grabbed the dyed calico tablecloth Hayako had just finished for the fall school exhibition. "So you're happy to go off and leave me with all this work! In that case—" And she tore the cloth into shreds.

Hayako had felt humiliation and rage. It was surprising, considering these incidents, how rarely she had longed for her real mother.

One night, her brother came home late and, without a word of apology, sat down at the one place left at the table.

"Where have you been?" her mother asked.

"It's none of your business," he replied.

"Oh?" her mother retorted. "Perhaps you'd like to try sitting on the floor, like your sister did, a few days ago? It works—doesn't it, Hayako?"

"It certainly does," Hayako answered, cheerfully.

There was no doubt that her brother was her mother's child, but time and again Hayako had the impression that she too shared her mother's blood. Not the thick, rich blood that flows peacefully through the veins, but the blood they sucked and licked from the scratches inflicted on each other when they fought tooth and nail—so passionate was their attachment.

Here was a woman who had been forced to raise the daughter of her husband's mistress, and with the same name as her own baby—whom she'd murdered with her own hands. It was only natural to vent her frustration on Hayako. At first, she must have looked at her adopted daughter with pure hatred; but as time passed, as she saw how Hayako, forced to suffer under her emotional outbursts, shared her unhappiness, she had come to feel a certain pleasure in her—a certain intimacy and love. Hayako remembered her mother telling her later, just as if they were secretly savoring some delicious tidbit of food, how tiny she had looked at kindergarten amongst the other children; how, on the day when she'd first been brought home as a little baby, she had wanted to hold Hayako, but her arms hadn't obeyed.

Hayako felt that her mother was the mainstay of her tenuous existence. Her father had been the one to rescue her from the garden that snowy day, but her impulsive violent mother occupied a special place in her heart.

It was about two years after learning the facts of her birth that Hayako started to suffer from her mother's malady.

She'd always known that her mother was troubled by migraines in winter, but she'd never realized they came because of the snow. Knowing they caused her mother's condition only increased her own hatred for snowy days, and made them twice as unbearable for her as before—not only because she couldn't help getting tense when her mother's mood darkened, but also because the snow seemed to taunt her, now, with a reminder of her own unhappiness. In all of these ways she was affected, and eventually she developed the same symptoms.

The first time she experienced a migraine, Hayako went and informed her mother.

"Since early this morning, I've had a pain here," she said, touching her right temple. This was the same side of the head which always afflicted her mother.

"Really?" her mother replied softly, clearly taken aback. Her voice held pity, but it was disturbed, too, by this adoptive daughter who insisted on sharing her malady.

But they avoided actually being together as they suffered from the same illness. To cling to each other was too much, for both of them. Although secretly longing to be with her mother, Hayako would stay out of her way. During the worst pain, her mother would take to bed, but Hayako felt too embarrassed to follow suit. I should stay up at least till nine, she would think, alone in her room. Her mother would come in, in several layers of nightclothes. "Aren't you in pain?" she asked, handing her a small bottle of medicine with a glass of water, and telling her to take some. She never inquired any further into Hayako's condition. Tilting the bottle, she would stare at the white powder inside. "Of course, it won't do much good," she would say, and leave.

When her headache was at its peak, her mother would snap at her father when he inquired how she was: "Why do you ask? It's always painful!" But if Hayako came to tell her that she was on her way somewhere, she would respond sweetly: "Oh, you're going out? Take care." Never once did she try to dissuade Hayako from leaving. She, too, preferred that they suffer apart.

Even after they lived separately, whenever Hayako's headaches came, the first person her thoughts would turn to was her mother. There was no need to feel constrained anymore, but this very freedom seemed to make Hayako obsessed by her. How was the weather in Osaka? Was it snowing there too? Perhaps there was no snow yet, but what about those horrible clouds? Were they looming over the horizon? As the pain came again, over and over, she felt that, miles away, the same pain shot through her mother's head.

"Aren't you in pain, Mother?" she wanted to call out. "Mother, I'm suffering too."

And now her mother had gone to a place where her old complaint could no longer trouble her—and for the first time in ten years, snow brought Hayako no sign of a headache. It could not be just a coincidence: surely, her mother was telling her something from beyond the grave.

The train passed through Ōiso and Ninomiya. The snow was still falling. White patches were beginning to form on the ground.

"How are you holding up?" Kisaki asked her.

Hayako shook her head. "I feel fine. Isn't it strange!"

"Maybe it *is* the heating inside."

"It's because we're taking a trip. My headaches don't want to get in the way." Hayako gazed boldly out the window. She turned back to Kisaki. "Why don't we get out at Hakoné?"

"Hakoné?"

"Yes, let's not go all the way to Itō."

"Why not? You know there'll be deep snow at Hakoné."

"Yes. Th-that's why I want to go there. I want to take the plunge."

"You're being foolhardy," he warned.

"I don't think so. I think my illness has left me for good," she replied. She explained briefly why.

"I still think it has something to do with the heating," Kisaki said.

"But I want so much to go," she replied.

She wanted to go to a place where the snow would be really deep, to be sure that the miracle had occurred. Why flee to Itō, where it would be warm, just for fear of her malady? That would be letting her mother down. If they went on to Itō she would never know whether this turn of events was a miracle or pure chance.

The train passed through Kaminomiya station.

"Odawara's the next stop. Come on." Hayako stepped out of her shoes and onto the seat to take down their luggage. Kisaki looked at her without stirring. Hayako laid their two suitcases on the seat, and put on her shoes again. "Please let me try," she pleaded. "It won't be too late to book a room, will it?"

"Oh, there'll be places to stay, but . . . ," he said, unconvinced.

"So you're getting out?" asked the man sitting next to Hayako.

"Yes."

The two men shifted their knees to one side.

"Thank you." Hayako took both their suitcases, gave Kisaki one more look, and set off down the aisle. Kisaki rose from his seat and followed.

The train came to a halt. As she stepped out of the warm carriage onto the snowy platform, Hayako shivered.

"I told you it would be cold," Kisaki teased.

Hayako said she wanted to go on to Sengokubara. They had once stayed at a hotel there in fine weather.

It was a Saturday afternoon, but only a handful of passengers boarded the bus, because of the season and the snow. At Miyanoshita, four alighted, making the inside of the bus that much more forlorn. Here, two policeman, their waterproof capes dark against the white snow, were waving down vehicles, inspecting them, and sending back the ones without tire chains.

"It'll get worse after this," Kisaki said. "Shouldn't we get off here? We'll be in trouble if we end up with no place to stay." Already one route change had been announced: the bus would terminate at Sengokubara, though it usually went all the way to Kojiri.

"Let's go as far as we can. I'm surprised the winter's so mild here!" Hayako remarked, looking outside. Snow was still falling, but dark patches showed through on the road and on the nearby bushes.

But Kisaki was right. On leaving Kiga, the bus progressed at a snail's pace, its chain-wrapped tires creaking and scraping. The land around them was rapidly turning white, and when the bus turned off for Miyagino, there was nothing but snow and more snow.

All they could see of the road were the tracks left by previous vehicles, and these were fast disappearing in the mounting layers of white. Snow clouds hung down low in the sky, merging it with the land at a point which seemed close at hand. Dusk was gathering. The gray world was growing darker, pressing in around them. The snow swirled in powdery flakes—in flurries that were whirled up again by the wind just before touching the ground. Some snowflakes fastened onto the windows, as if forgoing the mad joy of descent in order to move forward with the vehicle.

"I want a better view," announced Hayako, sitting beside Kisaki who was in the window seat. She moved to the seat behind him.

"Don't sit too close," Kisaki warned, looking back.

"I'm all right." Her headaches never came on that side of her skull, anyway.

"You're quite determined, aren't you!" he said, reassured, and turned to face the front of the bus.

But her headache had, in fact, started up soon after the bus left Miyanoshita. Had it been delayed due to the heating in the train? Or was it her excitement that had held it off? Was the delay of the pain just a coincidence, after all?

Already it was coming in short sharp stabs. With each assault, she had to hold her breath in order to bear it, and then, as soon as a lull came, take deep gulps of air. She had changed seats because Kisaki would soon have guessed what was happening.

They must be more than halfway there by now. But that was cold comfort, and only meant more snow up ahead.

The driver, his hands gripping the steering wheel, said something to the woman conductor standing beside him. She nodded, and turned to the passengers. Due to weather conditions, she announced, they would have to terminate the journey at the next hot spring. The hotel Kisaki and Hayako were heading for was a little farther on: they would have to walk.

Just as Hayako winced in pain, Kisaki looked around.

"So it's begun." He stood up, and stepping over her knees, he sat down next to the window and turned to look into her face. "You silly girl. Why were you hiding it from me?"

Hayako waited for the pain to go, and then, drawing a deep breath, she muttered: "I didn't think it would happen. I really thought I'd be all right."

"Well, not to worry. We only have to catch a bus back. I'll ask the conductor."

Hayako shook her head. She tried to keep her face calm as another wave of pain hit.

"No, let's go on," she said, when it abated. "I'll manage. It makes no difference now, anyway. It's started."

She refused to give up. Everything depended on getting to the snowbound outpost of Sengokubara. Perhaps she could force a miracle if they got there. Her old self had been too much under the sway of her mother and the snow. She was determined to part from that old self, once and for all.

Night had fallen. They borrowed coarse oil-paper umbrellas from the hotel, and went outside into the darkness and falling snow.

Shafts of light streaming from the windows cut through the snowflakes at several places around the building. Once they left these bands of light, it was as though they had plunged swiftly into the severest cold.

The hotel was a ten minute walk from the hot-spring inn, on the rise of Sengokubara. In front of them, the slope stretched down into the vaguely blue darkness to meet the rise of another hill. Only a single group of blurred lights was visible in the valley below, and beyond that, the sweep of winterbound hills—an immense vista of snow as far as the eye could see. Peering through the flurries to the distant hills, Hayako thought she could see the black shapes of trees. But then she realized the blackness was only more snow.

When they reached the bottom of the slope, they walked on,

bearing left, though with no goal in mind. About three inches of snow lay on the ground. Every step they took, the top layer yielded, after offering only a token resistance. The steady crunch of their footsteps added another, slow rhythm to the quicker, more caressing sound of the snow falling endlessly about them. The more she listened to the sounds' different beats, the more they seemed to exist only inside her head. She was still experiencing waves of pain. But though her breath came in fits and starts, her feet kept moving forward, impelled by their own steady rhythm.

"Aren't you in pain?"

Hayako let her breath out. "Yes," she said. "But I'll be better tomorrow. I should do this, just once. It'll be good for me." She was remembering the day of her mother's scolding when she had been made to hate the snow.

"Do you want to share my umbrella? Yours must make it heavy going."

She closed her umbrella. Snow slid off it and thudded on the ground. "I shouldn't have taken it," she said, joining him. She looked at it hanging in her hand.

"Let's leave it here," Kisaki said, grabbing it.

"But it'll get covered."

"We'll leave it standing up. We can collect it on our way back. Nobody'll take it." He drove the umbrella into the snow with so much force it sank in almost up to the handle.

They trudged on for a while. Their progress had become much more deliberate. Hayako's discomfort was obvious now; Kisaki was trying to take it slowly, and she was glad. The snow closed over her shoes, sneaking down inside and soaking her stockings. Her feet were chilled to the bone.

Kisaki stopped.

"Look how far we've come," he said, gazing over his shoulder. In the distance was a tiny blur of scattered lights—only a few guests were staying the night. "Shall we go back?"

"Just a little bit farther."

Kisaki shifted the umbrella as if bracing himself, and Hayako bent down to brush snow from her instep. As she did, she suddenly wished the snow to touch her bare skin. She took off a glove, crouched down, and scooped up some of the snow. She clenched her fingers, the coldness pierced them to the quick, and then she threw the frozen lump away. She was about to stand up when she noticed a little hollow in the smooth expanse of snow, and she stayed where she was, crouching.

"What are you doing?" Kisaki asked, above her.

"How about burying me?" she said. She scooped away a little more snow. "Yes, *me*. I just have to make the hole bigger—and get in. . . ."

"Bury you? In the snow?" Kisaki asked in amazement. The shock in his voice only exacerbated Hayako's desire. Just then, a sharp pain ran through her head. She waited for it to recede, then stood up and caught hold of Kisaki's wrist above the hand holding the umbrella.

"Please do it. I want you to!"

"But you'll die of pain."

"Yes, that's what I want! I want to die just this once. Please bury me. Go ahead—please dig!"

Kisaki was silent, his wrist pulling back from her hand.

"Bury me here, in the deep s-s-snow," Hayako begged him again through her stutter. "J-j-just cover me a little. Please do it!"

Kisaki staggered, and the snow fell from his umbrella with a soft thud, the thud of a dead bird falling out of the sky.

🏵 *Theater* (Gekijō, 1962)

THAT NIGHT, AN UNUSUAL EXCITEMENT—NO doubt over the presence of a foreign opera company—filled the theater lobby, particularly in the areas before the auditorium doors.

People trying to look like opera connoisseurs (though they were obviously perfect amateurs) were hemmed in by the too-intimate crowd, and here and there they tried with quick elbows to swim their way out. One young couple briefly observed the mêlée, withdrew to whisper, and then with self-assured, determined expressions plunged straight through to the auditorium doors. Some bachelors, taking up positions on the sofas, exhaled tall tales with their cigarette smoke, staring straight into it; and along the edges stood many middle-aged and elderly couples, mostly forming small circles, little smiles fixed on their faces, whether they were in conversation or silently waiting.

Everyone clutched garishly colored programs, bobbing here and there like little waves on a tossing sea.

Sugino Hideko surveyed the scene as she ascended the stairs. The friend who had invited her, a widow named Mrs. Yamashita, was waiting in the more expensive seats of the second tier.

"Thank you for inviting me," Hideko said, greeting her. "It was so kind of you to send the ticket express."

The widow moved to the next seat, indicating Hideko was to have her place. "Sit yourself down, dear," she said. When

Hideko was settled, she continued: "I haven't seen you in ages. The last time we met was surely . . ." she said, referring to her husband's funeral: "you remember. So you've still been coming to the concerts?"

"Recently, only to the touring production of *Carmen.*"

"With one of your friends?"

"No, by myself."

"But how did you get hold of a ticket?"

"I lined up and bought one."

"Really? That can't have been very pleasant."

"No, it wasn't. So I'd abandoned any hope of coming tonight."

"Well, why didn't you tell me, my dear? My husband may no longer be with us, but I still can take care of these things."

Hideko felt a twinge of guilt. She had scarcely thought about this woman since Mr. Yamashita's unexpected death six months ago.

Mr. Yamashita had been the music teacher at Hideko's girls' school in Kansai while she was in the lower grades. He had later given notice and gone on a scholastic exchange program to Germany, returning to Japan only after the war. By the time Hideko had moved to Tokyo with her brother's family for his company transfer, Mr. Yamashita was already a music critic of some acclaim. He had married Mrs. Yamashita in Germany, and the couple had had one child.

"The boy will be off to university soon," Mrs. Yamashita sighed when she telephoned Hideko to invite her. Rather than escort his mother to the opera, he'd gone hiking in the mountains with his friends.

Nearly ten years had passed since Hideko had run into Mr. Yamashita and renewed her acquaintance with him, or rather, with his whole family. All that time, she had never failed to visit the couple once or twice a month; and she had many times gone on shopping and theater trips with one or both of them, with or without their son.

After moving to Tokyo, Hideko had lived as an unmarried woman for nearly four years in her brother's home. Finally, thanks to her brother's mediation—a pure formality—she had ended up marrying Sugino, a man with whom she was somewhat acquainted. Neither of them was exactly in the bloom of youth. After two years, which had not gone very well, Sugino had been sent by his company for technical training to West Germany. By now he had been gone as long as they had been together.

Her unhappy circumstances and setbacks were doubtless the reason Mr. and Mrs. Yamashita had been so kind to Hideko for nearly ten years. The couple knew almost everything about her marital situation—though, of course, they never forced her to be explicit. Hideko no longer remembered precisely what she could have told them, nor in what circumstances; and the couple would probably have been hard put to say themselves. And though she'd received advice, even admonishment, from them over their long acquaintance, never once had they presumed to tell her how to live her life.

Hideko had adored being in the company of Mr. and Mrs. Yamashita. They had been so considerate, and such a very loving couple.

Mrs. Yamashita closed her program. "You must come and see me more often," she said. "I need company, too. Tell me, are you still hearing from your husband?"

"Yes, occasionally."

"I see. Well, dear, I think you should resign yourself. He's just a very peculiar man."

A buzzer announced that the opera would be starting soon.

Nearly every seat in the auditorium was occupied. Seated where she was, Hideko caught only a glimpse of the floor below, but it seemed, as far as she could tell, filled with foreigners. At the far end of one of the lower balconies she could see two couples—and one was foreign. The woman looked to be in her mid-twenties. She wore a white dress that exposed her shoulders, and long evening gloves.

Were those people here tonight? Were they sitting somewhere near? Hideko wondered, glancing around.

A little in front of her, down toward the left, sat two figures side by side with straight reddish hair pulled back in ponytails. There was nothing uneven about their shoulders, clothed in eveningwear. They had their heads bent toward each other, deep in conversation. They must be sisters, Hideko thought, or very good friends.

She was about to look away when the girls' heads drew apart. In the space beyond that opened up, she caught sight of a man's profile. The next instant, however, the heads came back together, blocking her view.

Straining to the left and right, and finally almost hoisting herself out of her seat, Hideko tried to get one more look at the man just to make sure. But the girls' heads were once more drawn tightly together, and for all her efforts, the man remained out of sight.

From his profile, he did seem to be the man she had met at the performance of *Carmen*. In that case, she wondered, was the woman who had been with him here tonight as well? She could only see men's dinner jackets flanking the man in question, however, and there was no sign of the woman sitting anywhere nearby.

The buzzer rang a second time. The girls' heads parted, opening a space again. This time, Hideko got a view not in profile, but of the back of his head, with its thick hair, just visible above the back of his seat. His head was much lower than any around him. It was also pitched forward at an unnatural angle. There could be no doubt. It was he.

Hideko gazed at the rapidly dimming auditorium lights, and felt a gnawing frustration at having been unable to catch sight of the woman. So she appeared not to have come.

An announcement came over the loudspeakers: Ladies

and Gentlemen, tonight we present for your appreciation *Rigoletto.*

Of course, Hideko thought: tonight was *Rigoletto.* And yet, she reflected, the woman hadn't seemed like the sort who would object to coming to an opera about a hunchback escorted by a man with that very deformity. Perhaps it was the hunchback himself who minded; perhaps he thought it too degrading for her and humiliating for himself. On the other hand, it was possible that the woman couldn't obtain another ticket. Or even that she was ill, or otherwise engaged. Or . . .

A burst of applause brought her back to the present. The conductor had emerged, and made his way to the raised platform in the center of the orchestra. The footlights dimly lit his face as he turned to the audience and, bowing, met another wave of applause. Out went the houselights. Now a shadow puppet outlined against his lit score, the conductor raised his arms, baton in one hand. A hubbub went muffling through the audience, as people cleared their throats for one last time. The instant it subsided, the baton came slicing down.

Yes, it was *Rigoletto* all right: that was the overture. Whenever Hideko heard an opera's first few notes, she always felt that the music wanted to tell her that, even if only for a little while, she could be liberated from all trivial cares. And she would eagerly seize the opportunity to be transported to another world.

But tonight, in Hideko's mind, the world of *Rigoletto* was occupied by another hunchback, the one in the audience. Did the woman know that the man was here? Or had he come on the sly? Was he such an opera devotee that, even with that deformity, he felt no compunction about coming to *Rigoletto?* Perhaps, since he'd been a hunchback all his life, the coincidence could no longer embarrass him. The absence of his companion began to obsess Hideko. She felt a craving to see them watch *Rigoletto* together.

It was the woman, alone, whom Hideko had first encountered, two months ago outside the ticket agency, standing in line to buy her ticket to *Carmen.*

That morning, it had started to rain before the doors opened at ten o'clock. Hideko was near the head of the line, but the doorway's awning provided shelter only to the person just in front of her—the woman.

The rainy season was nearly over, and earlier on the weather had looked fine, so few people had brought an umbrella or rainwear. The woman, however, was wearing an old, worn, off-white raincoat, with a belt. She also wore stiletto heels. She seemed about the same age as Hideko; nothing about her suggested she might be married—and yet she didn't look like a faded office girl, either. She had more the well-bred air of somebody who had graduated from college two or three years before, but whose family had recently come down in the world, and so she hadn't married and the years went by.

Turning up her collar, the woman peered at the sky from under the awning. "You're going to get wet," she remarked to Hideko. "Come in a bit." As she spoke, she tried to flatten herself to the wall. But the awning was very narrow and high, and she was right at its edge: the hem of her raincoat was already getting spattered with rain.

"Thank you. I'm all right," Hideko said, politely. "It's not raining very hard."

The woman didn't insist. Instead, reaching across her coat, she drew out a newspaper, folded lengthwise and peeping from her pocket. "Well, use this," she said, offering it to Hideko. "I'm done with it." The newspaper served to cover Hideko's head until the line moved inside, proceeding downstairs into the basement.

Here they found themselves in a long narrow room, or wide corridor. Fat pipes crawled along its low ceiling. The line formed again in front of big bins filled with discarded paper, faded documents bundled untidily together, and sundry bits of broken furniture.

Everybody waited, and grew bored.

"We have to get tickets for opening night," a young man announced to his neighbors in line.

Hideko was of exactly the same mind. The whole performance rested on the reputation of the lead soprano, but the woman would have an understudy, as would all the stars. Nobody knew which performers would perform on particular nights, but one thing was certain: opening night would feature the troupe's finest singers. Almost everyone who'd lined up early that morning wanted the cheapest possible tickets for that night.

A girl stepped out of line to count the people in front of her. "Twenty-one," she told her companion. "We should be all right." Well, Hideko thought, I should be too. She unfolded the woman's newspaper, now quite damp, and started to read it.

"That's where they'll sell the tickets," somebody said, and Hideko looked up. At the front of the line, two men were setting up desks. Another two brought a screen to use as a partition, and put up a notice: ONE TICKET PER PERSON, EXCEPT FOR SEATS IN SPECIAL CLASSES AND SECTION A. Hideko looked at her watch. Fifteen more minutes to go.

As she glanced through the newspaper, Hideko cast her eye occasionally on the young woman. Always standing in the same position, both hands thrust inside her raincoat pockets, she was carelessly leaning against the dirty wall. To judge from her profile, as she gazed at a spot on the opposite wall just below waist level, she was either lost in reverie or thinking about nothing at all.

The line began, very slowly, to move forward. Hideko saw people emerge from the partition and walk past, either putting their glossy tickets into the white envelopes embossed with the ticket agency's name, or taking them out to check them. But every so often, the line would come to a complete halt. In front of the screen an official stood admitting individuals or couples to the desk in a way that allowed people to take their time choosing seats.

Hideko gradually neared the partition—the young woman in front of her was allowed in. Reappearing with her ticket, she asked an official: "Is it all right if I get back in line, at the end?" People laughed. He chuckled awkwardly, replying, "I'm not sure what I should tell you." Then he beckoned to Hideko. "Next, please."

Hideko was sure she heard the young woman's pace quicken as she walked away.

The seat for *Carmen* that Hideko purchased that day turned out to be on the third tier, and one away from the aisle. When she'd taken her place, she looked around and recognized several people, now in their finery, searching for their seats—people whose faces in line she had grown tired of looking at two months before. Of course, no one gave a sign of remembering any of the others.

"Here's one of our seats," a voice said above Hideko's head. She looked up at the young woman who had stood in front of her in line. Noticing Hideko, she nodded a greeting—she remembered the incident with the newspaper—and Hideko nodded in return.

"Which would you like?" The young woman held out two tickets to someone standing beside her. Her companion did not reply, but brushed past her and dropped himself down next to Hideko, in the aisle seat. The young woman, going back, pulled down a seat two rows back, directly behind Hideko. Having made sure of where the woman sat, Hideko turned and discreetly scrutinized the man seated beside her.

He was a hunchback. This unusual aspect of his appearance made guessing his age difficult, but he seemed no older than the young woman, or, for that matter, Hideko herself.

Perched uncomfortably in his seat, his jacket pulling across the heavy-looking hump, the man slowly ran a rather under-sized hand through his soft hair. He had a dark and fleshy face, with well-defined features, and eyes that glanced around fiercely.

"Shall I buy a program?" came the woman's voice from behind.

The man took a cloth wallet from an inside jacket pocket and, without turning around, held it above his head. The woman reached over for it. After a while, she came back down the aisle and meekly placed the program, with his wallet on it, on his knee. The hunchback put his wallet away, and flicked quickly, without pausing once, through the program and then thrust it into the air. Again the woman's hand reached over.

She, however, perused it no more thoroughly, and very soon, the corner of the program was tapping at the man's shoulder. He glanced at it, and looked slowly around.

"Keep it," he ordered.

As he was turning back, Hideko caught his eye. "I could switch," she offered, unable to resist.

"Really?" he said. "Well, that's very nice."

During the first intermission, as Hideko sat staring vacantly into space, she felt a hand touch her shoulder. The young woman, who had slipped up behind her along the empty row of seats, asked: "Would you care to join us for a cup of tea?"

They went out into the lobby, where the hunchback waited—having either gone out first, or having sent the woman back to invite Hideko.

"Thanks for giving us your seat," he said, bowing awkwardly, his small arms hanging down.

"Yes, we really are most obliged," the young woman echoed, bowing deeply.

"So we can get refreshments around here?" asked the hunchback, already walking away. "We don't have to go downstairs?"

"I think there's a place over there," the woman said, pointing to one end of the lobby. So, Hideko thought, the woman had suggested inviting her out for tea.

Hideko could not help falling back half a pace to study the twosome as they crossed the lobby.

The clothes the woman was wearing tonight were just as threadbare as those Hideko had seen when they met. Her faded tan-colored dress of some soft material, which looked as if it had been washed a hundred times, was decorated with a brooch at the neck, and above it all she wore a dark brown hat that seemed to accentuate the brooding quality in her expression. Despite the touch of shabbiness, however, with her slender figure, and in those same stiletto shoes, all in all, she was quite a beauty.

The hunchback by her side barely reached her shoulders, but his clothing was obviously brand-new. Over his hump he wore a very dark blue jacket, almost black, with extremely fine green pinstripes. Though it didn't fit well, his outfit was clearly of a much finer quality than his companion's.

"Can you give me some money?" the woman asked at the entrance to the lounge. "What would you like?"

"Just see to it," the hunchback ordered, handing her his wallet, and leading Hideko inside.

In a short while the woman rejoined them. She placed three order coupons on the tabletop. The hunchback put away his wallet, glancing at the coupons: "What? You mean you ordered coffee?"

"I'm sorry. Was that wrong?"

"It's too late now, isn't it," he said and changed the subject. "That woman singing Carmen tonight, she's overdoing it, I'd say—she's a total hysteric." He blinked two or three times, and broke into a grin. "Her understudy is probably better, after all! What a pity for all of us!"

The beauty was silent, staring at the coupons, shifting them around on the tabletop. Was she upset, Hideko wondered, because coffee had not met with the hunchback's approval? Or was she just fidgeting as she listened to him?

Hideko couldn't puzzle out what connected this strange couple. Judging from how rude the hunchback was to the woman, she couldn't be his lover or mistress. But he was too aggressive with her to be her brother—and besides, there was no family resemblance. Nor did they seem to be husband and wife. For a couple roughly of the same age, and of their generation, the woman seemed far too subservient. And surely no wife would wear such high heels, only to accentuate how small her husband was. . . . No, Hideko decided, he must be a handicapped person who'd hired a beautiful chaperone.

Just then, the hunchback jerked his chin toward the coupons. "Well, why don't you call the waiter?"

. . . And tonight, the hunchback was attending *Rigoletto* alone.

At the end of the first act the lights came up, and people around Hideko started leaving their seats. She realized she had gone over into that other world, faraway, and she tried to savor the last moments of pleasure.

Mrs. Yamashita turned and said something to her. Hideko, however, who had just seen the figure of the hunchback loom up abruptly from his seat, did not reply.

The hunchback was seated three rows down, so he was bound to pass her on his way up the aisle. This was precisely what happened; and as he proceeded toward her, the spectators on either side of the aisle gaped in horror. No one had looked at him twice on the evening of *Carmen*, but tonight he was stealing the show.

As she saw what was happening, Hideko had an overwhelming desire to be by his side.

Mrs. Yamashita inquired, as if sensing her tension, "See someone you know?"

Hideko, unfortunately quite a few seats from the aisle, didn't bother to reply. Disregarding Mrs. Yamashita, she rose and hurried to get out of the row, squeezing as fast as she could past those who were still seated, apologizing, "I'm sorry, I'm sorry," as she went. The hunchback, however, passed her row of seats before she was free of it, and so she lunged forward, calling out: "Excuse me!"

The man lifted his head, and looked around.

"Well!" he called, catching sight of her: "We meet again!" He was about to continue walking, but stopped as he saw her trying to get out to reach him.

Hideko's haste was hardly discreet, and the person she so eagerly sought cut such a bizarre figure that many curious glances followed them as they struck up a conversation. Hideko wondered if he were uncomfortable. As she stood opposite him, she was hugely excited to be the object of so many stares.

"Where is your companion?" she inquired.

"Oh, the wife? She couldn't make it," he said, and then added, vaguely, as if the thought had just occurred to him: "Won't you come and visit us at home?" He handed her his card. On it she saw his name, Ōshima Ken'ichi, and an address in an old section of Tokyo, but no indication of his profession. Hideko did not have a card herself—she had no use for such things. She apologized and told him her name, but he didn't seem to take it in.

"Do come," he repeated. "We're both home Sundays. My wife would be so pleased." With that, he pulled in his chin, lowered his head, and walked away.

After the performance of *Rigoletto,* not two weeks elapsed before Hideko took up his invitation to visit their house.

Hideko's home was still the suburban apartment which she had shared with her husband prior to his departure for West Germany. Between the apartment building and the row of shops by the station, there was a medium-sized plot of land, now overgrown with weeds, which Sugino had bought for them to build a house on. It pained Hideko to see it every day, which was one more reason for her recent lengthy stays with her brother.

Her brother's family consisted of just three members: husband, wife, and child, a boy of primary school age. Hideko had always been on good terms with them. They didn't treat this adult baby sister who came home for such long stretches as a nuisance—or even as a guest; and she, for her part, was completely at ease in their company. What was more, though they probably sensed the state of her marriage—which was clear even to someone like Mrs. Yamashita—they never dreamed of asking awkward questions.

As she helped her sister-in-law with the housework, food shopping, or in supervising her nephew's homework, or as they all sat together in front of the television, Hideko often imagined that Sugino had gone to West Germany on a permanent visit, and she herself had come home for a permanent visit. She wouldn't have minded—in fact she would have preferred it. It was the state of being a divorcée, not divorce itself, that Hideko dreaded.

She received a monthly letter from Sugino, but hardly what one would expect from a forty-year-old man to his wife: they were "Essays from West Germany," written coldly and tastefully, like textbook compositions. His communications usually took the form of a stiff picture postcard, its horizontal lines filled with details of the weather, the countryside, his extremely heavy workload, his vacation in Italy, and the skiing there. Occasionally he added a word about a concert, or about cooking. He told her he hated having to cook for himself. Not as if he were longing for the dishes she used to prepare, but out of regret for the time he lost for studying.

To Hideko, these uninspired letters captured the spirit of the writer and his lack of imagination. Yet she could also sense an ulterior motive; their real intention seemed to be to advertise his orderly but varied life, and his great satisfaction with it: there was nothing more he could desire. But she also knew she was no longer in any position to demand more news from her husband—news, that is, with the slightest smell or shadow of him. And anyway, Hideko had come to like his impersonal letters. She liked them just the way they were.

Hideko set out from her brother's home that Sunday—a rare day for outings, especially when she was staying there.

Having met the hunchback only twice, and then briefly, Hideko didn't know what his profession might be, or even if he had a job at all. They'd both be home on Sundays, he'd said: so it was likely that one of them commuted to work during the week. Or they might be free every day, but the hunchback preferred to stay home Sundays because of all the crowds—this possibility seemed the most likely to Hideko, recalling the hunchback's words: "My wife would be so pleased." Doubtless he worried about his wife having to keep him company from morning to night, with nothing to amuse her except the occasional visit to the opera.

In any case, as she'd savored the pleasure of standing beside him, Hideko hadn't felt at all put off by the tender way he referred to his wife (despite being so harsh to her face), or by the way his *we* had subtly stressed that they were a couple. No, if anything, she was all the more intrigued. Was she impressed that a hunchback could have such a good-looking wife? Or was it the erotic appeal of the woman, heightened by the contrast with him? Perhaps it was the painfully sweet jealousy she felt toward both of them.

An old section of the city, a hilly area with pre-war dwellings—here was a short row of two-floor tenements: this must be the one. Having asked the way in a shop where she purchased fruit to take as a gift, Hideko finally located their house. It had a perfunctory gate with latticework at the top. Peeping through this, she saw a narrow garden with a path of five or six stone slabs leading to a glass-paneled door, and sure enough, a plaque with the name "Ōshima."

She went up the path and, sliding open the door, saw a tiny strip of corridor and a wooden door on the left.

"Hello!" she called, eagerly. "Anybody home?"

"Just a minute!" a voice replied, and as the wooden door rattled open, a woman stuck her head out. It was the beauty.

"Well, how nice!" she said, coming forward when she discovered it was Hideko. "Welcome to our home. My husband said that you might come. I'm glad you made it so soon." Turning to the archway at the foot of the stairs, she called up: "She's come, dear! The lady who was so nice the other evening at the opera."

Today the woman's outfit consisted of a dark red woolen kimono, so dark that it looked almost black, and a narrow, bright yellow sash.

"Do come in," she said, ushering Hideko inside. The room was small, four-and-a-half tatami mats, with a tea cabinet and a sewing machine against one wall. The adjoining room was larger, six mats in size. Here, the young woman set down a low table that had been standing up in a corner.

The hunchback made his entrance, dressed in a jacket, and nodded informally to Hideko. Just then came a sudden, violent crash: while removing cushions from the cupboard, the beauty had knocked down a ceramic foot-warmer.

"Idiot!" the man snapped. "Watch what you're doing!"

"I'm sorry." The woman blushed.

The hunchback sat down at the table.

"Ōshima Ken'ichi. Pleased to meet you," he blurted out. He scraped back the shock of hair hanging over his forehead. "Wait a moment," he added, "I gave you my name card, didn't I? That's how you got here." He beamed. "And your name is?"

"Hideko—Sugino Hideko. I'm very pleased to meet you."

"The pleasure is all ours," the man said, bobbing forward. The beauty bowed formally by his side.

"Shall we ask for her address?" He turned to his wife: "Get some paper."

She rose, picking up the fruit Hideko had given her a moment before.

"Of course, you don't need to go if you think you can remember it by heart," the hunchback teased, as, raising her hand to the door, the beauty smiled and went into the next room. When she returned, she brought a teapot, cups, and a piece of scrap paper.

"Oh, so these are the characters you use," the hunchback said, eyeing Hideko's name, which she wrote alongside her brother's address. "My wife's name is Haru, you know, short for Haruko—written with the second character of 'Meiji,' 'enlightened rule.' People always told her father that with that name she'd never find a decent husband. That worried him terribly— he was a doctor with a practice, you understand. I was his patient at one time. Haruko was in medical school when she decided she wanted to marry me. That didn't please him at all— he kept reminding her about her name, telling her she should be careful. Well, he was worried about my hump, that's obvious. Haru was quite determined, though. 'In that case, change your name!' was what he told her. I didn't let her. Not that I'm all that crazy about it myself, you know, but . . ."

The hunchback had struck Hideko as a difficult man, but he was turning out to be quite amusing. The next moment, however, he cast a threatening look at the beauty as she sat beside him preparing tea. "Happy you married me, Missus?" he asked. "What do you say?"

"Hmmm?" she asked, continuing with her task. "Oh, yes. Very happy."

The man rolled his eyes. "'Happy,'" he sniggered. "Say, Hidé," he continued (she felt a flutter of excitement at his familiarity), "I bet you're surprised by our house, aren't you? You don't find many houses this old nowadays."

"Have you been here long?"

"I have—ever since I was born. My father was a minor bureaucrat who rented the place. Even now I pay next to nothing. My parents have died, and my sister is married—-she isn't a hunchback like myself, of course. Haru and I have only each other for company. So you must visit us as often as you can."

The beauty had remained silent for some time, and Hideko began to feel obligated to draw her into the conversation. "You weren't at the opera the other evening," she said.

No sooner were the words out of her mouth than she realized

that she couldn't have chosen anything worse to say. She had already run through all the possible reasons why the woman had not come to *Rigoletto*. None, she knew, would be a pleasant topic for the couple. How could she have been so stupid?

But the beauty wasn't at all perturbed. "We didn't have enough money for us both to go," was all she said.

"But what a fine *Rigoletto* it was!" he exclaimed, and launched into singing some lines from the opera. He had a fine voice, if a little high-pitched for a man.

The part he chose began where Rigoletto enters the Duke's residence and, acting the fool to disguise his concern, sings, "*La-la! La-la! La-la!*"—keeping an eye out for his daughter Gilda, who has been abducted by courtiers. The hunchback went as far as the chorus's lines, "*Oh, buon giorno, Rigoletto!*" (which he managed with aplomb). One of the climaxes of the opera, this scene is also the point where an actor playing Rigoletto has to display his grotesque deformity to the utmost.

The beauty was silent, her expression as self-absorbed as ever.

Hideko's desire to see the couple together in front of her that night at the performance of *Rigoletto* now found itself more than fulfilled. She felt terribly envious of the role the beauty was playing—being forced to watch in silent humiliation while her hunchback of a husband sang the part of Rigoletto to a stranger. And her envy only drew Hideko on to desire the sweetness of outright jealousy. . . .

The hunchback stopped. "Now it's your turn," he said to his wife.

"But I'm a terrible singer," she said with visible distress.

The man took no notice. "What's the song you're so good at? Oh yes, it's '*Batti, batti, bel Masetto,*' isn't it?"

"No, no, I can't. Really."

"Of course you can. You're always singing it, aren't you, when you're scrubbing out your saucepans!"

"You know how bad it sounds when I do. My voice is terrible."

"Oh, but that's exactly what I adore," the hunchback glowered. "Go on! Do as I say," he commanded.

Finally the young woman began to sing the '*Batti, batti*' aria by the peasant girl Zerlina from *Don Giovanni*. No sooner had she started, however, than Hideko was overcome with embarrassment. The woman was right when she said she was a terrible singer. She sounded like a worn-out scratchy record lurching around on an old wind-up gramophone. The tune bore some semblance to the original, but her voice swerved, going too sharp on high notes and too flat on low ones. That the singer was such a beautiful woman made it all the more excruciating to listen.

His expression softening, the hunchback looked from one woman to the other. Both of them, singer and listener, were near the limit of their endurance. The singing became slower and even more out of tune, and the hunchback began to shake with laughter. Finally, when he was roaring, the singing broke off abruptly, and the man continued chuckling away.

"Well, what do you think?" he asked. "Isn't she a treasure? Don't tell me you're not going to applaud!" He turned to Hideko. "Come on," he urged, "Give her a hand! Clap your loudest!"

Blushing, the women exchanged sympathetic glances.

"You surprise me!" he said to Hideko. "You don't know how to clap? Do you want me to teach you?" Springing up, he tried to grab her wrists—and she recoiled. "There's no need to run away," he remarked. Still laughing, he sat down and put on a show of clapping wildly by himself.

What a way to behave in front of a first-time visitor!

But by the time Hideko left them, she was no longer judgmental. On the contrary, she thought of the way the hunchback and the beauty had treated her, and thought that she could not have asked for anything more.

The beauty accompanied Hideko to the main road.

"That was such fun," she said. "It's so rare that Ken gets to play. It's amusing, isn't it, when he does. You will come as often as you can, won't you? Please come, whenever you like."

"Are you home every Sunday?" Hideko asked. She wanted to make absolutely certain.

They were at home nearly every day, the woman told Hideko, since Ken did his work there.

Hideko soon became a frequent visitor at the house of the hunchback and his wife. She devoted herself to becoming their friend. She had never met a real man or woman before, she realized. Compared to them, anyone else was just a generic human being.

The hunchback's outbursts of temper and the beauty's cringing subservience that Hideko had witnessed at the theater and on her first visit disappeared completely. Soon they asked, even demanded, that Hideko participate; and they were glad to let her share in the pleasure that accrued. Yes, as far as dispensing pleasure was concerned, this fascinating couple certainly had a rare talent. The beauty was usually the one to direct the performance—either because of some unspoken agreement or a natural inclination on her part—and Hideko complied without a second thought.

Mrs. Yamashita had declared several times that Sugino was a peculiar man—and it was true. But then, Hideko had turned out to be more than his match.

"Ken. Go and take a stroll," said the beauty one afternoon. "You haven't been out for four or five days. You should get some exercise."

The hunchback was at work, designing book advertisements and posters.

"Do I have to?" he asked. "Just when Hidé is here?"

"Hidé will go with you." The beauty turned and faced her. "Won't you, Hidé."

"Will you come, too, Haru?" Hideko asked. "Please come with us." She would have loved a walk outdoors with both of them.

"Me? I want to tidy up his desk while you two are out. That's what you want, too, isn't it, Ken?"

"I guess so—let's go, Hidé," he beckoned.

"Will you wear shoes? Or geta?"

"Oh, geta, I think," he said, sitting down on the ledge of the hallway. Today, with his usual jacket, he was wearing traditional split-toed socks. The beauty squatted down in the entranceway on the cement floor, lined up his wooden clogs, and, one at a time, slipped them onto his feet. Once she'd finished, she gave him a little look, and then, with one geta-clad foot, he kicked the side of her face. Falling back, the woman caught herself with a hand on the ground.

Hideko stood rooted to the spot. The beauty got up and brushed the dirt off her hand: "Oh, we didn't tell you, did we? That's a little habit with my husband, before he leaves the house. His way of saying good-bye."

"Yes. Shoes do just as well," the hunchback said. "Come on, Hidé, hurry up."

When they were outside, the hunchback slipped a hand in his trouser pocket and looked up at the sky.

"What a lovely day," he remarked. "Shall we take a walk to the shrine?"

His whole torso seemed concentrated in his hump; and his feet in their geta were astonishingly light skimming past each other at his trouser cuffs. Struggling to keep up with him, her eyes riveted on his feet, Hideko recalled the spectacle she had witnessed a moment before: the agility, the accuracy of the man's kick landing on the beauty's face. The mud on her cheek; the two welts raised by the ridges on the underside of the clog, just like two thick parallel lines of crimson paint; that sudden sparkle in her eyes. . . . And it had all happened before her as she stood, swooning, on the porch step.

After a while they reached a quiet shrine. Before the main hall, an old woman was watching children playing in a pool of sunlight—the usual, predictable sort of scene.

"You wouldn't think we were in a city, would you?" the hunchback remarked.

"No, that's true."

"What's the matter? You haven't opened your mouth since we left the house. Are you thinking about Germany?"

"No, not at all."

"You know, Haru's quite worried about you. She wonders what your plans are. Next time, why don't you bring us some of his letters? We'll help you decide what to do."

"No, please." Germany was the last thing on her mind—she couldn't have cared less about that. "Don't talk about him."

She appreciated that the hunchback had brought her to the shrine, just the two of them, and that he'd expressed a kindly concern for her. And yet, ever since they'd left the house, she had felt a mounting frustration. Obviously, the beauty had sent the two of them out for a walk to encourage greater intimacy, and Hideko took pleasure in the feeling of obligation this incurred. But for any real effect, she was thinking, she needed the woman there, too, before her eyes.

And rather than this deserted spot, Hideko wanted a busy marketplace teeming with people—she wanted to be running after the hunchback and the beautiful woman, basket in hand, as they moved ahead, arms linked, ordering her around, scolding and shouting at her as she did their shopping. She would love it if the three of them could try that. . . .

"Welcome back." The beauty came out to greet them when they returned. There was an extra pair of women's shoes in the entrance. "Toshiko is here," she told the hunchback.

"Really?" he replied, stepping into the hallway.

"Hello!" a loud voice called out from the inner room.

Hideko went inside, and beheld a cheerful, healthy-looking woman in her mid-twenties.

"Oh, you have a guest!" the woman said when she saw Hideko.

"She's a friend of ours," said the beauty. "A very good friend." Then, in a way that was very deferential to the woman, the beauty introduced her to Hideko.

"Hey!" said the hunchback, glancing over the table. "Can't you even bring out some cakes for our visitor?"

"We don't have any at the moment, unfortunately. And since you were out, I couldn't go myself. I'll do that now." The beauty took the man's cup out of the tea cabinet.

"What do you think you're doing?"

"I was going to pour you some tea."

"Leave it. Just go, will you?"

"Very well." The beauty stood up and then she added hesitantly, "Do you have any money?"

The hunchback produced a single hundred-yen coin from a jacket pocket, and handed it over. "You can buy some cigarettes too," he said as the beauty was leaving the room.

She looked back. "Will that be enough?"

"How much more should I give you?"

The beauty stared silently at the hundred-yen coin in her palm.

"I said, how much more do you want?"

"Thirty yen should be enough."

The hunchback gave her that exact amount.

"High and mighty as ever, aren't you?" said the hunchback's sister after his wife had left. She turned to Hideko. "Don't you think so? He's a real tyrant."

The hunchback ignored this. "You've been well?" he asked his sister, with genuine interest.

"Yes. I've put on weight, though."

"Hubby and kids okay?"

"Fine. But I want to ask you a favor. I'll tell you about it in a minute."

"I'm not sure I want to know."

"Oh, come now. I've already had a word with Haru."

The beauty soon returned. She served some little cakes and began preparing the tea. These were tasks that Hideko had become used to doing in her place. Hideko had been agonizing over the hunchback's empty cup on the table, and over the tea cabinet, its drawer left pulled out, while the beauty was away. But she had hesitated to lend a hand. The beauty had given no sign of wanting her to do anything, as she usually did; and no encouragement had come from the hunchback.

The beauty poured tea into Hideko's covered cup, and placed it in front of her. Meanwhile, the hunchback's sister chatted on energetically about soaring prices, bargains she had found at department store sales, and her plans for getting a part-time job. What a proper little housewife she was. But to what absurd lengths the beauty was going in an effort to treat her sister-in-law with respect. And how kind and calm the hunchback was being—the classic older brother. The couple, every so often, would remember themselves and put on a little of their scolding act.

Hideko was completely thrown off balance. She could not say a word. For some time now she had been the couple's partner, but they had never before appeared as a threesome in front of somebody else. She hadn't received directions yet as to how she should behave.

But surely a "very good friend" would never sit there without offering to pour a single cup of tea. She was acting ridiculously formal—she must try to behave a little more naturally. But all she could do was grab the teacup she had been staring at ever since it had been placed before her, again losing the chance to join in the conversation.

Hideko couldn't help feeling that the healthy young housewife must have seen through their whole ménage. Cheerfully talking on, laughing away, the young woman looked at her brother, and at her sister-in-law, and every now and then she glanced quickly in Hideko's direction. Any minute now, Hideko felt, she would turn on her and ask them: "By the way, you two, what is *she* doing here?"

But their meeting finally ended with Toshiko having done nothing of the sort.

"Toshiko," the beauty said. "Have you spoken yet with Ken about that matter?"

"Not yet. Ken, can I have a word with you?"

"Shall I leave?" Hideko asked, relieved.

"No, that's all right. We'll go upstairs," said the hunchback. He left the room with his sister.

"Did you enjoy the walk?" the beauty asked Hideko.

On the way to her next visit to the hunchback's house, Hideko dropped by a department store to buy some specialty foods for a parcel she was sending to Sugino. She had been balking at this task, and putting it off from one day to the next, and now less than a week remained till sea-mail packages had to be dispatched to reach their destinations by Christmas.

She began at the counter that sold foods for export: choosing dried seaweed, packets of festive rice and red beans, pickled radish, various ingredients for fish-ball stew, and New Year's rice cakes. With each tin she dropped into her cardboard box, she felt her conscience, so heavy for the last two weeks, grow a little lighter.

"Would you like us to ship these for you?" asked the clerk, totaling up her bill at the register.

That would have taken an even greater load off her mind, but Hideko remembered the large padded kimono at home. She had made it for her husband and wanted to include it in the package.

Hideko slid open the door of the couple's house.

"Who is it?" the beauty called down from the second floor.

"Me."

"Hidé! I'm so happy you're here. Ken's out on an errand. Will you come up? We can listen to records."

When Hideko went upstairs, the beauty looked at the parcel in her hands. "What's all that?" she asked.

"Food—a care package."

"I see," said the beauty. "The room is a lot tidier than usual today," she added, glancing around.

The entire second floor consisted of this single six-tatami-mat room. The only two mats free of furniture, however, were littered with papers and design tools. A sofa bed took up one wall; and the next had a large desk with another smaller one beside it. This was where the beauty sat to help the hunchback at his work. The beauty was tidying up her own desk as she spoke to Hideko. Both desks were buried under papers, brushes, rulers, and pots of poster colors. Next to the desks were rolls of paper, a bookshelf packed with small mechanical tools, an old gramophone, and some records.

"This is as neat as it gets," the beauty said, sitting down next to Hideko on the sofa. She pointed at the book shelves. "Ken won't let me touch those. That's his task—when he can be bothered. If you could see what a sight he is, with a workman's towel tied around his head. I'm the one who really does the work, though," she added.

The two of them competed for a while in their praises of the hunchback's beautiful hair.

"Was it always so thick?" the beauty mused aloud. "It's strange, but somehow I don't remember. I don't think his hair was like it is now. His health has improved lately, you know. When he was ill all the time maybe I didn't realize how thick it was. Until about three or four years ago, he was very delicate. He'd had pneumonia so many times, and suffered from insomnia, and he was always breaking out in a fever. His sister—the one you met the other day—helped me take care of him. Even now, he tires easily. He works for a while, and has to lie down, here." The beauty patted the sofa. "If we could get rid of this thing, we'd have some room, but it's convenient, so Ken wants to keep it. He sleeps on it at night, of course." Then she added,

"That's where I sleep," tracing a long line along the floor with her foot.

"Don't you push the table back?" Hideko asked, eyeing the narrow two-tatami strip.

"No, it stays put. I'm quite happy with that. Ken stretches a leg out and kicks me, and then I'm allowed up beside him." The beauty stroked the sofa-bed again. Her words brought bitterly to mind Hideko's own marital relations.

Sugino preferred the more predictable positions, but Hideko would always balk at complying immediately. First, she would turn away from him onto her side, then slide up higher and higher in the bed. Finally coming back down, she would swing a leg over and thrust her thigh against his mouth, begging him, despite his lack of interest, to try even a little in that way to arouse her.

"Hey, that's enough," he would say, finally, after several attempts. "Let's go to sleep."

How many times had she had to hear those words? He would sound calm, but actually be very irritated.

Hideko would find it impossible to fall to sleep. Couldn't he, she would say all of a sudden, hold her, at least? Taking the limp arm he threw over her, she would wrap it tightly about herself. The desire to try again would rise up in her. Couldn't he, she would beg, grip the flesh on her back—with feeling? Sugino would do as she asked, but with so little enthusiasm that she only became more exasperated.

One night her frustration made her finally burst out: "I'm going to buy a whip tomorrow."

"A whip? You can count me out."

"Say what you like. I'm still going to buy one," she had retorted, stubbornly. "They sell dog whips for six hundred yen. I'm sure I could get a really superb one for a thousand. Black leather, with a square grip, tapering off at the end into a nice, pliant braid." She'd let herself get carried away. "They sell them in department stores with the collars. A while ago I had a look—I was thinking of asking you to buy me one. I'll get one tomorrow. Then, when we go to bed, I'll start by giving myself a whipping. There's nothing else for us, is there?"

What had she been saying?

When Hideko caught herself, her husband had already moved away. She was brought to her senses by the change in his manner, by the awful, frightening signs traveling silently over to her through the darkness.

"But you'd better not kill me," she added.

Hideko waited a while, but the space beside her kept silent so she reached for Sugino's arm. He lifted her hand off him and calmly pushed it away. She'd realized then that it was all over.

Of course, with Sugino you couldn't tell whether he resented what had happened, but in any case, she knew that their relations would never improve.

Why on earth had she let her mouth run away to humiliate him so cruelly? Whenever she remembered that night Hideko felt a horror that refused to let up. It discouraged her from seeking his attention, making her hesitant, until in the end she withdrew from him of her own accord.

Hideko paid a call on Mrs. Yamashita, whom she hadn't seen since *Rigoletto*. The last time Hideko had visited her at home was when she'd attended the obligatory seventh-day service after Mr. Yamashita's death.

The interior of the house had not changed. Sitting down in the living room she'd once known so well, Hideko felt strangely nostalgic.

"How have you managed to get in such financial straits?" inquired the widow, referring to the topic Hideko had broached over the telephone.

"It's just that I don't have a penny to spare," Hideko said. "And there's an emergency."

Sugino, before his departure, had put all his bank account

books under lock and key. His company was paying an allowance for his household expenses in Tokyo during his absence, but he had calculated the exact amount of money she would need as a woman living alone, insisting that she use no more, and arranged for the rest to go into a long-term savings account under his name. Of course, Hideko had no intention of telling Mrs. Yamashita these details. She explained that Sugino had left her with about fifty thousand yen for an emergency, but there were reasons why the money was unavailable now.

"And you can't ask your brother?"

"No."

"I see. Well, I'm happy to help you, of course." Hideko had begged her over the telephone not to ask why she needed the money, and Mrs. Yamashita did not press any further. "You're still so young, my dear," the widow added. "You can always count on me." She laid two ten-thousand yen notes on the table.

Hideko had learned that the hunchback's sister had visited him that day to ask for a loan: she and her husband had won the chance to buy some housing in a public development, but even after scraping together all their money, they didn't have enough for the down payment. If the balance had been large, they would have given up right away; but it was a trifling sum, and it seemed a pity to abandon the project now. The deadline for the payment was still one month away. She had asked if her brother could lend her just seventy thousand yen.

The hunchback and his wife had said they would. Hideko remembered the beauty telling her that Ken's sister had been especially kind when his health was poor; and it appeared that the couple was in her debt financially, too. They thought, since over a month remained, they would have plenty of time to come up with the money.

The hunchback was visiting various clients to ask them for loans. One day when Hideko had dropped by, she heard the beauty ask him anxiously: "Will we have enough?"

"Don't you worry," the hunchback boasted. "In just ten days I've collected thirty thousand yen."

But as the deadline drew near, he appeared to be having less luck. On her next visit, Hideko heard the beauty say when the hunchback came home: "If we can't do it, we should let her know soon—if we tell her now, they may be able to get the last twenty thousand themselves."

"Give me three days," the hunchback had replied. Witnessing this exchange, Hideko told them she thought she could help. And she had been sure she could get hold of twenty thousand yen.

Even this modest amount, however, had proved difficult for Hideko to obtain. The more she thought about it, the more hesitant she became about using the money Sugino had left her—or asking her brother for help. She was fully prepared to pawn some of her belongings to help her friends. But here, too, she let her doubts get the better of her. In the end, she had resorted to the kindness of Mrs. Yamashita.

The widow made Hideko stay at her home for hours. It had been ages since they last saw each other, she chided. Hideko suspected the woman was shocked that she dared to come ask for a loan after not bothering to visit for so long. Hideko knew how callous and impudent she must seem. Mrs. Yamashita had witnessed her talk with the hunchback at *Rigoletto,* but when Hideko returned to her seat, she had simply said: "Oh, that's someone I met last time I was here." The widow had probably forgotten the incident, but even so, Hideko felt doubly guilty thinking about whom the money was for.

During the past few months, Hideko had started to understand why she had neglected Mrs. Yamashita after her husband's death. It had happened naturally: had Mrs. Yamashita been the one to die, she realized, she would have dropped Mr. Yamashita in exactly the same way.

It was already seven o'clock by the time she left Mrs. Yamashita's house. She could take a train from the nearby station directly home, so rather than proceeding to the home of the hunchback and his wife as she'd planned, Hideko stopped by the main post office and sent the borrowed money by mail.

She received an acknowledgment soon. Though signed by the hunchback, the note had clearly been penned by the beauty; the handwriting and polite phrasing were hers. She thanked Hideko for the money, and invited her to attend a party at four o'clock on Christmas Eve. "We'll have all sorts of fun!" the letter read: "But no more visits until then." At the end came a P.S. scrawled in brash red ink, the only words from the hunchback himself: A GRAND TIME WILL BE HAD BY ALL!

Christmas was still eight days away, and more than ten days since their last communication, when she had sent the money. Lately, she had seen them much more frequently. What did they mean, "no more visits until then"? Was she forbidden to go and see them? That was a rude acknowledgment of a loan. Judging from the flourish of the P.S., though, they were not upset with her for anything. . . . Feeling a little out of sorts, she sent a postcard inquiring discreetly whether they were busy, but she received no reply.

When the day finally came, Hideko set out and arrived at the appointed hour.

The hunchback and the beauty were sitting at the heated table, which had been moved into the parlor from the larger room. They expressed a few words of gratitude for her loan, and then said, one after the other:

"Well, how did you feel?"

"Did you die from waiting? How patient you've been."

Hideko smiled and moved to join them. But they didn't let her: "No," the beauty admonished and pushed down the blanket that Hideko was trying to lift up. "There's no room for you, Hidé. We're the only ones allowed to warm ourselves under here. Right, Ken?"

They both burst out laughing. Hideko sat down with a pained look on her face.

"There's a chicken under the table," the hunchback said. "It's been delivered for tonight's dinner." He glanced at the other room. "Look. We've cleaned everything—even the glass."

Hideko saw that the glass doors, normally left just to gather dust, had been polished. Through them she caught a clear glimpse of the wintry evening sky.

"The two of us cleaned up just to welcome you, Hidé," the hunchback said. "It was quite a job."

"He's right," the beauty chimed in. "I had to drag out that enormous charcoal brazier. We're exhausted. So we're going to rest now. You can do the work. The mats in the other room still need help." She reached around behind her. "Here, catch!" She tossed two ragged towels at Hideko. "A light dusting will do."

She couldn't move freely in her kimono, so the beauty told Hideko that she should change into some of her clothes. The skirt the beauty brought out was far too tight, but somehow she forced Hideko into it.

As Hideko crawled over the mats on her hands and knees, she got an inkling of why they were welcoming her in this way, and what kind of time she was in for tonight. How wonderful they were to her, she thought. Meanwhile, sitting at the table, the two of them didn't stop taunting her.

"Don't try to skip anything. Remember, we're watching you," warned the hunchback.

"She's got tears in her eyes," commented the beauty.

"Dust underneath the brazier, will you? Hey! Don't just drag it. You'll ruin the tatami!" ordered the hunchback.

"You're warmer now, aren't you, Hidé?" teased the beauty. "See, you don't need to sit here with us. Maybe you're even a little hot."

When Hideko finished dusting, the beauty announced that it was time for a bath. The hunchback went into the room with the tub beside the kitchen, and the beauty followed.

"Hidé," she called after a while, "Come and scrub his back."

Hideko hesitated.

"Come on," the hunchback added softly.

Hideko did as she was told. Thick clouds of steam drifted up around the bathroom light. The hunchback was sitting with his back toward the door. The beauty, fully dressed, perched behind him on a section of the bath's square wooden cover.

"Now, put some water in the dipper," said the beauty. "And rub some soap on the towel. . . ."

Hideko found it impossible to take in all of the hunchback's body, even though he was puny. His hump, which she'd thought was set just below the nape of his neck, jutted up from a low, unexpected position and twisted around to the right. On either side his shoulder blades rose and fell faintly with each breath—and there was something indefinable that made them much more striking and raw than a normal man's. Hideko went up with a towel in one hand, touching his wet shoulder with the other, and tried to focus on his hump. But the whiteness foaming over the strange shape, and the slippery sensation of rubbing it with the warm wet towel was stimulating, and called all sorts of thoughts to mind.

"It's no good. She's just barely stroking it!" the hunchback complained.

"She'll get it. Come on," the beauty exhorted Hideko: "Use some force!"

This sent Hideko's head reeling; she found herself less and less able to comply.

"It's no good. You take over, Haru," the hunchback said, at last.

"That's enough now, Hidé. Go away."

Hideko rinsed her hands in the wooden bucket's hot water and stood up. As she closed the door, laughter and splashing sounds rang in her ears.

The beauty had already finished her own bath by the time the hunchback emerged.

The front door opened and they heard a delivery man call out his greeting.

"Ken," said the beauty, "let's use the cash we got from you-know-who." She took an envelope of money from the tea cabinet drawer, cut it open, and left the room.

She returned bearing a splendidly garnished fowl on a large china platter. She glanced at Hideko, tittered, and told her to hurry up and have her bath.

By the time Hideko came out, the table had been dragged back into the larger room and covered with a sumptuous feast.

"It's Christmas! We ought to be extravagant!" exclaimed the beauty, throwing a heap of red-hot coals on the brazier, her face flushed from the bath. She had removed her over-jacket, Hideko noticed, and now wore just a silk kimono with that same yellow sash.

It was time to gather around the Christmas dinner. Hideko started to feel intoxicated—the hunchback was filling her glass again and again. "You can manage it," he was saying. She knew he was trying to get her drunk, but it began to be too much of an effort to refuse him. Finally she just sat there, gazing at the rim of her wine glass, a twinkly circle that tipped up to meet the purplish stream.

"Hidé, you're getting a lot of attention today," the beauty was saying. "Don't you agree, Ken?"

"I do," the hunchback replied.

And then suddenly Hideko gasped—the beauty had sprung to her feet: "It's unfair! Unfair!" she was screaming. "What about me! Now it's my turn, Ken! I'm begging you, please!"

She was unwinding her yellow sash.

The hunchback obeyed. When the beauty had stripped down to her last piece of lingerie, he used the yellow sash to tie her hands behind her, binding her to the ring handles of the wardrobe doors.

The beauty began to gasp and moan. "There you two are

enjoying yourselves," she said, deliriously: "But I've hardly eaten a thing. I'm starving!"

The hunchback threw a gnawed drumstick at her naked shoulder. "There you are."

With all her might Hideko tried to think of Germany, about the town she had never seen, called G—. Was it snowing there tonight? Were the church bells ringing? Had her parcel arrived on time with its festive rice and red beans, and the ingredients for fish-balls and broth?

But it was no use. She let the fork fall from her hands with a clatter.

"What's up, Hidé?" The hunchback looked at her. There was a pause. "All right, all right," he said, getting up. "It's your turn now."

🏵 *Crabs* (KANI, 1963)

THE REST CURE YŪKO HAD INSISTED ON SO stubbornly did improve her health remarkably. Only ten days away from Tokyo on the Soto Bōshū coast, and all those feelings of enervation and helplessness had vanished completely. Day by day she sensed the strength returning to her body. Spring had finally come, and with it she could feel her own rejuvenation.

"Now, it's only to be for one month," Kajii, her husband, escorting her there on the train, had said once more: "You understand?" Beyond the window on the right side, the Bōsō sea, only glimpsed before in between huddles of cottages and cliffs, had suddenly burst into full view. All along, she reflected, Kajii had denied her need for a change of scene.

When she'd first talked about a rest cure, he had listened, humoring her, certain she was only half serious. But when he realized it was no joke, he had stared at her, amazed. Why, he asked, would anybody want such an old-fashioned remedy? Wasn't she already receiving the best possible medical treatment for her tuberculosis? He had then reeled off all the reasons she should not go. First of all, it would cost a great deal of money: she'd have to stay at an inn, or room with a family. He could accept that, of course, if there was any reasonable hope for a cure; but he would not tolerate wasting money on something that would probably not help at all. In fact, she would be lucky if it had no ill effect. What if, after having made such strides toward recovery, she acted on this whim—and then suffered a relapse as a result? And besides, she was bound to get depressed in such an isolated place: once that happened, she would never improve, whatever the climate. Why go to all this trouble, and waste money in the bargain? he demanded, now adamantly opposed to her plan.

Each point he raised was true enough, Yūko knew, but she couldn't bring herself to abandon the idea. So she persisted.

"I'm sure I'll recover completely if I go," she pleaded. "I just know it. I admit it's selfish, but please let me. It won't be for long."

It had been late autumn, two and a half years before, when Yūko's first symptom of tuberculosis had appeared. She had spat up a small quantity of blood. The winter that followed had flown by and she scarcely noticed it. The experience of being hospitalized for the first time in her life; her sense of panic at the disaster that had befallen her; and her impatience for the signs of recovery promised by proper treatment: all this had made her oblivious to the passage of time.

By the second winter, Yūko could only wonder at the miracles of modern medicine. Her treatment was working: the injections had had no side effects; and despite all her fears, her stomach had absorbed with no signs of strain the sandy para-amino acid she had to consume in such large quantities. With each new X-ray, she could see the TB lesions—at first three thick branches spreading out from the middle of her right lung—slowly getting smaller and fading away.

"You're responding remarkably well to the treatment," the doctor told her. "It won't be long now."

By the following autumn, Yūko was well enough to return home and commute to the hospital as an outpatient. Kajii had been having the elderly woman from the little cooper's store, Takara-ya, near their apartment complex come in twice a week to do his laundry and clean the house; she cooked dinner for him too, on the days she came in, and ran his bath. They decided to keep her on even after Yūko returned home. The woman took charge of the heavy housework, though Yūko could soon handle some tasks herself.

Yūko still caught colds easily, and would occasionally run a fever for two or three days during her period. But she refused to let it bother her. "There's nothing to worry about," she would say to Kajii. "I just have to accept it. It's all part of the recovery process."

Her health had greatly improved over the first year of treatment, but Yūko spent the next winter in a state of unbearable impatience. Her chest X-rays showed her three lesions very much reduced: now there were just two branches, their shadows on the negative no bigger than pine needles.

"I don't think they'll ever disappear entirely," her doctor had said the previous summer. "They're like scars left from a burn. But you're definitely over the disease itself. Once the weather cools down you'll feel completely well."

He had raised Yūko's hopes. But autumn had passed into winter, and she still hadn't regained her health. The very smoothness of her initial recovery now worked against her, increasing her anxiety. She started to get irritated by the erratic ups and downs of her physical state, which she'd been able to accept before.

"I still don't feel well," she grumbled to the doctor, as if blaming him. "Why's it taking so long?"

"Be patient," he replied, calmly. "You'll feel stronger soon. Even a little cold takes a while to get over, doesn't it? How can you expect instant health after coughing up blood? You're still taking a nap in the afternoon? Good. As long as you keep that up."

Yūko was hardly in a position to forget her nap. All day her whole body longed for the hours between one and three o'clock. She tried not to rest at other times during the day, because her doctor had told her that taking it too easy would delay her recovery. But she only really felt well in the morning, the first few hours after getting out of bed. As the day wore on, her sense of well-being would recede; her body grew heavy and her shoulders stiff. Sometimes the ache would extend up her neck all the way to her head, leaving her exhausted by noon. Some days she would marvel at how well she was bearing up; but then by late afternoon her cheeks would start to burn, and the thermometer would show her running a temperature.

When Kajii asked how she was feeling, she would have to report that there was no change. But she could no longer make light of it as she had done before, and she finally started to give full vent to her frustration. Sometimes she would sigh: "Perhaps I should have gone ahead and had that operation after all!"

"Don't be absurd!" Kajii replied, frowning.

In deciding against surgery, Yūko had followed medical advice, but there had, in fact, been considerable differences of opinion among the professionals treating her. The surgeon had argued that the only cure was to cut away the infected area. Her own doctor, however, had disagreed, pointing out that Yūko was over thirty, past the age when this operation yielded the best results. Besides, he said, though shallow, the lesions were widespread, which would involve excising a large area. His advice was to treat the lung with drugs. The loss of an organ through surgery, he added, takes a toll on the rest of the body until the day you die.

This last argument had been the one to finally sway Yūko. But there was no denying that other, personal, considerations also figured in her decision. She knew, though she made no mention of this to her doctors, that surgery would leave her with a large scar across her back, something Kajii, in particular, was opposed to. When the surgeon tried to explain to them the operation's advantages, he had replied, dubiously: "Well, if you really think she has no choice." But as soon as her doctor made his counterargument, he agreed with him: "I'm sure you're right. If three or four staff members were laid off at my office, the others would be crushed by the extra work. It's much better to keep everyone there, even if they're a little inefficient. The body must work the same way."

But when Yūko's body failed to recover beyond a certain point, even with all the medication, she couldn't help having second thoughts about having refused surgery. If only she'd had the operation, those shadowy pine-needle shapes on her lung wouldn't be bothering her now—she wouldn't be suffering these interminable aftereffects.

Kajii, however, disagreed: "If you'd had surgery, they might have had to operate several times, and you'd still be bed-ridden," he said. "You worry too much. That's the problem. Even people in the best of health have days when they run a temperature. They just don't realize it because they're not fussing over themselves all day."

One evening, after dinner, she reached for the metal medicine box to take her para-amino acid, and Kajii stopped her. "Can't you take that later?"

"Well, all right," she replied, and pressed the lid down. Then she rose, and put the tin away in a cupboard. Ever since bringing the box from hospital, where it had been placed at her bedside, she had left it out in plain view on the table. For more than a year now, she realized, she'd been subjecting Kajii to the sight of it—and to the ritual of her reaching for the box and taking out a sachet of the powder to swallow down. She had been so preoccupied with her illness, heedless of his feelings, she reflected; no wonder a long-term patient becomes an object of hostility. And yet it was probably only recently that he had openly started to resent her behavior. As these thoughts flooded into her mind, she began to feel the blood coming to her cheeks.

Yūko had never been able to be satisfied by ordinary love-making, and even now that she had fallen ill, she would demand that Kajii use violent methods of arousal.

"This'll only make you weaker," he would warn, when she

demanded that he use greater force. She refused to listen. Kajii would protest again, but despite his words, he would be doing as she asked.

For a time, this element of anxiety had heightened their sense of abandon and increased their pleasure. But now she knew that the need to be careful, coupled with her arbitrary point-blank refusals caused by the extreme mood swings characteristic of TB, was becoming more than he could bear. Whenever she did suffer a relapse after their lovemaking, he seemed to feel renewed disgust for her lack of shame and for the way she didn't hesitate to then complain about her health. Just the sight of her appeared to put him in a bad mood.

Meanwhile, the cold cloudy weather didn't change: she could rarely leave the apartment even for a stroll. On these days, Yūko's physical condition would be even worse, and it didn't help that their apartment was in a huge modern complex: she was beside herself with boredom. She longed desperately for spring. If only the weather would improve, she thought, she could recover, physically and emotionally. Before the month of January was out, however, she'd lost all patience.

"Why don't you go skiing for a few days?" she suggested to Kajii. He had always enjoyed the sport. "You weren't able to go last year, or the year before." She managed to get him to go skiing twice.

"My. And leaving the patient all alone?" the old woman from the cooper's remarked, when she found out.

"It was my idea!" Yūko retorted. The old woman was a hard worker and she meant well, but she could be annoyingly snide.

When Yūko told her she was thinking about a rest cure, the old woman replied: "Well, aren't you the lucky one!" And then, with a knowing air, she added something that left Yūko speechless: "But you never know what trouble a man'll get into left all by himself!"

Yūko grew weary, waiting for spring, and found herself thinking more and more of the warm Soto Bōshū coast, where they had once stayed together in Kajii's company's vacation home. She had vivid memories of warmth flowing up her legs as soon as she set foot on the beach, the soft seaside air, and the summery glow of the sunshine, in contrast to the weather in Tokyo, which at the same season had a distinct chill. And the people of the region had been so simple and kind, she remembered. One day she and Kajii had been waiting at a bus stop, when a young farm girl in pantaloons and smock passed by, pulling a wheelbarrow full of vegetables. They asked her about the bus route, and she replied in slow, unhurried tones: "Wait here. It'll come." After going on a few yards, she tipped down her wheelbarrow and came back to say something else, which they didn't understand, and she had to repeat: "The ticket costs ten yen."

Soon spring was nearly upon them, and still Kajii rejected the rest cure idea. By now, however, Yūko no longer cared what season it was: she wanted to go. She was determined to get to the seaside, whatever Kajii's objections—nothing would stop her. She didn't care if it did throw off their budget. Perhaps she never should have conceived this plan, but now that she had, it seemed to her that his refusal to let her go was actually undermining her full recovery. If only he'd let her go, she kept insisting, she would be completely healed.

Kajii finally gave his consent, begrudgingly, persuaded by Yūko's doctor, who encouraged them to give it a try. "A couple of months won't do any harm," the doctor said. "I'll give her a supply of medicine. We'll worry about a relapse if and when it happens. I'll soon get her on the mend."

"You don't need that long a visit," Kajii told Yūko. "I'm not having you fall into one of your depressions. I'm still not persuaded it's a good idea, you know. I'm only letting you go because you've worn me out. One month will be quite enough."

And now, here she was, looking out the train window at the Bōsō sea twinkling in the warm spring sunlight. The sea looked choppy today. White-crested waves were pummeling the heads of the low shoals jutting out from the shore, which was dotted here and there with houses. Even inside the train she could hear the crash of the waves breaking against the rocks and then sweeping back down the beach.

Perhaps the sight of the deserted coast prompted Kajii to insist again on her staying only one month.

"I haven't forgotten," she said to him, nodding. She wouldn't ask to stay longer, she meant to reassure him, no matter how much she might want to. She turned and looked out the window at the distant horizon, at the bobbing waves glinting in the sun, at the little green islands off the coast, and the wet sand on the shore turning dark and light as the waves pulled back and forth. And she thought to herself: I'm here. I've made it to the Bōsō coast! That alone sent the strength surging through her.

Yūko's room, located for her by the manager of Kajii's company's vacation home, was on the second floor of a gift shop, the last but one in the short row of such stores in the village. The smallest room in a set of three (all with reddened worn tatami mats, and separated by a small corridor), it was probably used to accommodate guests in the summer season. At the back of the house, it looked out over the sea. The man thought she would like this better than an inn, where the meals would be the same day after day, or a pension, where she would have to put up with the noise of locals gathering to drink. Yūko wouldn't have minded cooking for herself if he'd been able to find a suitable place, a small cottage, for example. But here she would have her meals prepared for her. The mother and daughter were at home all day running the shop, while the father of the family worked as a clerk at an inn.

As soon as Yūko arrived, she felt freed from everything that had been weighing her down—her listlessness, the heaviness in her shoulders, her depression, and all the bad feeling between her and Kajii. She could definitely feel herself getting stronger.

It had been so long since freshness and vigor had flooded every part of her body—this was exactly how she'd felt before falling ill. Several times a day, with a mixture of nostalgia and pleasure, she savored her emotional and physical well-being.

Here, though she continued to take her nap every day, Yūko spent the mornings and late afternoons outdoors. Sometimes she would go to look at the large fish farm just along the shore, or, slightly farther away, to a flower nursery, where she'd buy marguerites or wallflowers in a bunch of three for ten yen. But most of her time she spent down on the beach. Sitting on the decks of deserted beach huts, on the last swing in a buckled row (apparently the work of the typhoon two years before), or on a rock ledge overlooking the sea—she never tired of watching the rollers. They broke in any number of ways; and then there were the small black periwinkles playing in the rock pools; and masses of torn seaweed thrown up with the waves that rushed between the low rocks, only to be swept away again. As the sun went down, the sea became a clear indigo blue. Yūko would stay and gaze at the sunset, until suddenly the breeze came up, and she would realize it was time to go in.

She could still only take the briefest of baths in the evenings, and often at dusk she would watch children playing baseball on the beach in the distance beyond the covered veranda. They carried their games on late, well after dark; it was a wonder they could see the ball. On and on they played. She would leave the room for a minute, and come back to find the beach deserted. It was strange how she never caught sight of the children actually leaving the beach.

Yūko did not mind having to dine alone. Sometimes as she sat eating, her landlady would come in with some fresh raw sea urchin, delivered a few moments before. "Would you like some?" she might ask, and set them down, cracked open and still bristling with spines. The woman would stay, chatting on interminably, but this too Yūko did not mind.

She had hardly touched the embroidery, books, and radio

which she had brought along with her. After eight o'clock at night, she was too tired to do anything. She had worried a little that the sound of the waves might keep her from falling asleep, but it did nothing of the sort. Every morning she woke up at 5:30, refreshed and ready to face the day, just as she had as a young girl.

It was so wonderful to be there. Paradise, Yūko thought. Before she arrived, she had expected to be able to get some perspective on the days she and Kajii had spent squabbling. But once here, maybe because her nerves had relaxed so completely, she found she couldn't bother trying to locate the source of their tension. Occasionally, something came back to mind, but only a vague and blurry memory, which refused to come into focus and soon faded away. Even matters of love and sex seemed to belong to a distant, previous existence.

Yūko began to daydream about settling down in a place like this, alone. Perhaps she could run a small gift shop. She wouldn't need to stock much: a few picture postcards, kokeshi dolls, candy, net bags of natural seashells, wakamé seaweed wrapped in paper and marked by hand with "50 yen" or "100 yen," sazae shellfish, dried clams. . . . One day, when she returned from a walk, a customer in front of the shop had mistaken her for a clerk. "Hey, give me one of those, will you?" he said, pointing to a packet of wakamé. "Certainly," she replied, handing it to him and receiving a 100-yen coin in return.

Schools were already closed for spring vacation. It wouldn't be long before people started arriving on holiday trips. For the moment, though, even on Sundays, gift shop customers were few and far between. The saleswomen didn't bother standing out in front to hail people. Their only sales ploy was to drop an extra sazae from the big box into the customer's basket. "This one's free." If that was all there was to it, even she could manage. If she could only move to this beautiful, warm seaside town, if she could have her fill of all this peace, all this freedom and good health—then, surely, Yūko thought, she could live without any other consolation.

And then Kajii's younger brother, who was a school teacher, came with his wife and little boy to visit the place and see how she was doing.

Yūko was returning from a walk around midday when she heard a shout over the road's grassy bank from the beach below, and she saw a child down there, waving. It was her nephew, Takeshi.

"Well, how nice!" Yūko said, leaning over the bank. "Didn't anyone come with you?" The boy didn't reply but immediately started to clamber up the embankment, scrambling as fast as he could through the shoulder-high grass, his little legs pumping up against his chest, and finally emerging up on the road.

"Where've you been?" he asked accusingly, pulling on her hand. "We've been waiting."

"Oh, I'm sorry. Who's 'we'?"

"Oh, both of them." Takeshi started to walk, still holding her hand.

"Did you come on the semi-express?"

"The 'Bōsō No. 1!'" he replied. Then he faced straight ahead, pulling the visor of his brand-new school cap to the left and right. "I'm a first-grader now!" he announced.

Yūko, who had been about to comment on his uniform, realized she was being asked for congratulations, and duly complied. "I bet you can't wait to start school!" she added. Then she slowed down a little, and leaned over for a look. It was adorable. The hooks under his little chin; the white collar of his shirt, just visible within his jacket's black collar; the two neat rows of gold buttons on his chest; the square cuffs, with a line of three small buttons accentuating the manliness of his chubby little wrists. Everything was there, in miniature. He was like a little doll. Yūko was enchanted.

"Did we surprise you?" Takeshi asked, pulling her along to make her hurry.

Yūko's brother-in-law and his wife were waiting in her room, sitting at the low table, empty teacups in front of them.

"You look so well!" they both exclaimed when she appeared with Takeshi. "You even look as if you've put on weight!"

"It's because I made Kajii give me this time all to myself," Yūko answered. She looked over at Takeshi, who had gone to stand next to his mother. "Well *what* a nice surprise!" she said, with a touch of formality. "And doesn't your school uniform suit you!"

Kōji looked at his son, proudly.

"All right, Takeshi," Fumiko said. "Let's get you changed. You've had your chance to show off in front of Auntie." She pulled her traveling bag toward her. Then she exclaimed: "Oh! You *are* a dirty boy! You've got it dirty already!" Dragging him by one elbow over to the window, she began brushing off the dirt from his climb up the bank.

"When are we going to have our lunch?" the boy asked, undaunted.

Fumiko looked over her shoulder. "We've brought lunch for you, too, Yūko, if you'd like."

Yūko proposed that they all have lunch down on the beach. On their way out, she bought sazae from the shop, and got her landlady to fill an empty bottle with soy sauce. Once they were down on the beach, she started to make a fire in the shelter of an overhanging rock, sending Takeshi, beside himself with excitement, to collect dry sticks and driftwood.

"What a great idea, Yūko!" Kōji said. He brought out a small bottle of whiskey.

"I've been wanting to do this for so long," Yūko said, wisps of smoke blowing past her eyes. "I couldn't do it all alone."

"Really? I would have, every day."

At last she got a good blaze going, and they placed the sazae around the edge of the fire.

"Auntie, do you need any more?" Takeshi asked, bringing up another four or five pieces of driftwood and setting them down.

"No, that's all right," Yūko said. "Thank you. Here, come

sit by me." She spread a sheet of newspaper next to her, keeping it from blowing away until Takeshi settled his little bottom on it.

"This one's huge!" he exclaimed and pointed at a sazae in the basket: protuding out of its shell was a particularly thick, slightly spiralled twist of flesh. Takeshi fearlessly stuck out his finger and moved closer to the fierce-looking thing. Suddenly it shrank back inside and Takeshi, snatching his hand away, jumped back. They all burst out laughing.

For the first time since she arrived, Yūko went without her afternoon nap. Once the picnic was over, she continued to keep her guests entertained. She wasn't conscious of having to make an effort. She was exhilarated; and yet she felt no onset of a fever. Just offshore was a little island that she hadn't set foot on yet. They were rowed across, and wandered about from rock to rock, and then the boat was rowed back, and they walked along the beach away from the village, gathering shells and taking photographs of one another. Still Yūko was quite content, not in the least bit tired.

Kōji and Fumiko had no way of knowing about her afternoon nap regimen, but they did voice some concern. "Are you sure it's all right for you to be so energetic?

"Let's go back to the house. You mustn't overdo it."

Yūko took no notice. If anything, she felt irritated by their words.

"Don't you think it's a nice spot?" she exclaimed, learning it was their first visit to the area. "Aren't you glad you came?"

The sun was beginning its descent. They had been sitting on a ramshackle boat for a few minutes, Kōji having insisted that the adults, at least, take things more easily. Yūko looked toward the sea, glowing now with the first rays of sunset.

"Look how blue the sea gets," she said. "Always around this time, it turns a beautiful deep blue."

The three of them sat there for a while longer. Finally, Kōji, who had his arms wrapped around his knees, turned his wrist and looked at his watch. Fumiko glanced at it too, and nodded meaningfully.

"We should be going," she said.

"We'll be right on time for the train if we pack up now."

"Are you taking the semi-express?" Yūko asked, staring at Takeshi, playing a little distance away.

"That's what we'd planned."

"What if you stayed the night?" Yūko proposed.

"That's out of the question," replied Kōji. "We just came to see how you're doing. My brother would never forgive me if we stayed."

"Oh, he won't mind," Yūko said. "Please stay. You're on vacation, aren't you?"

"We'll be coming again," Fumiko said flatly. "Do you want me to go and get him?" she asked her husband.

"Takeshi!" Kōji shouted. "Come along!"

Takeshi stood up, clutching the handkerchief with all of his spoils that he had set down beside him on the sand. Instead of turning around, however, he stuck up a chubby forearm and waved his hand a few times, as if to say: "I'm not coming!" Child though he was, he knew perfectly well he was not being called back to be shown something new and exciting this time.

"Poor boy!" Yūko said, "Just when he seems to like it so much." His little gesture, which seemed to her to speak volumes, made her remember all the other things he had said and done during the course of the day. She could see his pure white undershirt peeping out of his brick-red wool shirt. Not for one instant had his small body stood still. How he had hopped and skipped about when he discovered a pile of sea shells, busily picking them up! When she had found a dried up "box fish" lying in the sand, a rare variety of blowfish (she'd been learning about such things since her arrival), he had come running up to look. After staring at the weird object for a while, he had put both hands behind him, and said, "No thanks." And when the boatman who took them to the island had huffed and puffed, pulling on the oars, Takeshi had asked him, "Are we that heavy, Sir?"

Now he was scampering even further away and stopping to examine something else.

"It's no good. Go and get him," Kōji said to Fumiko.

"Oh, why not leave him?" Yūko said, just as Fumiko got up.

"But we'll miss our train."

"No, leave him with me," Yūko said. "Just for a couple of days. It'll do him good. Besides, the day after tomorrow is Saturday, when his uncle's coming. He can take him back."

"But he's still so little," Kōji said.

"And he'll be too much for you, Yūko," Fumiko chimed in.

Yūko took no notice. "Takeshi!" she called. "Are you coming?" Seeing he was about to dash away again, she added: "I've something nice to tell you!" At this, Takeshi stopped, turned round, and started heading toward her.

How could she persuade him? Yūko wondered, keeping her eyes on him. Kajii was going to visit her the day after tomorrow. She felt no joy at the prospect, despite being able to show him how much her health had improved. They had been apart for two weeks now. The prospect of having to deal with him weighed on her mind. But Kajii was very fond of Takeshi. If only the boy were present when they met again, perhaps they'd be able to spend a day like today, in innocent enjoyment. This idea made her all the more unwilling to let him go.

Takeshi was now by her side.

"What is it?" he asked, and immediately poured the treasures from his handkerchief out onto the sand.

"What are you doing that for!" Fumiko scolded. "You'll only have to pick them all up again!"

Takeshi crouched over his pile of shells, and started scouring through them. "Where's it gone?" he cried. "My crab's disappeared!"

"What crab?" Yūko asked, poking at the shells with her finger. "It must have run away."

"No, it was a crab's shell," Takeshi said, combing through his collection again. He brought out two or three thin crab legs, in pieces and bleached white by the sun.

"This must be what you're looking for," Yūko said, picking one up. "It must have broken apart."

"Oh no!"

"That's too bad," Fumiko said. Kōji chuckled. "You shouldn't have crammed them in all together."

"Takeshi, do you want to stay the night here?" Yūko asked. "You're a grown-up boy now, so you won't be afraid without Mummy and Daddy, will you? I'll find you some crabs: live ones, with bright red pincers. You can bring them back with you to Tokyo. Uncle Kajii will take you home. He's coming the day after tomorrow."

Takeshi tore his eyes away from the pile of broken shells.

"Where will we find them?" he asked.

"Well—lots of places."

"But why didn't you take me there today?"

"Because I forgot. Let's go and look tomorrow."

"What about Mummy and Daddy?" Takeshi asked, looking at them.

"Us? We're going home," Kōji said.

"Can we come again to hunt for crabs?"

"But there might not be any around then," Yūko said quickly.

"I don't know what to do!" Takeshi wailed.

"Well," Kōji said, "It's up to you to decide."

"All right," Takeshi declared, suddenly. "I've decided. You go on home." He waved his hand at his parents.

Till the very last moment Yūko was on tenterhooks about whether Takeshi would have the courage to stick to his decision. She was still prepared for him to back down when they reached the front of the shop and it was time to part. Her hand on his shoulder, she almost winked at them, as if it were all a joke.

"Well, this is goodbye, then."

"Thank you," they murmured, bending over briefly for a look at their son's face. "Do look after him." They walked away a little, looking back again. Whether he had forgotten them or he was trying to look as if he didn't care, he avoided their gaze and concentrated on pulling the rubber bands around the rows of wakamé packets on display, making them go snap. Yūko lost no time in turning him around and steering him inside the shop, where she could finally relax.

She did not feel tired, but because she had walked around more than usual, she refrained from taking a bath, though it would have been more than welcome. Asking the landlady to prepare a bath for Takeshi, she watched over his ablutions from the side of the tub. By the time he was washed and clean, and she brought him upstairs, it was dark outside. She slipped him into the fresh underwear his mother had brought in case he got wet wading, and then hastily closed the rain shutters, not wanting the sea under the dark night sky to scare him.

"Could you bring in an extra bed?" she asked, when the daughter came in with their evening meal tray. It was some time since her tuberculosis had been contagious, but she felt hesitant about letting the boy sleep with her. His parents were bound to make inquiries later.

She tucked Takeshi into bed dressed in his shirt, and began preparing to lie down herself.

"Where are my shells, Auntie?" he asked, turning his head on the pillow.

"Don't worry," she said, over her shoulder. "They're safe. They're all on the veranda railing."

She slipped into bed with the light still on, and stole a look at the boy lying by her side. He was gazing up at the ceiling. His child's head seemed very small, sticking out from the adult-size bedcovers. What was he thinking about? Was he thinking about home?

"When are we going crab-hunting?" he asked.

"Tomorrow."

"I know, but can we go after breakfast?"

"If you want to."

Now that was decided, he twisted over onto his side and wiggled toward her to the edge of the bed.

"Tell me a story."

"You've forgotten your pillow."

He pulled over the cushion she had wrapped in a towel, and laid his head on it. "Come on," he said. "Tell me a story."

"A story. . . . A story," Yūko said, hesitating. "Let me try and think of one." She had no experience telling children stories. She could recollect two or three tales, but there was a special way to begin, wasn't there, and she didn't remember that.

"Don't you have one you could tell me?" she said, feeling too uneasy. "What about a story you've seen on television? What's your favorite? 'General Pon-pon'?"

"No."

"Well, which one?"

"I don't like television," he answered. He flipped his body over one more time so that he was now on his stomach, face down, and put one arm under his pillow.

"Scratch my back," he said.

Yūko sat up in bed, and put a hand down the collar of the boy's shirt, feeling the warmth of his skin inside. "Where does it itch?" she asked. "Here?" Her curled fingers moved around.

Takeshi buried his face in the pillow. He nodded slightly.

"How long has it been itching? Were you bitten by a bug?"

"I always have my back scratched when I go to sleep," he said. "Go a bit higher."

Yūko complied. Takeshi closed his eyes, clearly enjoying the sensation. "Don't always scratch the same place," he said, after a while.

First one spot, and then another came up for request. For all its smallness, his little back never seemed to run out of scratchable places. Holding back the covers with her arm, Yūko scratched his firm flesh in small circles with her fingertips—to the right, to the left, down the middle, and then back up again. Her hand started to get a little tired.

"One more time, where you were scratching before."

Yūko moved her hand as she had been told.

"A bit further down. No, further."

"Here?"

"No," he replied, eyes closed, his little eyebrows frowning in irritation. "Not there. I mean nearer the floor."

Smiling wryly, Yūko hastened to follow his command.

It wasn't long, however, before Takeshi's requests became softer and fewer. Finally, they lapsed into silence. His breathing showed he was fast asleep. He was still only a baby really. After gazing for a while at his innocent sleeping face, with its lips pouting peacefully, she moved him back to the center of his bed.

Yūko slipped back into her own bed, and laid her head on the pillow, only to realize that the ceiling light was still on. She threw off her covers. Then her eyes fell on Takeshi's school uniform hanging on a coat hanger against the wall. Its front unbuttoned, its stubby little sleeves thrusting sideways, its gold buttons twinkling in the yellow light, the little uniform was looking down on her, imperiously, from on high. Lying back on her pillow, she let her eyes linger over the uniform for a while.

Some live lobsters were being kept in a shallow wooden tank. Most of the time they stayed stretched flat out on the bottom, as if stuck there; but every now and then, with a violent twitch, one would start to thrash around in the water. Yūko crouched over the tank with Takeshi by her side. Rather than the lobsters, she wanted him to look at the baby turtle in there with them.

They had been walking past the shop, when they'd seen three men peering into the tank, remarking, "You don't often see those!" and "What a rare catch!" Her curiosity piqued, Yūko had taken Takeshi over to see. "It's a sea turtle," one of the men explained. "Hatched yesterday evening."

The baby turtle was just like an adult in shape and coloring, but its shell was only about three centimeters wide. It was swimming near the surface, going first to the left, then to the right. Covered with webs of skin, its feet were without toes.

"Is this the type that grows really big? Big enough for people to ride?" asked Yūko.

"Yes."

"Remember the fairy tale about Urashima Tarō?" Yūko asked Takeshi, who stood gripping the edge of the tank, staring into it. "This is the kind of turtle that took him to the Dragon Palace at the bottom of the sea. People will be able to ride on its back when it gets big. Look. Its legs are just like paddles, aren't they?"

Takeshi nodded, without saying a word. The turtle paddled through the water, moving its legs one by one, its shell veering this way and that, as if still unsure of itself.

Yūko hesitated. "Do you think you could let me have this?" she asked the men.

"It would only die. You have to live here to know how to take care of these things."

"But we only want it for a while, to play with."

"Sorry. We don't own it."

Yūko had had no idea that the turtle, rare though it was, would be treated as such a prized object by the locals. "All right," she said, and apologized for having asked. She was also sorry for having raised Takeshi's hopes. "Well, thank you," she said to the men. "Come along, Takeshi." She was worried that he wouldn't be persuaded to leave, but he followed her quite meekly.

They hadn't got very far before he asked: "Where are we going to look next?"

Yūko had spent the entire morning looking for a crab for Takeshi, but to no avail. The sight of the baby turtle trying to swim had perked her up. If she could get the men to give it to her, then even if she and Takeshi still had no luck, she would have made up the loss. Surely it was beginning to dawn on him that crabs were turning out to be more difficult to find than she'd thought; maybe he would forget the crabs if he had a turtle to play with. Judging from what he'd just said, however, even if she had managed to get possession of the turtle, he wouldn't have given up the search for a crab. He was determined to go on till they found one, a live crab, one that scuttled from side to side waving a bright red pincer. And he seemed utterly confident of success.

"Takeshi, it's nearly lunchtime," she said. "Let's go back and eat, and take a nap."

"But I don't want a nap."

"But you must. You won't grow up unless you take a nap. Even crabs take naps in the afternoon. There's no point in looking for them now."

Yūko was determined not to skip her nap today. When she had risen this morning, if anything she'd felt better for all yesterday's walking. But she felt anxious about breaking her habit two days in a row. Takeshi was here, and Kajii was coming tomorrow. She couldn't afford a relapse.

They had lunch, and then she finally managed to persuade Takeshi to settle down to nap.

"What time can I get up?" he asked, pulling the blanket over his head, and kicking it away.

"At three. I'll tell you when it's time, so be a good boy and go to sleep."

Takeshi shut his eyes.

"Auntie," he said, opening them again. "Do crabs sleep on their backs, like we do?"

"What do you think?"

"I don't know."

"Well, neither do I. Now be quiet and go to sleep." Yūko closed her eyes.

"Auntie. I think they do sleep on their backs."

Yūko pretended that she was no longer awake. In the afternoons, Takeshi did not seem to require his back scratch. When all was quiet, she took a peep. He was sound asleep. Yūko closed her eyes again.

When Yūko napped in the afternoon, she hardly ever fell asleep: she usually just lay down and closed her eyes. When she had first started taking her naps, all sorts of worries would come crowding into her head; but in time she had learned how to reach a state almost as good as sleep, even with daylight streaming down on her eyelids.

But today, relaxing was difficult. She felt tense knowing that as soon as the nap was over they would have to go crab-hunting again. She wanted to be sure to find one for him. The thought made her both eager for three o'clock, and apprehensive.

Many times that morning, she had asked the same question: "Do you know where we can find some crabs?"

The first person she had queried had been her landlady. "It's for the boy," she had added.

"I think I do. Try down by the sand flats."

"You mean by the sea?"

"You should find some there. We're always coming across crabs when we go clamming."

It had been down at the beach that Takeshi had first found his crab shell, Yūko remembered, even if it had been dried up, in bits and pieces. Yūko decided to take the boy there.

For a while they had tramped along the wet strand, the morning sun pouring down. It was a beautiful sandy stretch, with no dead cats, bits of radish, or wooden clogs with broken thongs strewn up by the tide to mar the scene. Theirs were the only footprints, a line of dots trailing behind them by the water's edge.

"I'm going to try digging a hole, Auntie," Takeshi said, stuffing the nylon sack he had brought into Yūko's bag. Legs apart, he cupped his hands and started to scrape at the sand, throwing it out in front of him.

"Wait." Yūko stopped him, and unbuttoned his cuffs. She took hold of each wrist and, as if she were peeling his short little arms, pushed the sleeves of his shirt and vest up as far as the elbow.

Takeshi returned enthusiastically to his task. Soon sea water started seeping into the hollow.

"Well, there aren't any here," said Yūko, as she stood and watched him.

"I'll try somewhere else." He continued to dig more holes, tirelessly, but all that turned up was water. "Maybe they're higher up." He ran to a drier part of the beach and resumed digging.

Still no crabs were to be found. After letting Takeshi gather shells for a while, Yūko called him, and they climbed up the bank to the road. Now they headed toward the other side of the station for the fish farm, which had been built using the natural features of a rocky inlet. Apparently the farm was owned by wholesale dealers in fish, but one corner was used by local fisherwomen as a harbor for their boats and a place to drape their nets—so it was pungent with the smell of the sea. Yūko was sure it might be a likely spot.

When they arrived at the farm, there wasn't a soul to be seen.

"Let's go and ask inside," she said, taking Takeshi over to the warehouse built toward the rear on top of the rocks. Opening the rattling wooden door, she saw a dingy dirt-floored room filled with coarse baskets stacked one on top of the other.

"Excuse me!" she called. An old woman appeared.

"Do you happen to have any crabs?" Yūko immediately inquired.

"You want saltwater crabs, is that it?" the old woman replied, making a circle with her hands. "But they're no good to eat, you know. And they're difficult to catch. No, we don't sell any of those."

"Well, we're not interested in eating them," Yūko said. "You know those small ones, with—"

"With red pincers? The ones children play with?"

"Yes, those," Takeshi answered.

The old woman looked down at him, kindly. "Hmm, I see. But where would you find them, I wonder? There are hardly any to be found here, I'm sure. Would you like to look round our hatchery, instead?"

"Would you like that?" Yūko asked him.

"What's a 'hatchery'?"

"There's a big hollow beneath these rocks filled with sea water, and they keep fish there, with abalone in pots and things like that. Want to take a look?"

"I don't care," he answered.

"Well then, we'll be on our way." Yūko thanked the old woman on their way out of the shop.

They went back to the road, and it wasn't long before Takeshi repeated: "Where are those crabs?"

At this moment, Yūko saw three middle school students coming toward them along the road, with their arms thrown around each other's shoulders.

"Let's ask those big boys," Yūko told Takeshi. She waited till the students were about level, and then called out: "Do you know where we can find some crabs? The little ones that children play with?"

"What?" they asked, crossing the road, still linked up together.

Yūko repeated her question.

"Oh, crabs!" the students exclaimed. They looked at each other. "Must be some somewhere around here," they said, moving off, with smiles playing on their lips.

"But where?" she almost pleaded.

The students looked back over one another's shoulders as they crossed the road again. "How should we know?"

Were they embarrassed because they had no idea? Or were they making fun of her?

As she stared at their receding backs, Takeshi said resentfully: "Why didn't they tell us where? They told us there were some."

"They probably didn't really know," she told him. "Come on. Let's ask somebody else."

They began walking again. The students had reminded Yūko that there was a middle school at the end of the road. They must have just come from there. Its spacious grounds, on a hill up above the beach, afforded a spectacular view of the sea. A couple of times, when out on a walk, she had slipped inside to use the toilet in one corner of the grounds. Each time she'd thought how nice it must be to teach in such a place. Bicycling to work every day, and going fishing on Sundays. . . . Perhaps the biology teacher researched the local marine life in his spare time. He would be able to tell her immediately where the crabs were. But now it was no good. School was out.

From the tall grasses edging the road a young woman emerged, with an empty basket under her arm. She had probably just finished spreading wakamé out to dry on the beach. Yūko took Takeshi by the hand, and repeated her question.

"Oh," the woman answered, "You'll find those crabs up in the hills."

"In the hills?" Yūko's voice rose. "I thought they lived by the sea!"

"You mean the ones with the red pincers, don't you?"

"Yes."

"Scarlet crabs, they're called. They're freshwater crabs, they live in streams. That's the kind children play with. They tie strings to—"

"—So there are none of those around here? No crabs at all?"

"Well, there are really tiny ones."

"What color?"

"Oh, I don't think they have a color. They scuttle out when you lift up rocks on the beach."

If there are so many, Yūko thought, surely one would be a reasonable size, even if colorless.

"Thanks," she said.

On second thought, however, it occurred to her that hardly any stretch of the coast here had the right size rocks—large enough to hide a crab and small enough to lift up. It was all sandy stretches or large boulders. The smaller rocks were deeply embedded in the sand and right in the waves.

Yūko made her way with Takeshi to still more beaches. They trudged down various paths: a well-worn grass trail; a gravel road with a sign indicating a large inn farther along the shore; a street of houses and on their roofs tall antennae pointing up into the sky—but each time the result was the same.

"We're out of luck," she had to tell him. "These aren't the right kind of rocks."

As they turned back, he asked: "Where did that lady mean, I wonder?"

Finally, they did find a beach with the right kind of rocks. Several the size of footballs lay scattered along the highest, driest stretch of sand. The waves probably reached them only during a storm. Of course, that was no guarantee they hid any crabs, but Yūko wanted Takeshi to at least try one, so she took him down.

"We've found some at last," she said.

"I'll lift a rock, Auntie. And then, can you catch the crab when it comes out?"

"All right."

They mustn't let any crab that came out get away; it was a very delicate operation. . . . Takeshi placed both hands on the rock of his choice and began, very slowly, to lift it, craning his neck as far as he could at the same time to peer underneath. Their heads almost touching, Yūko looked from her side, her eyes riveted on the crack that was slowly widening.

"Well, Auntie? Do you see any?" he asked, his voice breathless with excitement.

No matter how impossible it had been to find crabs, no matter how many false trails they had followed, not once had

Takeshi considered giving up. For every time he complained, "Why aren't there any there?" or "Where did that lady mean?" he also always came back with, "So when are you going to find me one?" or, "Where do we go now?" Was he unwilling to abandon the search simply because each failure sharpened his disappointment? Or was this the innocent cruelty of a little boy who believes adults can accomplish anything? She couldn't just tell him to give it up when he was asking her so earnestly. And yet by continuing to go along with him she continued to feed his hopes.

How she longed for that moment when, grabbing hold of a crab brandishing its pincer as it scuttled sideways, she'd be able to say: "Careful! I don't want it to pinch your fingers!" And then she would drop it for him into the clear plastic bag.

"Auntie, haven't any come out yet?" Takeshi was asking her, a second time.

"Not yet. Lift it a bit higher."

Bending her head, squinting into the depths of the crack, Yūko wanted so much to see a crab wave its bright red pincer at the sudden light breaching its abode that the back of her eyeballs began to ache.

Takeshi was still napping and Yūko shut her eyes again.

Really, why were crabs so difficult to find? If only she could have persuaded those men to give her the baby turtle. But even if she had managed that, they wouldn't have been able to give up the search. Not unless Takeshi said and really meant that he did not mind.

She hadn't lied to him yesterday, persuading him to stay by promising to find him some crabs. Somewhere along this coast, she was sure, there must be one crab that would come out when it heard her call. That had been the opinion of all the people she had run into, hadn't it? Every one who had given her directions had said there must be crabs somewhere.

But perhaps they were only imagining them. She remembered her landlady's reaction when they'd returned empty-handed: "Really? There weren't any? I'm sure I saw some when I went clamming. But then, it isn't April yet. That's the start of the harvesting season. Well, maybe I saw them later."

If that's the case, Yūko thought, the students hadn't been kidding her when they had replied to her question about where exactly the crabs were with "How should we know?"

So were there no crabs to be found at all? There was still one rocky part of the shore that they hadn't investigated, but that didn't seem very likely. Perhaps she really would have to go up into the hills.

Yūko suddenly remembered the stone embankments around stepped fields she had seen here and there in the area. Hadn't she seen some patches of water there? They weren't exactly up in the hills, and the water wouldn't be fresh. But perhaps scarlet crabs preferred such places. . . . She decided to go and have a look now, while Takeshi was still asleep.

"Going out?" the landlady's daughter asked, as Yūko came down the stairs.

"Yes," she answered. "My nephew's asleep. Would you keep an eye on him? I won't be long." She was reluctant to say any more than that. The woman was hardly likely to understand her obsession.

Slipping on her sandals, Yūko started to cross the dirt floor. Just then, in the front of the store, the landlady, sitting on her haunches next to an elderly man who was peering into a bucket, glanced over her shoulder and saw her.

"We'll have some raw sea urchin for dinner tonight," she said.

The wet sea urchins lay at the bottom of the bucket, their dark brown, spiky, ball-like bodies moving faintly. One by one, the man took them out, placing them on the ground, and gradually the rest of his booty came into view: smaller creatures, about the size of ping-pong balls and covered in green bristles, filling the bottom of the bucket.

"What are those?" Yūko asked.

"They're sea urchins, too," the man answered. "They're inedible, but I still collect them. They're used to make kokeshi dolls."

"Where do they live?" She had no idea where ordinary sea urchins lived, let alone these strange things.

"On beaches where there are lots of rocks. They're some under every stone, if you look."

Yūko hesitated. "There wouldn't happen to be any crabs under those rocks, would there?"

"Of course! Hermit crabs, starfish. Everything."

"Ordinary crabs, too?"

"That's right. Just lift up the rocks, and they come running out like crazy."

Lift up the rocks: that was exactly what the young woman had said.

"Are you talking about small crabs? Do you find any bigger ones—say, this size?" She spread her fingers about a match stick apart.

"Sometimes."

"What do you mean?"

"Well, there aren't all that many, you see. Today I must have seen, oh, perhaps ten."

"And they had a red pincer?"

"Oh no, you won't find red-clawed crabs in this parts. They're the same color all over."

Well, she could do without the red pincer. She wouldn't be too fussy.

"Where is this beach you went to?"

The man told her the name of a port about an hour's train ride away, where ferries went to and from Uraga.

"And how far is it from the station?"

"About twelve or thirteen minutes' walk. It's on the other side of the docks."

"So you're planning to go?" the landlady broke in.

"I'm not sure," Yūko replied, evasively. "I was hoping to go somewhere tomorrow. . . ."

She decided to skip the stone embankments around the fields. She would take Takeshi to this new place in the morning. After all, Kajii wouldn't arrive till late. But she wanted to move cautiously after her morning experience. The crabs were living creatures: there might be ten today, and none tomorrow. Besides, it might very well rain, and they'd have to cancel—it might rain for two days. She resolved not to tell Takeshi anything beforehand. Of course, that meant she'd have to carry on pretending to search for the rest of the afternoon.

It was past three o'clock, and Takeshi was still asleep. As promised, she roused him. She gave him some cakes from the shop, and then they went out together to a rocky stretch of the shore.

The tide was beginning to come in, but some pools of water remained in hollows around the rocks. Yūko pointed toward them.

"You know, Takeshi, there might be some crabs there."

Next she pointed to a broad horizontal crack in the face of a rock. "This might be a good place. Keep your eye on it."

But her enthusiasm had waned since hearing of the better place which must have been obvious even to the child. Having failed yet again to find the object of his desire, he started to collect small black periwinkles from rock pools. Finally, he stood up, clutching his plastic bag of shells, and approached the ledge where she sat.

"Let's go back," he said. "There aren't any crabs."

Then, in the next breath, as if Yūko's lack of concern was somehow to blame for their day of bad luck, he added: "I'll ask Uncle to catch me some, tomorrow."

"Oh, Takeshi! How can you say such a thing!"

She said this so vehemently that the boy blinked in surprise. Her own face had gone red, she realized. It was not simply because she was jealous. She went on more gently:

"You won't do that, will you, Takeshi? Please don't ask your uncle to take you looking for crabs. And don't tell him we went looking today, and couldn't find any. Okay?" The boy had hung his head.

If Kajii ever found out how keen she'd been to find crabs to please this little boy. . . . At the possibility, Yūko was overcome with embarrassment. But Takeshi was a child; he couldn't possibly know what she was feeling. He had been terrified by her sudden display of anger. Eyes lowered, he nodded obediently at everything she said, not daring to ask why.

"And if we still haven't found any crabs when you go home, Takeshi, we'll catch some the next time you visit, after I make sure where they live."

"But I might not come again."

"Well, I'll bring some back when I return to Tokyo."

"Okay." Takeshi was beginning to brighten up.

"Auntie," he said, finally raising his head.

"What?" Yūko put her hand on his shoulder.

"Can I tell Uncle about the baby turtle?"

Yūko pretended to think. "Yes, you may."

"And that we made a fire, and ate fresh sazae?"

"Of course you may."

"And that we went in a boat?"

"You may."

"And can I tell him about the crab I found yesterday?"

This time, Yūko really did pause to think. "Yes, you may."

But she'd already started wondering whether she should take him on that trip to the beach tomorrow. She was quite ready to take him if Takeshi could then tell Kajii they'd found a crab. But would that be all he learned from the boy?

❀ *Ants Swarm* (ARI TAKARU, 1964)

FOR A MOMENT, FUMIKO THOUGHT OF SINKING
back into that deep, free world she'd just been immersed in. But
no, she couldn't go back to sleep; she had to get up. . . . She
pushed the thin quilt away with one hand, and then paused,
reluctant: it worried her to think how her body might feel if she
changed her position. Enclosed in the warm darkness, she lay
on her side without moving, her body curved like a bow, her legs
strictly aligned.

Her husband Matsuda was still fast asleep, his breath deep
and powerful. The clock on the wall reverberated with each
swing of the pendulum, but this didn't tell her the time. Lying
there, keeping her body as immobile as a person being forcibly
held down, Fumiko began to feel her chest constrict; it became
difficult to breathe. Laziness and hesitation kept her there for a
while, but she finally stuck out a hand to help raise her upper
body. This didn't seem to make any difference in how she felt,
so she let her legs relax out of their strict line, bent one knee,
and slid the other onto the cool tatami mat. Still she felt nothing.
She moved both feet firmly on to the tatami.

Sliding open their bedroom door she was surprised to discover that it wasn't night after all. The corridor was hushed and
still. Various objects were dimly visible: the white patch of
frosted glass on the door of the bathroom met her eye. She was
hardly ever awake this early, she realized. If anything, this was
when she slept most deeply—worry had awoken her. Her hand
touched the knob of the door to the toilet.

Fumiko's period was overdue—by almost a week now. This was very unusual for her. From the start, her period had always been regular, so punctual as to be almost amusing. Even the time of day it came—the evening—was usually the same. She had been married to Matsuda, a man one year her junior, for six years now; and all that time her period had been as regular as ever. The two of them had agreed to avoid having a child, and until now, nothing had ever happened to concern them.

After her period didn't come, she had waited three days before telling Matsuda. He responded with a surprised grunt.

"I told you, didn't I?" she continued. "I told you I felt something that time."

In fact, though they did not intend to ever have children, their only precaution was the regularity of Fumiko's periods. Fumiko worked at an American law firm—there wasn't any overtime, she could leave the office at five, and she had Saturdays and Sundays free. Matsuda, however, was a journalist who covered political affairs: his hours were unpredictable. When things got hectic, he would stay all night at the office, or for days at a stretch, come home at dawn. Often when he did get a breather, Fumiko would be entering a risky phase in her cycle. Reluctant to have sex at these times, she still felt guilty; but the one time she suggested that they use another method of birth control, he had flatly refused.

"I can hold back if I want to," he told her. "Like a lion— lions only need to feed once in a while."

Well, she could see it his way.

Whenever Matsuda started to caress her before making love, Fumiko's body would feel a craving for physical pain. Matsuda seemed especially aroused by the sight of her imploring him to hurt her, and he would direct his efforts at her arms first, then her legs. Eventually, with increasing force, he would use various objects to give her pain. Before she knew it, she would be moaning in a voice hoarse with excitement: "So, you'll do this much for me, will you?" This would spur him on all the more, as a result of which she would madly beg for more—only to plead in near delirium, "Forgive me! Forgive me!" until, in the end, Matsuda would have intercourse with her, inflicting pain all the while. It was not unusual for him to want them to spend the following night in the same way.

When Fumiko entered an unsafe time of her menstrual cycle, however, Matsuda amazed her with his ability, as he said, to hold back. Occasionally their lovemaking would leave a few bruises on her body, but he never demanded anything more. She'd always loved this controlled side of his nature, which coexisted with the more unrestrained side.

So she had felt quite annoyed when, one morning two weeks earlier, as she got out of bed, she suddenly found herself being dragged back. It was risky, she warned. "I know that!" was all he replied. She frowned. This wasn't like him—the Matsuda she knew stayed sound asleep in the morning, even when it was safe to make love—only waking up when she placed his stack of newspapers by his pillow; and he would go straight back to sleep after reading them. Perhaps it was the contrast with his usual restraint that she found shocking, but then again, since this behavior was so unusual, she couldn't reject him too adamantly. When she realized he still had apprehensions despite his eagerness, she even urged him on.

But the truth was, Fumiko from start to finish was not pleased. For an instant, she managed to persuade herself that she didn't care, and was able to gain a sense of release; but the fear of getting pregnant was always there, weighing her down. It was also almost time for her to go to work, and besides, he was making love without giving her pain, which made it impossible for her to get carried away.

She got out of bed, and as she hurried to get dressed, she felt even more irritated and indignant. She looked over her shoulder, and saw Matsuda, the top of his head peeping out of the blankets.

"I think I conceived," she said. "It felt different than usual."

"Think so?" he replied from under the covers.

She couldn't suppress a sour smile, but the next moment a strong premonition overcame her—what she had just told him would come true. In the middle of zipping up her skirt, she froze. Yes, now carefully thinking about all the sensations she could remember, she did recall, though she'd experienced nothing like pleasure, having felt something special—something different.

As she waited for her period, Fumiko grew more and more nervous. When the day at last came around, there was no sign of her period—not then, and not on the following day. So, she had been right, she thought, nodding bitterly. Even if it were impossible, rationally speaking, for a woman to feel the moment of conception, she was sure she'd had a presentiment. That knowledge couldn't have arisen simply from fear.

When she informed Matsuda her period was late, and referred again to "that time," there was a touch of rebuke in her tone: "What should we do?" she demanded.

"This is bad," replied Matsuda, hugging his knees.

"Of course it's bad!"

"But surely you don't expect me to apologize?" he countered.

Fumiko sensed he was chiding her for the way she had spoken. "You're right," she said. "I guess I got carried away, too. But we are going abroad. What bad timing."

In July, the two of them were supposed to go to the United States for a year: Matsuda had won a Fulbright to attend C— University. Since he'd applied in good time, he had managed to arrange for Fumiko to enroll too, in her own right. She had completed all the paperwork and entrance procedures. Before the start of the fall semester there was an orientation program, so only a month or so remained before they were due to leave the country.

Fumiko wasn't certain, as she didn't have any experience, but surely, she told Matsuda, they didn't have enough time left for her to have an abortion and recover—and she'd heard it was difficult to get an abortion in the States. And anyway, even if she could get one there, it would be impossible to arrange as soon as they arrived.

Matsuda listened in silence.

"Anyhow," he said, after a while, "you're not certain yet, and—"

"—It's been three days! This never happens to me."

"All right. Calm down."

"But what if I really am pregnant?"

"Hmm." Matsuda thought for a minute, and then raising his eyes to hers, he said: "Can't you give up the trip to the States?"

"If I really can't get rid of it before we go."

"So you would stay?"

"I suppose."

"Well," Matsuda said. "Why not have the baby?"

Fumiko was stunned.

"Do you really mean that?" she asked, eventually.

"Why not? It might be nice to have a kid. One, at least."

"Since when have you . . . ?" Fumiko broke off, staring at him. "You mean, that was on purpose that time?"

"No. It wasn't."

"I didn't think so. But when did you change, and decide you don't mind?"

Matsuda was silent.

"Was it after I told you about my period being late? It was, wasn't it?"

"Well, yes, but . . ."

"I see." Fumiko sighed, and looked away.

Fumiko had her job when she met Matsuda, and she kept working after they were married. At first they had avoided having a child without really thinking about it, but soon they realized that neither of them was particularly fond of children or felt the need to have any of their own. Then they started being explicit about her never becoming pregnant.

"Not many men get obsessed with kids," Matsuda would say

to her: "It's women end up insisting on having them. I know two couples like that. I'll be okay, as long as *you* don't change your mind."

Fumiko would always assure him that she'd stick to their resolution. For the past few years she had assumed that they were both so used to the decision that they no longer needed to discuss it.

Fumiko loved it whenever Matsuda talked about his childhood.

"When my grandmother died," he'd told her once, "nobody knew where to find me. I had my air gun up on the roof—I was shooting pigeons. Nobody heard the sound of the gun, they were all too caught up in their own grief." Another time he had told her: "I'm average now, but I was small when I was in primary school, the second smallest in my class. In lineup I'd always be number two. It made me want to cry." Matsuda would jump up, hold his arms out straight, and pretend to be standing in line. "'Line up,' the teacher would say. I hated those words." Fumiko would feel so attracted to him when he acted like this. And in bed, sometimes in the middle of tearing off her clothes, he would suddenly become calm and press his head up against her chest like a child. The next moment he might produce a button he had ripped off her blouse and place it on her pillow, saying, "I found it!" Fumiko would feel so happy she had to laugh out loud.

But she had never once wanted to have a child of her own. The very thought of giving birth and having to raise a baby repelled her. Even now, when her period was late, all she felt was fear, resentment toward Matsuda, and worry about how she could get an abortion. She had never once wondered longingly about what it might be like to be a mother. Matsuda's announcement that he wanted a child shocked her: so, she thought, despite all their promises, he had secretly started to want one. Seeing him excited about being a parent made her feel deceived and jealous—contemptuous, too, when she recalled how boyish he was. How could such a boy imagine that he was mature enough to be a father? She forgot that he was thirty years old, only one year younger than herself.

Nevertheless, in the evenings, before going to sleep and after laying out their futon when he'd asked her to, she would make a final trip to the bathroom, come back to bed, and tell him: "It still hasn't come." The tone of her own voice would surprise her: she sounded so calm. It seemed naturally that the number of times she visited the bathroom increased. She didn't go to the toilet so much at the office, but at home for some reason she made frequent trips. She made sure to give Matsuda an update if he were home. Though he never asked, she knew just from looking at him that he was waiting to hear.

But that didn't mean that if she turned out to be pregnant, she had decided to have the baby. If in the next few days her period still didn't arrive, she would start investigating how to get rid of it. And if she could have that all over and done with by the beginning of the semester, she fully intended to go abroad. Surely, if an abortion were possible, Matsuda would give up the idea and consent. But then again, if it were not . . . Her only option would be to stay behind. But even then, she couldn't imagine she'd want to have the baby. And in that case, why was she bothering to keep Matsuda so informed? He would only assume she'd come round to his way of thinking.

Fumiko saw his face shine every time he learned her period had not come.

"Imagine," he would say. "You've got this little thing inside you—just a speck at the moment—about the size of a sesame seed. We'd better look after our sesame child."

Fumiko found herself affected by this. She gave up saying, "It still hasn't come," and started telling him, "It's still all right." Sometimes she would add, despite herself: "Are you happy?"

"Of course!" Matsuda would reply.

"You really want me to have it, don't you," she would sigh. He would put his head against her chest and nod two or three times, looking just like a child who wanted something with all his heart but was worried that his mother might not allow it. This look made him irresistible to Fumiko. But he also seemed to be playacting, which made it easy for her to answer him insincerely. "You want me to have it, don't you?" she would repeat, wanting him to do it again. Matsuda would nod again, still pushing up against her chest.

"All right, then: I will, just for you."

Hardly even a week had gone by, but already Matsuda's fantasies had reached ridiculous proportions—and her attitude removed his last compunctions about sharing them with her.

Fumiko couldn't help being dismayed, seeing Matsuda like this. She still privately prayed that her period might start. It wasn't only that she wanted to go abroad to study: she simply had no interest in a baby. She could not bring herself to want one. It seemed such an unending, hopeless thing to do—to have to carry a child around inside her, to give it birth, and then to look after it. And yet, on the other hand, there she was, letting Matsuda entertain these fantasies, which seemed to have taken on a life of their own.

The fact was she quite enjoyed it when Matsuda talked to her about their baby. Sometimes, as if to be a double hypocrite, she would even start the conversation herself.

"We'll have a baby, this time next year," she would say.

"That's right," Matsuda would reply. "I'm sorry I'm not going to be with you when you're in labor, though. I wish you could have a baby easily—have it pop out from between your fingers, say."

"I'll be fine. Don't worry about it. By the time you come back—"

"—There'll be a baby. That's great. He'll be the apple of my eye. You just see how many presents I buy him."

"What kind of things?" Fumiko asked. She took out a cigarette, but then, seeing Matsuda's anxious look, put it down without lighting it.

"Oh, toys, a tricycle. . . . I'll take him to the zoo. I wonder if you can buy season tickets."

"What for?"

"For the zoo—it'd be cheaper that way. When he grows up, I'll make sure he can charge his drinks at bars. If he's a drinker, that is. I hope he will be."

"Well! The doting father!"

"That's me," Matsuda declared: "And I'll go to his PTA meetings."

"Good. It'll save me the bother."

"I'll have to bow when I meet his teachers, won't I? Like this." Matsuda almost knocked his head on the table. "But just let one of them punish my son: I'll beat his brains out!"

Fumiko wouldn't be able to stop laughing. As she laughed, she thought how much she'd love to see him act that way. She could not bring herself to have a baby, and she was not broad-minded enough to let him have one with another woman, but to watch Matsuda act the father . . . That was something she longed to see.

Her period had started, she discovered, just a moment before. Pure relief was her first emotion. Anxiety and stress must have delayed it. Well, at least her immediate worries were over, and the matter of her study trip abroad returned to occupy her mind.

As she left the toilet to return to the bedroom, however, Fumiko paused in the silent corridor, and glanced back. She looked at the wash basin and at some of Matsuda's discarded razor blades on the little shelf above it. A few feet away, through the open door of the kitchen, she could see a cupboard. Directly ahead was the entry, where the thick winter curtain they used to keep out the cold still hung. The hallway, their bedroom door, the door to the sitting room . . . They had moved to this rented house over a year ago now. But for the past week, after she had told Matsuda that her period was overdue, life here had utterly changed.

Mourning, Fumiko reflected on the past few days. Matsuda's footsteps as he came in at night had sounded different. While she prepared his dinner, he would be eager to talk about the child. When she headed to work in the morning he'd see her off, whereas before he'd just gone straight back to sleep. And even in this room, she thought, looking behind her at the toilet, there had been a difference. She did not want to dismiss everything that had happened as a silly delusion. The curtain, the corridor, the door, the walls . . . Everything in their daily life had been filled with a special significance. Now, she realized, the significance was fading away.

She slid open the bedroom door. Matsuda was still sound asleep. As she went back inside, she saw by the light in the corridor that it was about six o'clock.

Slipping her body back into bed Fumiko considered in the darkness whether she should tell Matsuda about her period. He would be so disappointed. But no sooner had her head rested on the pillow, than she raised herself and leaned over against him. The sound of his breathing faltered, he mumbled something, and his arms moved, as if they would wake alone. His cheek was warm. She pulled his head toward her, embraced it, rubbing her nose against it and sniffing in the smell of his ears, which she loved.

"It was all a mistake," she whispered, pulling her head away. She started to sob. She felt Matsuda rise abruptly. "It was a mistake," she repeated.

"Was it?" He did sound disappointed. "Well, but that's all right. It's all right. Wait." There was the sound of the light going on.

"Oh, don't do that."

"Okay." He reached again for the switch.

"I shouldn't have said anything. I spoke too soon," Fumiko

said, laying her head on his pillow and crying again. Her tears flowed naturally, but one part of her mind was conscious that she was acting like a woman who had been desperately hoping to be pregnant.

"No, it's good you told me. We had a trial run," Matsuda said.

"But you were so happy."

"Well, you can make me happy next time. We have to go to America first—we'll do it after that."

"All right. But I mustn't wait too long," Fumiko said, realizing her voice sounded as if she meant it. But then, she did want him to have a child. "I don't like children, though," she added.

"You'll come round—I didn't like them, either."

"But what if I don't, though? What happens if I have one, and I still don't like it?"

"That's all right. I'll see to the diapers."

"You'll spoil it wildly, I bet. I won't. I might spoil a boy, but if it's a girl, I'll just be mean and cruel—I'll be so cruel, people will think I'm her stepmother."

Suddenly, a picture flashed into her mind of the child she would treat like a stepdaughter: this whole event had had quite an effect on her. She no longer had the worry of the last few days, and once the image rose in her mind it began to stimulate all sorts of fantasies.

"If it's a girl," she continued, "let's not allow her too much education."

"I agree," Matsuda answered. "Too much schooling is no good anyway."

"Of course, we'll have to send her for the compulsory years."

"No, they're the worst. Let's hire tutors."

"Far too expensive. I'll never agree to that," Fumiko replied. "No, she can just go to the local school. When she graduates from junior high, I'll keep her at home and treat her like a maid. By this time of the morning, she'll be up cooking our breakfast. I'll be lying in bed like this, taking it easy with you."

"That sounds nice."

"So it appeals to you. In that case, I'll make her cook breakfast when she's in grammar school."

"Will a first-grader be able to cook?"

"She won't have any choice. And she'd better get the rice just right."

"The poor little thing!"

"But it's best to be strict with girls—better for them."

"True."

"I'm not going to have a girl who thinks too much. Let's raise her so she'll never talk back. I don't mean just so she can restrain herself—I want her incapable of talking back—a girl who has no opinions of her own. A girl who does what she's told, automatically, like an idiot. Even her face must be an idiot's face."

"A girl like a doll."

"Yes. When she's small, I'll train her to serve other people, like a good little wife—like the girls in ancient China. As soon as she gets out of school, I'll marry her off."

"I'll go and visit her. I'll take her some of that sugar we got as a present, behind your back."

"Will you indeed."

"But you never use it to cook with. There's too much, anyway."

"How do you know?"

"You told me."

"Did I? Well, take it, then."

"I'll go and see her every Sunday."

"Her husband won't like that."

"That's all right. He'll understand. I'll find her a kind husband."

"He won't stay that way. I'll encourage him to be cruel and mean. You must encourage him, too—to have affairs and drink. If you meet any beautiful women, you mustn't keep them for yourself. Send them over, lots of them, to him, just like the sugar. She won't get any sympathy when she comes over to complain. I'll show her my body. 'Look!' I'll tell her: 'Look at what your father does to me. *I* can bear it, and so should you!'"

The clock chimed.

"What time is it?" Matsuda asked.

"Half past six."

"Go and look. I bet it's seven-thirty. You'll be late."

"No, I won't: it's six-thirty."

For their conversation to end when she was having so much fun was the last thing Fumiko wanted. She wanted to pick it up where they had left off—as soon as possible. Matsuda, however, got out of bed, unlocked the window, slid a panel aside, and opened the outside shutter.

"You see?" Fumiko said, looking at the clock. "Half-past six."

Matsuda slid the window back, left the shutters open, and drew the curtain, the way she usually did for him as he lay in bed. Then he left the room.

When he came back, still in his pajamas, he was carrying his newspapers. Putting them on the floor, he sat down, crossed his legs, and started reading them one after another. She couldn't object, considering his profession. But after a while, it was obvious that nothing was particularly catching his eye.

"There's nothing urgent," she said. "Can't you leave that till later?"

Apparently he could.

"What about the time?" he asked, putting down a newspaper and coming back to bed.

"It's all right," replied Fumiko though it was ten to seven. Ten more minutes, and she would have to get up.

"You're so lucky that you get to leave later," she sighed, and suddenly remembered they'd run out of butter. "We don't have any butter for breakfast. Do you mind? I forgot to get more."

"We have jam, don't we?"

"Yes. And cheese."

"Well then, that's plenty."

In the gap between the doors, which she noticed Matsuda had not bothered to shut, Fumiko glimpsed a short fluttering skirt: their daughter—the girl whom other people might mistake for her stepdaughter.

"I won't allow our daughter to forget to buy butter," she told Matsuda. "I'm very strict with girls. I punish them cruelly. You won't be able to stand seeing what I do to her—despite what you do to me. You'll have to go hide in a closet and cover your ears. . . ."

The door slid open, and the short pleated skirt came in. Fumiko pretended to be asleep.

"Mother," said her daughter. She was about seven years old. Fumiko didn't acknowledge her for a long while, until finally she said with her eyes closed: "You didn't close the door. I scolded you the other day for leaving it open."

"But Father never bothers to close it. . . ."

"You think you're the same as your Father?" Fumiko shouted. She jumped up and rushed at her daughter, grabbed the sides of her mouth, and pulled. *"Are you talking back?"* The girl tried to free herself, but she couldn't, Fumiko had her in such a tight grip. *"I'm sorry!"* the girl begged. *"Forgive me!"* The same words that Fumiko uttered at night making love with Matsuda.

"I won't forgive you!" Fumiko retorted. She started pinching and jabbing her. *"And not only because you talk back, either. Think about how badly behaved you've been—in the last few moments. Addressing your mother without getting down on your knees. Who taught you that? And when you came in—just entering, without even knocking."* Fumiko began to strip her of all her clothes—the short pleated skirt, her blouse, her underwear— and pinch her all over her body.

And there was the butter, she remembered: something else to berate her for. Fumiko pushed her toward the kitchen.

"Do you have butter for breakfast?"

"No. I wanted to go buy some, but I needed some money, and that's why . . ."

"You forgot, didn't you."

"Yes."

The girl immediately cowered by the gas stove, hiding her face: on her back there were several small round scars like cigarette burns.

"Go out and buy some."

A stick of butter slid down from the ceiling to rest cold and heavy in Fumiko's hand. She unwrapped the translucent wax paper from the fresh butter, took a large scoop with a big metal spoon, which she set on the gas ring over a flame. When it melted the butter would be boiling hot. She threw a proprietary glance at the back of the girl crouching at her feet, and then peered at the butter in the spoon. The yellow lump was changing from a congealed mass to a liquid grease.

"You'll be late," Matsuda was warning her. Both hands of the clock were pointing down—it was long past seven.

"Yes, I will," Fumiko mused.

"Aren't you tired?" asked Matsuda. "Why don't you stay home today? I'll call the office."

"I've never taken a day off," Fumiko replied, trying to hint that she wanted to.

"Well, maybe you should." Matsuda's hand groped for her breast—Fumiko was already excited. Unlike the other morning, she had no objection today.

"When do you want me to have your baby?"

"How about when we come back from America."

"How soon after?"

"There's no hurry."

"The earlier the better, I suppose. I do want to have a baby for you, but . . ." She broke off: Matsuda had her nipple between his forefinger and thumb and was pulling it toward the center of her chest while with his little finger crooked he searched out her other nipple. His finger slipped over it two or three times before catching it. The next moment, a terrible pain seared her: Matsuda was pinching both nipples, and pulling back at the same time. He pulled harder—as hard as if he were trying to lift a heavy bucket by its handle. Fumiko gasped, arching away and burying her face in his shoulder. This worked to increase the pain, and her pleasure.

"I do want very much to have a baby for you," she continued, when she could draw a breath. "But I don't like babies; you know that. So you must tell me to do it—order me when you want one. If you don't, I'll never . . ." Again, she had to gasp and hold her tongue. Shivering all over with pleasure at the pain, she choked out, "You'll have to tell me to do it. You've got to force me!"

"I will, when I think the time is right," Matsuda said. He pulled again, harder. "I'll say: 'Give birth to it, even if it kills you!'"

"I will," she gasped. "Even if it kills me. So you must stay with me, by my side."

"I will."

"But I may want you to do more. . . . The pain might make me scream and struggle. Then you'll have to tie me up. Maybe I won't stop screaming—in that case, will you beat me, please? Tied up and beaten as I have my baby: that sounds better—I wouldn't mind if I could give birth like that. How about letting me try now. . . . Please . . . ? I want to. Now!"

Matsuda sprang out of bed to open the closet door. Fumiko became aware of an oblong strip of sunlight on the curtain over the window. By the time she heard him take out their bamboo fishing rod (neither of them fished), she couldn't have cared less about the time or about whether anybody up and about would hear the noise.

Matsuda, his shoes on, was already in the hallway. He drank the bottle of milk Fumiko had brought him, standing.

"You all right?" he asked, moving the bottle away from his lips. Fumiko smiled, not saying anything.

"We won't be able to do that when you're pregnant, you know. We'll have to go easy. You'd better bear that in mind."

"But after we have the baby . . ."

"Don't worry." Matsuda tipped his head back, and drained the bottle. "I'll make us a soundproof room. We need one already, if you ask me." He handed her the empty bottle. "I'll call your office," he said over his shoulder, as he left.

The futon had yet to be put away; the only difference in the room was that the shutters were fully open. It was the rainy season, but the sun managed to find its way through the clouds, along with a breeze.

Fumiko sat down heavily on the edge of the veranda. With every fiber of her being she concentrated on her physical sensations. Everywhere on her skin she felt heat, then stinging pain, then heat again—alternating sensations which were gradually diminishing in intensity. Her whole body responded in successive waves to every breeze, a feeling she liked very much. Matsuda had left without breakfast since they had run out of time, and she hadn't eaten yet, either: she could feel hunger pangs. She went on sitting there, however. In a while, drowsiness overtook her and lying down on the futon, she closed her eyes. Such a pleasant early summer breeze.

She awoke to find it was nearly two o'clock. What, she thought suddenly, if a child were to see her in this state? She tidied the futon away, and went into the kitchen.

As she opened the window, a strange object on the inside sill met her eyes. Jet black, and oval in shape, it seemed to be squirming. On closer inspection, she saw that it was a lump of raw meat, alive with crawling ants. Oh yes, on the cutting board. She remembered putting it away herself in the refrigerator.

This was one of the slices she had gotten Matsuda to press up against some of her wounds this morning—though of course there hadn't been any ants then. She had had him do this several times before: from the kitchen Matsuda would bring in the slices of meat to the bedroom, using chop sticks, and she would lie and watch, and burst out laughing each time a piece approached her shoulders or haunches. He must have forgotten to put the board of meat back in the refrigerator.

Now, hundreds of ants covered the slice, swarming all over it, crazily. Hardly any ants were wandering around on the board itself, and, strangely, not one was making its way toward it, so she couldn't tell where they had come from.

Well, she was in no hurry to brush them away: nothing could be done about the meat now—the ants could do what they liked with it. Fumiko stayed there and gazed at them, all squirming and wriggling together like a single organism. She was amazed to find so many ants living inside her house; she hadn't ever before caught a glimpse of one. Their absence she had attributed to the lack of sweetness and sugar in their household—and that, in turn, she linked with her own lack of domesticity. After all, the last thing she wanted was a baby drinking milk, or small children leaving caramel candy wrappers lying around. Neither she nor Matsuda took sugar in their coffee; she preferred smoking to snacking between meals; and she rarely spent time boiling up stews in sweet gravy.

And yet all these ants had been living here, the whole time. These ants must have forgotten the taste of sugar—or else had never sampled it. But perhaps they found a certain sweetness in the vinegary taste of the blood in the meat, putrefying slightly in the warm air. . . . It was just like ants, wasn't it, to have detected the meat so quickly and gathered around.

Fumiko concentrated on observing the movements of the ants individually, each one burrowing away, its body trembling while it pushed its head eagerly into the meat. After a while, however, her eyes grew tired and she had to give up trying to focus on them singly. There were just too many, and all so close together. As she gazed, they formed a single writhing mass again before her eyes, a black lump squirming obscenely, teasing and goading her on.

❀ *Final Moments* (SAIGO NO TOKI, 1966)

SHE HAD TO DIE AT SOME POINT, SHE COULD accept that; and to die in that particular way might even be her fate. But so suddenly, so quickly—Noriko couldn't begin to face the possibility.

"Give me a few days," she begged.

"You mean you want time to get used to the idea," a voice said.

"Who ever 'gets used' to dying?" she retorted. "I'm not an old lady—I'm not terminally ill: I'm middle aged. I'm healthy—and nothing is wrong with my mind, as far as I know. And anyway, there's not a drop of samurai blood in my veins: I know I won't want to let go of life—I'll be exceptionally unwilling—unless you manage to kill me on your very first try."

"I thought you said you believed in spirits."

"I do. But that doesn't mean I'm happy to die!"

"Well, that's better than not believing at all."

"I don't know if I agree with you. Spirits and ghosts are probably powerless creatures, you know. I know they're supposed to be able to influence humans—to be able to read their minds, and so on. But they don't have physical power over people, or objects; I don't think they can even see them. And what happens when from the other side they try to reach people whose minds are insensitive, and who don't react? Or who are too sensitive, so they overreact? I'm sure lines get crossed all the time: it must be easy for a ghost to get frustrated, and lose interest. Besides, after a while, seeing into people's minds must get quite boring and annoying. And aren't ghosts supposed to be bundles of irritation and resentment? No, I dread dying all the more when I think of such an eternally painful existence. If anything, I envy people who can believe in nothingness after death."

Then she cried out: "Oh, I wish that my spirit could stay with my body forever! Or at least that when I die, my spirit would go too!" She so fiercely wanted this that for a moment she forgot about the reprieve.

"Anyway, the point is," she resumed, "I don't want to die. I have to, I know, but you could at least give me some extra time."

"You can't get out of it, you know."

"I know. That's exactly why I'm asking. I only need two or three days. . . ."

"Out of the question."

"But it's not as though I was born in a matter of seconds. How can I just suddenly die? There are so many things I have to take care of before I . . ."

"Such as?"

"Look at me," she said, holding the edges of her kimono sleeves as she spread her arms out. "You can't expect me to die like this. I was on my way to a friend's funeral. I wouldn't have dressed like this if I'd known."

"That's good enough—better than house slippers and an apron."

"But this is black—the color of the dead!"

"The color of the dead is white. Oh, you're right, so is black. But so much the better—think how impressed everybody'll be by your wearing black: they'll think you died very tastefully, in a mood of calmness and acceptance."

"But that's the last thing I want! I don't want to give the impression I went calmly and peacefully!"

"Well, what would you wear to show them you held out to your very last breath?"

"I don't know! I need time. Time to think about it, time to change."

"All right. You have a day to get ready."

"Can't you make it two?"

"What difference will that make? One day, and no more."

Noriko looked at her wristwatch—1:17. The ticking seconds were suddenly very loud to her ears.

"I expect you here in exactly twenty-four hours," the voice said.

The ticking grew even louder. At 1:17 tomorrow, Noriko thought, trembling, she would probably still be alive—but by 1:30 or 1:40, she'd be dead. The fatal time was getting closer by the minute, and once it came, she would never experience that time, or any time of day, ever again.

"Can't you make it twenty-six hours?" she pleaded.

The tiny hand continued on its way round the watch dial. Seconds were passing; already it was 1:19.

"All right—3:19 tomorrow!"

Noriko bowed, and began hurrying away.

"So you're not going to the funeral, after all?" the voice said, behind her. "Your friend's ghost will be sad—don't you care?"

Noriko didn't pause to look back, but walked even more quickly toward home.

As Noriko turned off the street for the road to her house, the red public telephone in front of the corner bread shop caught her eye. She went over, dialed the number of her husband Asari's office and, staring blankly at the broken cradle for the receiver, listened to the urgent ringing. It would seem odd, she reflected, if she asked straight out when he was coming home. First she'd pretend to consult him about how much money to take to the funeral as a condolence gift.

The switchboard operator came on the line.

"Mr. Asari in sales, please," Noriko said.

"Who shall I say is calling?"

Noriko was silent.

"Who is calling, please!" the operator repeated, her voice rising. Noriko cut the connection, and replaced the receiver.

Arriving home, she unlocked the front door and turning the knob to go in, her eyes fell on the yellow milk-bottle box by the step's wooden wainscoting. Its lid was half up, propped on the two empties from breakfast. After tomorrow, she reflected, one bottle would be enough. Her habit was to attach her order for the milkman to an empty bottle with a rubber band whenever Asari went away on business, or the two of them took a trip. "Please leave one bottle till such-and-such a date," she would write; or "Please cease deliveries until further notice."

It occurred to her as she went inside and slipped off her sandals that she should write a note before she forgot, telling the milkman, "Starting the day after tomorrow, please leave one bottle only." Taking a ballpoint pen from the letter rack, she sat down at the dinner table and searched in her bag for the condolence envelope. She found an unmarked part of the envelope and, after taking out the money, tore off a rectangular strip.

"Dear Milkman," she wrote. "Thank you for delivering the milk every day. From the day after tomorrow . . ." But here she paused. She intended to take proper leave of her husband, but discreetly, without his actually being aware of it. If she put this note on the bottle now, and Asari saw it, she'd destroy her whole plan. No, it would have to wait till tomorrow morning, after her husband had left the house.

Any number of things would have to be put off until her husband departed tomorrow: the key, for example, there on the tatami next to her purse. Whenever she left the house knowing he might return before she did, she hid it on her way out in the drainpipe by the kitchen door. On occasion, she forgot, and Asari was locked out. That must not happen tomorrow, but she couldn't attend to it until she left for the very last time.

Noriko tore another strip off the envelope. After scribbling *key*, and *milkman*, she folded it up in her powderpuff box on the low table before her mirror. She would definitely open that tomorrow.

She untied her obi and took off her kimono. After changing into a sweater and skirt, she threw open all the windows as well as the connecting doors between the parlor, the living room, and the corridor. A fresh breeze and spring sunshine flooded the rooms of the small house. She wondered: should she leave her kimono out for a while? But according to her watch it was already nearly two o'clock. If she wasted energy on tasks like that—and she had scarcely worn it anyway—she wouldn't get anything important done by the deadline tomorrow. She would only regret it, so she started to fold up the kimono. She glanced at the undergarments lying beside it, her hands moving busily. She could put those things in the garbage, she thought. It would all be collected tomorrow.

Once the kimono had been tidied away, she took the neck band off her chemise, wrapped it and her other undergarments in newspaper, and stuffed them all in a large plastic bag. Everything she had to discard could go in the bag. The garbage truck would come at eleven—the underwear she changed out of tomorrow morning could be thrown away, too. She took some freshly washed underwear from the wardrobe and laid them ready on the quilt in the closet. On second thought, she didn't want to leave her worn nightgown lying around to be found. She wrapped the nightgown she'd worn last night in a newspaper, put it in the bag, and chose a fresh one for tonight—this one would go in too, eventually. She placed some clean underwear and a pair of pajamas for Asari on the quilt. Opening the other closet door, she took out pillows and changed their cases. From the bottom half of the closet, she dragged out the two folded futons to strip off their sheets. Then she put them both back, set two clean sheets on top, and closed the closet.

She would have to do something with that, she realized, eyeing the mound of dirty clothes at her feet. But laundry would be a waste of precious time now. The man from the cleaner's might come round tomorrow. . . . But then again, he might not. True, she could always call to tell him to come and collect it, but there was no guarantee she would be there to receive him.

"I have to get everything sorted out—as soon as I can," Noriko told herself.

They had six sets of sheets and pillowcases, the extra set for guests. Surely it would be all right to throw these two sets away; she wasn't going to be around any more. She stuffed them in the plastic bag. Asari's pajamas, however, made her hesitate: he only had three pairs. But she discarded these, to save time. And noticing her tabi, which she'd worn with the kimono, she added them to the bag—by now, it was filled to bursting.

There was no risk of Asari noticing a garbage bag, and even if he did, he would hardly check its contents. Noriko tied it up, carried it out through the kitchen door, and deposited it next to the plastic trash bin. Countless other things still had to be thrown away, but unfortunately, they'd have to wait, like the key and the note for the milkman, until tomorrow.

Noriko went upstairs. She tore a piece of paper from a pad in Asari's desk to make a list of things to dispose of.

"My pillowcase," she wrote, "sheets; nightdress; and today's clothes (skirt and sweater)." Then, under a separate heading for Asari, she wrote, "underwear." After thinking for a while, she added, "socks and handkerchief." But then, where was she going to hide this list? Some place that wouldn't catch Asari's eye, but where she would see it once he had gone, before the garbage truck came by. The harder Noriko tried to think of a place, the more elusive it became. Well, for the time being she could conceal it in her can of dried sardines: she'd open that up tomorrow, to make miso soup for breakfast. True, Asari would still be home; but she could move it somewhere else then, and in any case, a better spot might still occur to her.

As she made her way down to the kitchen, Noriko was still pondering what to wear when she left home for the last time tomorrow. She was determined to die in a way that clearly showed her will to live. She was even more set on leaving traces of the most appalling death agony. It would be best if blood spewed out, if it left the most gruesome stains. She would struggle to her very last breath, thrashing about horribly with her arms and legs, slipping and rolling in her blood, smearing it everywhere. . . . Come to think of it, blood would never have shown up against the black kimono she'd been wearing this morning. Thank goodness she hadn't had to go dressed in that.

Noriko recalled a white outfit that she had had made two years before. The fabric seemed slightly yellowed; she hadn't worn it once this season. But it was basically still the same color. It would set the blood off nicely. But then she remembered: white was a color for the dead. One more minute, and she would have opted for what she least desired. Well, the only other garment that would do, considering the season, was her beige suit. A simple jersey skirt and jacket, she hardly ever wore it. She knew the suit would be in the wardrobe, but she opened the door just to make sure.

Yes, there it was: it would contrast shockingly with the blood. A purple winter suit was also hanging there, as well as a raincoat, an overcoat, a light green spring suit, and a folded blouse sharing its hanger with a cardigan. None had been cleaned since she last wore them; these clothes would have to be thrown away too. Come to think of it, there was also the shoe cupboard in the hall—she would only need one pair now. But all the other shoes, sandals, and rain clogs had been kicked off and thrown inside. She didn't want to leave them in that state. But Asari also used the wardrobe and the shoe cabinet, and again, he might notice if she cleared them out too soon.

Noriko headed toward the kitchen—*wardrobe* and *shoe cabinet* had to be added to the list in the dried sardine can—but halfway there, she stopped in her tracks. I must not forget, she told herself firmly, that I was the mistress of this household. If I get rid of everything, the house will look like a place left by a daughter who has run away to get married, or a maid who has stolen everything and gone off. She retraced her steps, draped a tortoiseshell necklace over the beige suit on its hanger, and closed the wardrobe. On her way back down the front hall, she let herself glance inside the shoe cupboard. Her brown shoes, and several pairs of Asari's were, all of them, clean enough.

Cutting down the number of her tasks was a relief, but the next moment it occurred to her that she would never have thought of such things if she hadn't started preparing her outfit for tomorrow. If she didn't keep her wits about her, she thought anxiously, she would forget so many things—she would die without completing important tasks. . . . The more she worried, the more impossible it became to keep track of where one task ended and another began.

Already it was nearly three o'clock. The front door of the bathhouse was just being thrown open. Noriko imagined selecting one of the wooden basins stacked just inside the bathing area, and hearing its hollow echo as she set it down in front of a deserted row of faucets. The afternoon sun would stream in through the high white-framed windows and reflect off the bottom of the tub. . . . Her very last bath, Noriko thought. She wanted to hear the clap of the wooden basin; she wanted to see the sunlight hit the tub.

But there was still a much more important task: she hurried upstairs, opened a closet, and from behind some cushions at the bottom removed a wicker basket. She took out of it Asari's three yukata. She replaced the basket and cushions. Standing up, she looked at the yukata in her arms: one more month, she thought, and it would be time to wear these. Asari would be sure to find them if she put them in the chest of drawers downstairs, with his underwear. And then it occurred to her that it might be nice to leave him a little message in one of these yukata. That way he'd discover it one summer evening, the first time he put it on. Yes, she wanted to whisper just a few words to her husband.

Noriko laid the yukata down, and sitting at Asari's desk, took out some writing paper and a pen. She contemplated the garments on the tatami, and the yukata-clad figure of Asari rose to mind—not on his way out to the bath, nor on his way back, but off to see a movie, on one of his evenings of not drinking.

Every ten days or so, Asari would declare, as he was changing out of his work clothes, "Tonight, I'll do without." This was his way of saying that he wouldn't have any drinks with dinner. When Noriko replied with comments like "Great!" or "I'm impressed!" he'd snap back: "I didn't say I wouldn't have any later!" On the other hand, if she only said, "I see," or "All right," he'd look hurt and resentful, and accuse her of indifference. Whatever she said on the nights he tried not to drink put him in a foul mood. She remembered infuriating him one evening: he'd asked her where the hammer was, and she'd told him to go and look in the saké cupboard. On these evenings, Asari always felt the need for some distraction, and often ended up at their local movie theater. He hardly ever invited her, but then she didn't particularly want to go. If anything, she felt relief when he told her that he was going out, after a short supper without saké or beer; she would busily help him get ready. The tense set of his shoulders as he left showed that he was fuming about having said he wouldn't drink. Rather than money she would put books of movie tickets in his yukata sleeve, so he would not be tempted on the way home. She felt sorry for him, but she also found the whole thing a little amusing.

Noriko gripped the pen.

"Good evening, dear," she wrote. "So you've put on your yukata. You must be feeling cool and comfortable. Are you on your way to the Shōwa Cinema? Perhaps they're showing one of your favorite sexy comedies tonight."

She signed her name, folded the note twice, then slipped it into the sleeve of the yukata on the top of the pile—a navy blue one with white horizontal stripes made up of small circles like sliced macaroni.

But the prospect of greeting her husband from his yukata sleeve after her death like this made her want to give him a winter surprise too—perhaps from the pocket of his overcoat. She took up the pen again.

"It's gotten so cold, hasn't it!" she wrote on the next sheet of paper: "I expect you'll stop off for a drink on your way home tonight. Here's a little pocket money, from my own secret supply. Well, I wish that were true. You always said, didn't you, that I was no good at saving—that's why you could trust me. Well, you were right, dear: this is only household expense money, plus the condolence gift for my friend's funeral, which in the end I didn't attend. You're fussy enough about money—except when it comes to drink—to have been wondering what became of this small sum. Didn't I see you, the other day, rummaging around in the chest of drawers for it? I'm glad you finally have it—sorry there's no interest. Well, say hello to your friends for me. . . ."

She would have to remember to enclose the money with the note. She tore that page off the pad, set it on the desk, and took up her pen again. It did cross her mind that perhaps she should be writing her will rather than these little notes. But no, she decided, that could wait; it wasn't as if she could forget that. If she began to run out of time, a simple letter of testament to Asari would suffice. These messages were much more precious, at least in her opinion.

"So you're off on a business trip?" She would put this one in his suitcase. "You really are devoted to your job. Should I come with you? Or shall I stay home? Well, maybe I will stay. I should look after our house, after all. Well, when you are leaving, don't forget me—that way, you'll remember to shut off the gas and lock up. Have a safe trip."

She should next appear, she decided, from their bundle of New Year's cards. Asari would look them over again, before writing his own cards for the coming year. "I hope that you will marry again, and that your new wife will make you happy," she would write. "You won't be seeing me any more now. This is goodbye forever," and with these words, she would disappear from his life.

But it occurred to her, as she finished writing, that Asari might very well remarry *before* the year was out. Even if she could count on surprising him from his yukata sleeve, there was every chance that an appearance from his overcoat pocket might bring her face to face not with Asari, but with his next wife.

A widower, just past forty, with a steady job and no children (even if he drank too much and wasn't likely to be promoted), Asari wouldn't have much difficulty in finding a new partner. He'd probably remarry as soon as he could, Noriko thought. He hadn't had much luck with wives, as her own death would shortly prove; and she was his second. From what she knew of his past and personality, though, bad luck would not make him give up on marriage altogether. He wouldn't search high and low trying to find the perfect partner this time either; he would get married again, not because he couldn't bear being single, but simply because there was no reason not to.

When Asari had first met Noriko, about eight years ago, he had been quite open about having already been married once. His wife had affected traditional tastes, he said. Their marriage hadn't lasted long; they had divorced three or four years before. Noriko hadn't any idea of the woman's name or her age: Asari had gotten a completely new family register drawn up when he married her.

Noriko knew, because he had told her himself, that he had had several affairs after his divorce, before meeting her. It seemed he'd even lived with one woman. When Noriko first moved in, she came across all sorts of feminine accessories among his things: a bright red fountain pen, a set of automatic pencils, a little wickerwork purse, a lady's scarf. . . . They were mostly imported, hardly likely belongings of a woman with traditional tastes. Asari didn't seem particularly bothered that she discovered them; and Noriko herself had been quite unconcerned. She'd even appropriated some, though the fountain pen she was using now was Asari's.

Once, a year or two after they were married, Noriko, looking for wrapping paper, had discovered a department store package with a mailing label on it. It had been sent to Asari at the address where he had lived with his first wife. Though he'd told Noriko he had been divorced for three or four years before meeting her, it had been postmarked just the year prior.

"Would you like to see what I've found?" she asked, showing it to him.

"Where did that come from?" he asked, staring at the address label.

"It must bring back memories," Noriko teased. "It was in the closet, with the wrapping paper."

"That's strange. I wonder how it got there."

"It is strange, isn't it?" Noriko pointed at the postmark: "Especially this."

Asari didn't seem to know what to say.

"Oh, I remember," he said, suddenly reassured. "Look. My brother sent it to me."

"Oh yes. He was in Hakata by then, wasn't he."

"I'd been too busy to tell him I'd moved. . . . So he mailed it to my old place."

"And then?"

"And then it was forwarded. I got it here."

Noriko started to laugh. "So it was in the mail for years?" she asked. "The post office forwarded it three years later? Don't worry—it's all right. I'll let it go."

"You're just like the secret police," Asari said, scowling. He returned the package to her with a show of indifference.

Noriko suspected, judging from the quantity and type of items left behind, that they had belonged to the woman Asari had lived with for a while after his divorce. If so, since he'd been divorced later than he'd originally said, he must have married and divorced one woman, lived with another, and then married her—all in a short space of time.

But she didn't think Asari had actually been unfaithful: true, there'd been signs that he had been dragged off certain places by disreputable friends a couple of times. Maybe she'd let herself be fooled, but she basically trusted him.

And this trust might account for Noriko never having felt any jealousy about the women in his past. She herself had had a lover before meeting Asari, though they'd broken up completely. The fact was, neither had a right to object to the other's past—and anyway those relationships weren't worth getting upset about.

If anything, Noriko felt a certain intimacy with Asari's first wife as well as with the imported accessories' owner, which only increased when she learned that he had been involved with all three in such quick succession. She came to think of the three of them as some harem in a primitive land, all sharing the same husband and coexisting in harmony.

Asari must have sensed her feelings: "Hey, Noriko," he would say, showing her some little thing he had come across. "Look what I found—would you like it?" He didn't go so far as to say that it had belonged to a woman with whom he had been involved; but he didn't have to, it was obvious.

"Oh, yes," she would say, gratefully, "Give it to me." And the truth was that she'd also been gratified by the discovery of the package with that mailing label.

Noriko now started to feel that same sort of intimacy toward Asari's future women: surely his third wife wouldn't object to meeting her amid Asari's things. The two of them might enjoy reading her messages together. The new wife might even declare that, of the three women in his past, she liked her, Noriko, best of all.

Thinking this, Noriko wanted to send a little note to Asari's wife-to-be. Since he hadn't discarded the packaging or the other woman's things around the house, he would probably be just as lax preparing for his third spouse. Noriko didn't worry that her note wouldn't be found.

"Hello, how do you do? I'm so glad to meet you. I've been

wanting to have a chat. There are so many things I'd like to share with you.

"Perhaps I should start by telling you the bad things about Asari. He won't buy you anything, you know, unless you ask him a thousand times. As you must have realized, he's very tight with money and for some reason, he's particularly stingy about our clothes. He's very clever in the way he gets out of it: 'Don't buy that,' he'll say. 'Let's shop around and get something that really suits you.' So you must make him buy you as many clothes as you can—get him to buy you what he didn't buy me.

"Also, please help yourself to any of my things, though I doubt they'll be of much use to you. I used his other women's belongings—I'd love it if you did the same with mine."

Realizing that Asari might again renew his family register for his third marriage, and that her name would mean nothing to his new spouse, Noriko signed the note: "From the deceased wife."

She tore off the page, and left it on the desk with the other notes. Later she would put it in the crate of her summer glass-ware. She took up the pen again and started another note: "Well, I see that you are now quite settled in. I'm very happy to see you being so good to him. I hope you won't spare any effort to see to his every need. . . ."

Writing this, a picture began to form in Noriko's mind of the way Asari and his well-settled-in wife would live. The living room would be much more cramped—cramped and untidy. They would have rented the second floor to an office worker and Asari's desk would have been brought down, and all sorts of objects would be piled on top of it, and around it. One of his wife's soiled workaday kimonos would hang on the wall. The table would be laid with food, a strange combination—curry, and then squid cooked with radish in soy sauce. Asari and his wife would be eating in silence, their eyes on the television.

"This singer looks like our lodger," the wife would say.

Asari would not reply.

"Oh, speaking of the lodger," she would continue, "I think he's going to get married soon. Something tells me."

"What makes you say that?"

"I don't know. Just something. He's got his nerve—staying on all this time, paying the same rent. You can tell he's a hick."

"You were the one who wanted to rent it out."

"Well, we need the money, don't we, if we're going to build a house. We'll never do it on your salary."

"The rent doesn't make that much difference, does it?"

"Every little bit helps. We couldn't hope to buy a house without it. Look how little you earn. And you like to drink."

Asari, who that night would be abstaining, would grimace, his chopsticks moving, his eyes on the screen, but his wife would continue, undeterred.

"You know how much last month's liquor bill was? Eight thousand yen!"

"So what!" Asari would snap, finally facing her, and a violent altercation would ensue.

But a few hours later, in the bedroom, the wife would say: "You know, the sooner we have our own house, the better."

And Asari would reply: "Well, I probably can't even find a plot of land within an hour and a half of work."

Noriko had never grumbled about Asari's meager salary. They had no children, after all, and she'd been able to make ends meet. It was true that they were only renting. Asari was always regaling her with grand plans about the dream house he would build for them in the future, and so she'd stopped even thinking about owning their own place. As a result, both of them seemed tacitly resigned to renting for the rest of their days.

In other words, Noriko realized, she had never, not once, broached the subject of owning their own house. Was it appropriate, then, to consider themselves "husband and wife"? She found herself forced to look at her life with him in a new light. She went back to the letter she was writing.

"Thinking about it now," she wrote, "maybe Asari and I weren't really married, after all. Maybe we were only lovers who happened to end up living together. Legally speaking, we were married; we lived together for six years—a record for Asari; and we loved each other, or so I like to think. But I have a feeling that we lived together the way lovers do, not like a husband and wife. People often say that couples who don't have sex can't really be married, but it's in the opposite sense that we weren't really married. I would guess that some of those other couples were more truly husband and wife than we were.

"You will try, won't you, to be really married. Please let him experience this—contrary to appearances, he never has before. . . .

"Why do I say we were not husband and wife? Well. . . ."

Noriko let the pen fall from her hands. The truth of her life with Asari was bearing down upon her so closely, she had a hard time assimilating it.

Yes—that was right, Noriko admitted, still lost in thought. They hadn't been husband and wife; they had simply chosen to live together. Sometimes they were like brother and sister, each in turn playing the older sibling, and at other times like parent and child. But they had never been husband and wife. Their life together hadn't been what marriage is supposed to be.

Yet as Noriko looked back over her relationship with Asari, her strongest impression was of their happiness. And so was it really that important, not having been husband and wife? She couldn't help being disturbed, though, by having been all this time under the illusion that they were truly married.

They were both at fault for not becoming a true married couple, it seemed to her: perhaps they simply hadn't bothered. Of course, they hadn't been young when they met; Asari had been married before; and they didn't have any children. But all these factors didn't get at the root of the trouble. Their dispositions—Asari nonchalantly giving her former lovers' belongings, and her eager appropriations—she wasn't certain, but

Noriko suspected their dispositions were somehow to blame. All she knew now was that all sorts of evidence was suddenly assailing her that their marriage had been a sham.

All the time they'd been together, Noriko had seen to Asari's every need—if he washed his face, she'd be there to hand him a towel. Every day he had a choice of clean underclothes, a variety of dishes to eat, and freshly aired sheets and futon. She tolerated his drinking, hardly ever losing patience with his coming home late after an evening out, in his cups, and still eager to hit the bottle; or when he got so drunk that he was throwing up and kept her awake all night. She never sulked the next morning. Asari, who didn't seem to know what a hangover was, would get up looking reinvigorated, and just at the sight of him she would feel refreshed. Far from discouraging him when he wanted to go out for drinks with his friends, she let him have all the spare money.

But now she knew a wife wouldn't have been so tolerant or devoted. A husband returns in a drunken stupor in the middle of night—a real wife would be angry the next day, and resentful, and refuse to speak to him. He'd have to sit there, suffering a terrible hangover, in silence. Perhaps more than his constitution played into Asari's freedom from hangovers.

Had she been a wife, she would never have given Asari all their money when he went out drinking: she'd been more like a doting mother spoiling her son. Of course, the roles were often reversed, and she was the daughter looking after the house for her father.

Sometimes, toward the end of the month, she'd ask Asari in the morning: "Can I have some money?"

"You've run out?"

"Yes, I have."

"You've got to be more careful. Well, on my way back home tonight I can buy meat or something—or we can eat out. Asari would search in his pocket, and leave two hundred yen: "This should do for lunch."

She had no interest in hoarding up the monthly household account money, the passion of so many wives, and he didn't have affairs, but didn't both these facts really mean they were united only by love and nothing else? If they'd loved each other as husband and wife, surely, he would have been thrilled by the prospect of love affairs, and she by hoarding money.

And they never fought—there just didn't seem to be anything worth fighting about. True, she thought he was stingy; she'd written as much to his next wife. But perhaps she'd exaggerated, hoping to get a taste of conjugality. All in all, their life was extremely calm and harmonious. Except, of course, when Asari got terribly drunk, or irritable because he was trying not to drink. They had been happy. She hadn't assumed that for the rest of their days they would never know any sorrow. But it had never crossed her mind that she'd find herself rethinking their relationship in the final moments of her life.

"I'm home," Asari called, opening the front door. She went out into the hall.

"There's an odd letter in our mailbox," he added, with a wave toward the front gate. He threw the evening paper, which she'd forgotten to bring in, at her feet. Slipping on some sandals, Noriko pushed past him taking off his shoes, ran out, and opened the mailbox flap to find the red-topped salt shaker inside.

"You didn't do it?" Asari asked, as she hurried back in with the shaker. He stopped unknotting his tie and mimed sprinkling salt on himself.

Noriko's parents had taught her the custom of shaking salt over oneself before going inside the house after a funeral. Her mother and father never forgot this act of purification. She remembered one summer evening her mother had called from the front door: "I'm home. . . . Can someone bring me the salt?" She'd been on her way to the theater that night, not a funeral: Noriko had gone out to the hall. Her mother's face was deadly pale.

"Where's the salt? Quickly," her mother had repeated. Noriko brought a jar of coarse salt from the kitchen. Her mother scattered handful after handful over her shoulders and around the hem of her kimono. When she finally entered the house and sat down, she explained that a young woman had committed suicide by throwing herself in front of the train.

"She was about your age," her mother had told Noriko, then just twenty. "Not married, apparently. It was so awful, I couldn't look. But I heard them saying, 'That's a leg,' and 'That's an arm,' and 'There's a lump of flesh.' And such a smell . . ."

It was probably the memory of that incident which caused Noriko to carry on the salt ritual herself. Her mother's white face at the door, the young woman her same age whose body had been turned into lumps of flesh in the space of a second . . . Her mother's ghastly expression made Noriko imagine she might be possessed by a ghost. The look was gone by the time she came inside and Noriko could see her in the light. But who could tell whether, had she come straight in, that thing might not have come in too, and still be hovering in the air?

Whenever Asari returned from a funeral, Noriko would make him wait at the door as she hurried to fetch the salt.

"Don't bother. It's silly," he would say, coming straight in to remove his shoes. But Noriko would insist on taking him back outside and shaking salt over him. Her parents had always used coarse salt, which wasn't available these days, so Noriko made do with the ordinary table variety, though it left something to be desired.

One day as she sprinkled him with salt, Asari had asked her: "What'll happen if you die before I do? Will you shake salt down on me from somewhere in the sky when I come back from your funeral?"

Whenever Noriko knew that she'd have to purify herself, she would leave the salt shaker in the mailbox as she set out—as she had done today.

"I must have forgotten," she told Asari, putting it back on the dinner table, and forcing a smile. "Which do you want first: dinner or a bath?"

"What would you prefer?" Asari said, adjusting the front panels of his kimono before tying his sash.

"I don't mind either way."

"I'll go later, then—I'm starved." He added: "Tonight, I'll do without."

But Noriko didn't want him not drinking tonight: the last thing she wanted was for him to go off to the Shōwa. On the other hand, if he stayed home, he'd only get irritable, and it would be even worse if he started after dinner: he might get very drunk.

"Well," she replied, "Feel free to change your mind." This was her habitual response these days when he announced that he'd do without. But tonight she chose to say this for a special reason: she wanted him to drink, not too much, just enough so he'd stay and talk with her.

In the end, Asari did break his resolution—not through weakness, but at her suggestion.

"Would you mind if I had a beer, though?" Noriko asked, using the same embarrassed tone Asari adopted if he changed his mind. "I'm really thirsty."

"All right," he said. He grinned. "Since it's a request from someone who rarely indulges, I'll make an exception and have some too."

"But we'll have to go at my pace."

"What do you mean, your pace?"

"You know what I mean."

"Whatever you say."

Noriko brought over the bottle, and Asari reached out to open it.

"Let me do the honors," he said. "Now, you can purify yourself with beer, since you forgot the salt."

Noriko silently gazed at the filling glass. Asari stopped when it was half full.

"Is that all I get?"

"I'll give you some more in a minute. You're not a drinker, after all."

Noriko took the bottle from him, poured his beer, and by the time she'd set it down, he was already swigging. "Aren't we going to toast, since I so rarely indulge?" she asked.

"Oh, that's right." But all he did was put down his glass and seize his chopsticks.

Noriko took a sip.

"How old was your friend who died?" Asari asked.

"My age."

"An old lady like that?" Asari covered his mouth, pretending that had slipped out. "Who let her get behind the wheel?"

"She gave me a ride once."

"That was stupid. You've got to be more careful. What if you'd been in the car when she had the accident? You'd have died, and I'd have had nobody to sprinkle salt over me after funerals."

Noriko picked up her glass, and drank a little beer.

"It was safer then. She had a sticker in the window that said 'I just got my license. Thank you for your cooperation.'"

"People don't pay any attention to those stickers."

"No, but that's how careful she was."

"Anyway, I don't want you to ever get in a car with a woman driver."

"You don't mind if the driver's a man? Even on a very long long trip?"

"I'm serious."

"I know."

"I hope so. But you know, going so unexpectedly like that—I think that'd be the worst."

"So you'd rather I came and said goodbye?"

"I meant if *I* died. Well, it would be pretty bad if you did, too. . . ."

"You think so? Tell me, what would you want to take care of before you died? Do you have a mistress?"

"Possibly. Actually, at one time I thought a lot about what would happen if I did die unexpectedly. Right after I got out of school my father died, and my mother divided up the family property for the children. Some land was bought for me in Setagaya—Mother planned on my building a house there, and moving in with me when I got married, but it was years before I did marry, and in the meantime I sold the land and squandered all the money."

"You've told me this story."

"But she never knew. Every time I went home, my mother would tell me to go ahead, get married and build my own house, she'd help me financially. And then prices went up. I'd sold my land when it was cheap, and there wasn't any left. Back then, you know, I really drank—I don't drink at all now in comparison—I ended up not being able to pay the rent. I brought all my things to the pawn shop, my suitcases and trunks were empty. Once, I counted up the tickets from the pawn shop, you know, and I had eighteen. But I kept hitting the bottle. Sometimes I'd wake up on a bench in some train station: what would happen if I died now, I'd wonder. Those pawn tickets would loom up before my eyes. I couldn't stand the thought of Mother finding out I drank the land away, debts piled up, and had nothing but a stack of pawn tickets. I'd have to get rid of those tickets, I'd have to have time for that, at least, I'd tell myself."

"What would you do if you were going to die now?"

"Well, first of all, this, I suppose." Asari raised his glass, and gulped down some beer.

Noriko picked up hers. It was nearly empty. As she drank, the foam on the top sank down to the crystal bottom, the bubbles dispersing. Asari's face, the size of a bean, came into view.

"Want some more?" he asked.

Noriko held out her glass, and as he started pouring, she warned, "Oh, not too much."

"You were complaining a minute ago how little I gave you," replied Asari, deliberately taking his time complying.

Noriko took two sips in a row. Her glass was more than half full.

"You sure you're all right?"

She paused. "Yes," she answered, glass in hand, and the next moment, she finished it off. Pretending to be engaged in draining it to the last drop, she immersed herself again in that distant, miniature, cheerful world sparkling in the bottom of her glass. Seated at a cute little table scattered with dishes, Asari looked small enough to hold in the palm of her hand. What would he do, she wondered, if she told him she only had a few hours to live? Would he kill her before 3:19 tomorrow, with his own hands?

"I see what you're doing," said Asari, who was copying her. "You look so tiny."

"So do you. It's pretty, isn't it?" And then, after a pause, she asked: "Tell me, did you ever think of leaving any notes behind for people to read after you died?"

"No." Asari put down his glass and Noriko did the same. "My only hope was that my mother would die, so she wouldn't see me end so miserably. That was my one try at filial piety. Now," he changed the subject: "How about some saké?"

Usually he found it difficult to stop once he got onto saké.

"If we're going at my pace," replied Noriko, "that's it, I think. But we could eat. How do you feel?"

"That's fine with me," Asari acquiesced, mildly.

As they ate dinner, Noriko asked: "I wonder how we'll turn out, growing old together, you and I."

"What do you mean, how we'll turn out?"

"You know, how we'll lead our lives."

"Same as we do now, I'd guess."

"You mean like young newlyweds, or like friends who get together over a cup of tea—for the next twenty, thirty years?"

That's not a true married life, she wanted to say. But Asari seemed oblivious.

"What a great way of putting it!" was his reply.

He glanced at the clock above the cupboard. "Guess what— it's not too late for the movie at the Shōwa. I don't mind taking you, if you'd like to go."

Taking the ticket book from the letter rack, he flipped open the red cover. "Only one left. Want to buy me another booklet, and use one yourself?"

Noriko said yes.

They set out, walking along close to the hedges that lined the neighborhood roads. In the gardens they could see light from the houses, soft lights that spoke of spring evenings. These houses all looked so peaceful and assured to Noriko's eyes. In the past, she had once been terribly lonely after being abandoned by her first lover, and she remembered that the light from other people's windows had always looked so warm and inviting. When she returned to her lodgings and switched on the light in her small bare room, she would think that nobody, not even a person dying of cold and hunger, would look with envy and longing at her window. Now, as she strolled along with Asari, she wondered about the light from their living room window. Did it glow, calm and confident, like these? Or was it the weaker, uncertain kind that shines from an inn or dormitory?

They reached the shopping district and crossed the railway tracks. The Shōwa Cinema was a small theater beyond the station, specializing in foreign films.

"Hmm, I wonder what's playing," Asari said aloud to himself, looking at the movie stills in the window: a western and an Italian film, apparently.

"One book of tickets, please," Noriko said, handing over the 500-yen note she'd tucked into her sash.

"I thought you were going to buy me a few," Asari grumbled next to her.

They went inside and as Asari opened the door, Noriko made out lines of backs ranged in all the seats. But when her eyes gradually adjusted to the darkness, she saw several empty places near the front.

"Let's go over there," Asari said. Crouching, he headed down the aisle. Once seated, they looked up at the screen: the Italian film was playing. A shot of a peaceful country village in beautiful muted colors; then a train station; and in the next scene appeared a woman, obviously recovering from a serious illness, accompanied by her husband: they were leaving a health spa. Not long after they got home, a visitor came, a friend of the husband. From what the men said when the woman was out of the room it became clear that the marriage was no longer passionate—in fact the couple hardly felt anything for each other any more.

Not like herself and Asari, Noriko thought: they still felt strongly about each another. Not one day passed without her being aware of his heart beating, and it was surely the same for him. Yet she did wonder about the kind of light shining out of their home. A legal bond, cohabitation, sex, and love were supposed to be the four pillars of marriage. But they don't alone suffice—any more than four pillars constitute a house. Neither of them had bothered to do any work on their four pillars, it seemed to her. They hadn't put a roof over them; they hadn't even painted the walls—the things that would keep a house up when a pillar got wobbly. But their marriage had nothing supporting it. Their life together only amounted to a simple succession of days.

In other words, she reflected, they hadn't known the hardship or the happiness of true conjugal life. But if only they'd been aware that they were lovers, and not husband and wife, and lived out their relationship as it really was, their experience might have been totally different. True, they might have been ostracized, and they would have lost their easy tranquillity—but they might also have felt a keener, more intense kind of joy.

If she did write a letter to Asari before her death, Noriko told herself, she'd have to be honest with him. "What I regret," she would say, "is dying without ever finding out what our relationship might have been, had we tried to be husband and wife—or known that we were, in fact, simply lovers living together."

The movie was still depicting the husband and wife becoming more and more estranged. One or the other would occasionally attempt a reconciliation, but each time both felt betrayed and ended up feeling more hopeless than ever.

"Your wife will never get better unless you encourage her more," the husband's friend told him. The husband immediately followed this advice.

"You look wonderful this morning," he said to her. "Your cheeks are so rosy. The worst must be over by now."

The wife took this as a sign of his impatience with her weak condition and forced herself to pretend that she did feel better. At this, her husband said that since she was doing so well, he would be able to take her to a party he'd been invited to the following week.

A few days later, their little boy ran a fever. They both nursed him through the night.

"Mummy and Daddy are here, sonny," the husband told the boy, his arm around her shoulders.

"Darling," the wife said, addressing their son. "How many days do you want to stay out of school? Daddy can do everything; if he can cure people, maybe he can arrange for you to be ill as long as you like."

The man's arm fell from her shoulders.

"I want to get better quickly," the son said.

"All right. I'll make you get well very soon."

On the day of the party, the wife came into her husband's

room, dressed up and ready to go out. He had forgotten all
about the party, and hurriedly started shaving.

Despite how badly they got along, there were no fights:
only short ironic exchanges between this husband and wife
showed how distant their hearts and minds had become. And so
the days passed, without any incident that might have led to
divorce.

Noriko turned her now heavy head to look at Asari sitting
beside her. His eyes fixed on the screen, his face was bathed in
its light. Would he understand if she told him she didn't think
they had ever truly been married? They were nothing like the
couple in the movie. But their bond of simple love and affection
had allowed them to interpret each other's words in purely
positive ways—the way that he had taken it as a compliment
when she said at dinner they were half like newlyweds and half
like friends visiting over a cup of tea. The couple in the movie
drifted farther apart because they always interpreted each
other's words negatively; but she was Asari's accomplice in a
similar sort of crime, continually inferring only good things in
what was said, without really listening.

She could imagine the way he would reply if she did say to
him, "Please listen to me. I'm wondering now if it's a good thing
that we've never had a fight."

"It is a good thing!" he would say. "Trust me. I know." And
the urge to tell him what she wanted to say would fade, just as it
did for the screen couple who never bothered to explain any true
state of mind. . . .

They got home just past ten o'clock, after staying to watch the
western.

"I think I'll go take a bath," said Asari.

Noriko stopped herself from saying she'd go too.

"That's good—see you when you get back."

When he left the house, she went upstairs, sat at the desk,
and took out some paper.

"I must tell you that if I had to die now, I would have regrets and disappointments," she wrote.

She went on to describe her fears that, even though they had been legally married and lived under the same roof, united in mind and body, they hadn't been a married couple. After listing her reasons, she continued:

"Today, waiting for the bus on my way to the funeral, I looked at my watch: it was just past one o'clock. At that time the day before yesterday, my friend was still alive. She'd eaten lunch, and left the house, just as I had. The thought of death was probably the furthest thing from her mind. When I imagined her driving, without the faintest idea of what was going to happen, I got so frightened that the ticking of my watch scared me. As you said, it must be the worst thing to die unexpectedly. My friend would have had so many things to do, had she known her fate—if she could only have had one more day. . . . That idea made me think about what I would do if I had to die tomorrow afternoon. I didn't stop thinking about it, even after I'd come home. I started to wonder about your next marriage, which I imagined as something quite different from our own; and then that made me reflect on our life together.

"My dear, our choice was either to become husband and wife in the true sense or consciously live out the relationship that we have—simply a man and a woman who love each other. And I want us to do one or the other now—even if it brings conflict and pain. What I don't want is to continue to believe that we're living a married life when we're not. . . .

"And you know, when I do finally die, I think I would like a few final moments. Because even if they bring on other regrets and disappointments, at least I'll be able to feel that I've lived my life fully.

"In any case, I'm sure I won't regret my friend's death making me reflect on the life I've led with you."

As soon as Asari came back, Noriko said that it was her turn.

"What? You didn't go yet?" he asked. "We could have gone together."

"Only we would have had to lock up the house again," Noriko replied, gathering her toiletries.

"There's an odd letter in our mailbox," she called back to him, the moment she was out the door.

No sooner had Noriko put her shoes in the bathhouse locker and taken the key, than the outside light over the entrance was turned off. A few people remained in the changing area, putting on their clothes: only one other person was undressing.

"Good night," a woman called as she was leaving to the girl tidying up the baskets.

Wooden pails lay scattered over the bathing area tiles. Four or five women, at some distance from each other, were washing themselves, and one started to wash her hair. That's nice, Noriko told herself, stretching out in the tub. Thanks to her, she could take her time.

At that moment, over on the men's side of the bathhouse, someone started whistling. It was a straightforward happy tune, a children's song from a well-known musical. Whoever it was, he was whistling very exuberantly.

Noriko tried to conjure up a picture of the man who was whistling. Perhaps he was a young manual laborer from one of the better factories—maybe he had worked overtime tonight. His shift finally over, all that he had to do now was go home and sleep, without a care for tomorrow. . . . That was why he could be so happy-go-lucky, whistling. As Noriko listened, he came to the end of the song, managing the instrumental part with skill. Then, he started all over again with even more enthusiasm. Noriko felt her own heart ease and lift.

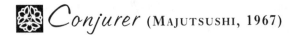

Conjurer (Majutsushi, 1967)

On stage, the conjurer, a Western woman in a skimpy costume, lifted a large green jar off the table. Holding it over another vessel, she turned it upside down: a stream of water poured from the one to the other. She placed the jar back on the table. Her assistant, a man, took hold of the second container and poured the water straight back into the jar, holding it up high so the audience could see. The conjurer, lifting up the jar a second time, pretended now to stagger under its weight—much to everybody's amusement. Meanwhile, her assistant pulled the table back onto two legs to expose its underside, rapped its top smartly, and set it down again. Placing the jar on the table, the conjurer drew back a few paces.

"What do you think will come out of it now?" she asked the audience, pointing to the green jar.

"Doves!"

"Flags!"

"Colored paper!"

Children yelled suggestions, one after the other, and the conjurer replied to each in English, "No." This didn't mean, of course, that she understood everything they were shouting: she only had to know the Japanese for whatever object she was about to produce.

"Panties!" a man shouted from somewhere, as the children's voices died away. Everybody laughed.

"Panties?" repeated the conjurer, jerking her head back in

exaggerated surprise. As if deciding this was quite enough audience participation, she approached the table and picked the jar up by the rim as if it weighed nothing at all. Wrapping one arm around its belly, she plunged her hand inside and, bringing it out, released a fistful of cherry blossoms. There was a burst of applause. The woman dipped her hand in again and again, scattering petals all over the stage and exciting more cheers and clapping from the crowd.

Then she gave the jar to her assistant, who went off with it into the wings, wheeling the table ahead of him. He returned with a Japanese parasol. This the conjurer took, and showed to the audience, after snapping it open: a simple waxed-paper parasol. Next she held it out with the handle extended toward them, displaying its underside. Then she closed it. As she re-opened it, the strains of a waltz, "The Voice of Spring," came over the loudspeakers. The woman started to step back and forth on the petal-strewn stage in time to the music, opening and closing the parasol. There was another burst of applause: a dove had fluttered out. One after another, a whole flock of pure white doves rose up into the air—though it was difficult to tell when they emerged, so fast was the parasol's fluttering.

The curtain fell. Hisako realized she had been fascinated, watching this scene. Japanese performers, of course, were capable of this kind of trick, as well as the preceding numbers in the program, simple sleights of hand. But these foreigners' gestures were so polished, and their costumes so eye-catching—their performance had extra élan. Come to think of it, how long had it been since she had last seen a live magic show? Discounting the ones on television, it had been years and years.

She remembered as a child having watched conjuring tricks at some dance hall or other: a hand of cards that shrank every time it was spread, finally disappearing altogether; a Manchurian flag drawn out of a bowler hat. She also recalled watching three dog couples—in tuxedoes and gowns—waltz in a traveling fair. Then there was the time she went to the German circus when it toured Japan. Her parents had gone twice, taking their children two at a time. Some of the acts had involved scores of lions and tigers in the ring, and in the event of an emergency, they wanted to be able to escape each carrying one child.

But she couldn't remember having gone to see anything like this magic show since then. And that had been when she was still in grammar school—a good twenty, no, thirty years ago. She had almost forgotten such things existed. Hisako smiled wryly: so what did she think she was doing, coming to a show like this at her age, and by herself?

At least half the seats in Hisako's section of the balcony seemed unavailable for purchase. A whole block of vacant seats was cordoned off by ropes with tags saying "Do not enter." The same went for the opposite side of the balcony and the first five rows from the stage on the floor below. No doubt it was necessary to keep people from seeing the tricks' secrets, but it seemed a pity as far as the theater itself was concerned.

All the available seats had been taken. The place was so full, in fact, that she wondered whether some people hadn't been turned away. If they'd timed their run to overlap with spring vacation, it was a successful strategy: the audience buzzed with the voices of grammar- and middle-school students. Several groups looked like tourists who'd come to town specially for the show. She was the only one who'd come alone, of course; every other middle-aged person was accompanying a child. In the audiences of the foreign magic shows and circuses she watched on television, Hisako always saw several middle-aged, even elderly, couples. But not here—here the couples were all very young.

Noguchi and Tsuneko had told her that they had come without their children. Last Sunday they had seen this show. She wondered: what would they have looked like, sitting there in the audience? Generally speaking, a middle-aged Japanese husband and wife who go out on dates would have to be very happily married. On the other hand, one could, a little cynically, reach the opposite conclusion. A couple on terrible terms might decide on a whim to go, after say, being persuaded by a friend that they should try going out—to try enjoying something together just once in a while. Where could they go, they would wonder, as they stepped out the door. Not to visit friends. Shopping would be irritating; and it would be depressing to face each other over a long drawn-out meal. We don't have any amusements in common, they would realize; how can we just invent one on the spot? Neither would object to a film or a play; but how uncomfortable if one was moved to tears—and bothered by the other's lack of reaction. The poster for the magic show would catch their eye, and each would sigh with relief. *That* was what they should go and see: at a magic show, they wouldn't need to talk—and unlike a movie or a play, it wouldn't make any emotional demands. As they watched, deceived into feeling that they were in a happy mood, they might even have the illusion that they were enjoying a moment of harmony together as man and wife.

The next number—a kind of circus act—had begun. A slender steel ladder, placed sideways, rose straight up out of the stage floor. Advertised in the program as Spanish, a man dressed in a sequined toreador's costume of white and yellow came bounding out from the wings, striking two steel swords together. Aiming one sword at the stage floor, he tossed it away and it landed with its point embedded in the wooden boards. Bending it back like a bow, he released it, and the sword flashed upright vibrating loudly, shivering, and eventually coming to rest still stuck in the floor. After doing the same thing with the other sword, he plucked them both out, and then held them out horizontally, one on top of the other, in front of him. One blade clattered to the ground—he had dropped it on purpose to prove that they weren't magnetized.

Now holding each by the flat of its blade, he aligned the swords together at their points, and then swung them round so they were positioned vertically in front of him, and raised them into the air. As the two swords joined tip to tip moved up, he took his hand away from the higher one. Using this hand to grip the handle of the bottom sword, he lifted the whole thing still higher. Then he turned his face up toward the ceiling, placed the handle of the bottom sword between his teeth, and took both hands away. Balancing the swords with his mouth, he started to climb the vertical metal ladder.

With every step he took, the precariously balanced swords swayed together, threatening to come apart. When he got half-way up, the delicate ladder began to teeter and sag. The higher he climbed, the shakier the ladder grew, and the more danger-ously unstable the swords. The man waited patiently after each move for the shaking to cease, and then took one more step up. He was a handsome man, with Mediterranean features, which seemed to make the possibility of the top blade slipping and running him through the throat all the more exciting. The glints of light thrown about by the trembling swords and metal ladder—and the man's tense concentration—were thrilling.

The man reached the topmost rung, and swung a leg over. Still balancing the swords in his mouth, he started his descent. As he approached the bottom of the ladder, Hisako saw that his upturned face was drenched in beads of sweat glittering like specks of gold leaf. Finally he was off the ladder and down on the ground. He turned to the audience, and with a jerk of his chin, tossed away his swords which separated, landing straight up in the floor. He was met with cheers and applause.

"What a wonderful performance!" Hisako suddenly wanted to exclaim to somebody, not that she actually looked around for anybody to say it to. Instead, she imagined what a happily mar-ried middle-aged couple might say to each other—and then, what the unhappily married might say.

A little while after the applause, a happily married couple might say:

"Oh, look! There's a dove up there."

"It probably flew out as the curtain fell."

Or else:

"Imagine if the ladder had snapped!"

"I'd sort of like to see something like that."

But an unhappily married couple could easily have the same conversation. And then, having exchanged such simple remarks, both couples would turn their innocent faces forward, blank for the beginning of the next act.

An announcement came over the loudspeakers:

"In a few minutes the high point of today's show, an act entitled 'The Beauty under the Electric Saw,' will start. Since this is an especially frightening act, will pregnant women, anyone with a heart condition, anyone who is nauseated by the sight of blood, or who does not want her child to see what is about to occur, please leave now."

Hearing this, the happily married couple and the unhappily married couple might say:

"Do you think they'll actually cut her up?"

"You'd rather leave now?"

"But you want to see it, don't you?"

"The warning is probably just part of the act."

"Oh I see. Of course."

And they would go on sitting there.

Hisako had no special gift for determining the marital relations of a couple who went out on a date to watch a magic show. At first sight, such a couple would seem to get on very well; but on second thought, one might conclude that in fact such a couple would have to either get on very well or not at all—and this would probably be closer to the truth. But she was just thinking about it in a general kind of way. The reason she'd even started was her curiosity about her friends Noguchi and Tsuneko's relationship. Of course, how well a couple get on is something that even the two concerned, let alone a third party, find hard to judge. But even so, after witnessing their fight the other night, she couldn't help doubting whether Noguchi and Tsuneko were getting along as well as they had always seemed to.

Hisako had long known that Noguchi and Tsuneko went out together on a date once or twice a month. This last time, they'd left the house to go to the movies, but then, catching sight of a poster in the train for the magic show, Noguchi suggested that they go to watch it instead, and Tsuneko had agreed.

A few nights later, Hisako visited and they'd started to tell her about the performance. When they reached a certain point in their story, however, their opinions diverged noticeably, and they began to argue.

According to Noguchi, the entire show consisted of one spurious deception after the next. Tsuneko insisted that the magic was real. There are, in any case, two ways to appreciate magic shows: you either try to figure out how the tricks work, or sit back and enjoy the illusion. So their argument might have boiled down to a simple difference of opinion reflecting these two sorts of enjoyment. But both of them stuck so stubbornly to their points of view. Tsuneko couldn't possibly have believed that all the tricks were real magic, but she refused to admit this, insisting that even the most farfetched things had been genuine.

Even Hisako on the sidelines thought she was being a bit irrational, and Noguchi flatly contradicted her. But he went to the opposite extreme, insisting that even the most convincing tricks were all sham.

"It was so obvious," he told Tsuneko. "You're the only one who didn't realize—that's typical of you. You're so easily taken in. And yet you won't believe your own husband!"

Tsuneko had retorted: "Oh, what's the point of even talking to you!"

Hisako had interrupted three times: "Come, come," she'd said. "It's not that serious. I'll go and see it. I'll be the judge." But her words didn't make the slightest impact: their faces were white with anger and excitement, and far from seizing the opportunity to stop quarreling, they wouldn't even look at her. Even when they appealed to her—"Listen to him, Hisako" or "Can you believe anyone so stupid?"—they kept their eyes fixed on each other, not sparing her so much as a glance.

But her offer didn't go entirely unnoticed. When the time came for her to leave, Tsuneko had said, "You will go and see it, won't you? Go with your husband, and tell us what you think—I can't wait to hear."

"Me too," Noguchi added. "Because I know I'll win."

By then, they seemed all made up.

Nevertheless, Hisako had been deeply disturbed by her friends' fight. She'd felt just like a little girl witnessing her parents violently quarrel, people who had always treated each other with nothing but affection. She hadn't ever seen her friends argue before; she'd been told by them of some of their squabbles, of course, but never about such an out-and-out altercation. Perhaps they just didn't mention such things, but she couldn't imagine them quarreling like that every day. She'd gone to school with Tsuneko, who'd also worked in Hisako's husband's company. Hisako had known her through several periods of her life: she was not a contentious person. Hisako felt she was partly to blame for letting the fight go on for so long, but she had been so taken aback.

She couldn't help thinking, even in retrospect, that the fight had been unbelievably obstinate and acrimonious. Noguchi had started it, she recalled; but Tsuneko had reacted with a defensiveness that was quite out of character. Surely it wasn't just because she was there that they had stuck to their positions. And it didn't seem as if they'd simply discovered something in the other of which they'd been previously unaware. No, it seemed more like they'd been forced to acknowledge something in each of them and also something about their very relationship that they'd been unconsciously avoiding, and, forced to become aware of it, they felt betrayed.

The deep impression of her friends' quarrel had set Hisako's mind to wondering about the marital relations of middle-aged couples who went out to magic shows.

But she hadn't really come tonight in the belief that she could deliver a judgment about the show, or, for that matter, her friends' marriage. She had come simply to see for herself the cause of so much disagreement, and out of a childish curiosity about magic itself.

Two days after their scene, Sumita, her husband, had returned from a five-day business trip. Hisako told him all about the quarrel, expressing her amazement, and said: "Tsuneko wanted us to go see it. Will you come?"

"You've got strange tastes," Sumita smiled. "Thanks, but no thanks."

But that didn't mean it was possible to say where their own marital relations lay on the scale of good to bad.

The curtain rose for "The Beauty under the Electric Saw." The stage was deserted, without a single prop. As Hisako watched, several people in starched white coats hurried on stage. Four women in nurses' uniforms, foreigners, wheeled on an operating table. A blonde woman lay on it, face-up—no doubt this was the Beauty.

"She must be drugged," voices whispered.

"Probably."

A hush fell over the audience. The blonde girl, her arms tied down, her torso covered in a white sheet, had an oxygen mask on, the type used for anesthesia.

This mask was something they'd disagreed particularly vehemently about, Hisako remembered. Noguchi had contended it was just for the sake of appearances, but Tsuneko insisted they must really have anesthetized the girl. No conscious person could stand to be used for that act, she said; and sleeping pills wouldn't have been strong enough to conquer her nerves. Then Noguchi had demanded: what sort of sense did it make to anaesthetize a person for something that was not going to happen?

As she watched, Hisako found herself agreeing with Tsuneko here, even if that meant she too was deceived. The girl's arms looked too limp for her just to be pretending. She'd probably been made up to look pale, as Noguchi claimed; but she looked so deathly white, without a trace of life or warmth, even though directly under the hot lights.

Three foreign men in white surgeons' coats and masks came on stage, pushing a large mounted circular saw up to the edge of the operating table. The performers in this act were obviously not going to acknowledge the audience.

Next came a group of four Japanese men in shirtsleeves, carrying a long fat column of something white, which they dumped down in front of the table and rolled out forward. It was a thick white plastic tarp.

The three surgeons maneuvered the saw, placed at a right angle to the table, to the right and left, backwards and forwards, then up and down, correctly positioning the blade. The circle of men widened a little. The saw emitted a buzzing noise, then rotating at terrific speed, groaning away, it drew closer and closer to the blonde girl. All of a sudden, the sound changed to a high-pitched whine, and the men drew back. The blade was visible only as a blur, but as it whined it grazed the stomach of the blonde girl, and that part of her torso turned scarlet.

"That's blood!" somebody in the audience said.

The next instant, the wound split open.

"Oh no!" a woman screamed, covering her eyes. Over the whining of the saw a continuous sound like the tearing of cloth could be heard. A red rain spattered over the plastic tarp covering the floor. The saw was issuing a scarlet spray, Hisako realized, which went curving through the air like a fan held sideways to the back of the stage, and then fell down in a bloody rain.

The blonde girl slept on, her white masked face utterly still. According to both Noguchi and Tsuneko, the girl's arms twitched when the white sheet covering her abdomen turned scarlet, but this, too, had been cause for disagreement. Tsuneko claimed that had the girl been faking unconsciousness, she would have jerked her arms away; she must have been anaesthetized; she had hardly moved at all. Noguchi countered that this was either a trick to fool idiots like her, or a mistake—the girl was tense. At this, Tsuneko brought up the anesthesia mask again: well, if the girl was tense, what was the mask for? Even if other things might have been fake, she couldn't stay silent when he denied that *that* was real.

Nevertheless, they both agreed that they'd seen the girl's arms twitch. Today Hisako paid special attention: the girl's arms were utterly still. It was clear at least that she wasn't pretending.

The circular saw was still producing its high-pitched whine and large pool of blood had collected on the plastic tarp. Hisako's seat was toward the back, so she didn't have a very good view, but the wound in the girl's blood-soaked stomach seemed to gape wide open. Something appeared to be pushing out of it, suggesting the force of what was inside. The electric saw gave no sign of stopping, however. The seven men and women in white uniforms stood stock still, at some distance from each other, their arms folded.

"She's done for," said somebody. A lot of stuff seemed to have come out of her belly.

Then the saw noise ceased. Everything went quiet. The three men in surgeon's uniforms gathered around the operating table and stared down into the bloodied torso. The four men in shirtsleeves reemerged in a line, and raised the far edge of the tarp to collect a pool of blood in the center. Then, each at one corner, they dragged it to the side. They pushed the saw off into the wings.

One of these men remained on stage, and announced that twenty people from the audience would be permitted to view the body. Would anyone interested please raise their hands? Hands shot up here and there.

"All right, you, and you," the man said, pointing at people and counting them off on his fingers. "The gentleman by the aisle. The lady behind. Come on, get into line. You, and you too, sir."

Rising from their seats, the volunteers were directed to use the steps on either side of the stage. No children, but several women decided to go. The foreign surgeons and nurses stood motionless behind the operating table. The man instructed the volunteers to line up between the table and the plastic tarp, and wait their turn.

There were various reactions. Some people paused, staring straight down at the body. Others sneaked a glance before their turn, only to avert their faces as they passed by. Nobody laughed. When the last person stepped down from the stage, the curtain fell.

Hisako didn't tell Tsuneko and Noguchi that she had gone to the magic show. Not because she lacked confidence in her judgment, or because she feared starting another quarrel, or even because she thought Tsuneko might laugh at her.

"What?" Tsuneko might say. "Oh! You mean you really went to see it, just because I . . ."

She did inform Sumita that she had gone. But she took pains to talk as if it hadn't amounted to much: "Even 'The Beauty under the Electric Saw,' the high point of the evening, was just an act," she said. "It was so obvious." Though she'd found herself in agreement with Tsuneko, she refrained from saying so. "But if I say I thought it was faked," she told him, "it'll seem as if I'm on Noguchi's side. I don't want to hurt Tsuneko. I'll just say I didn't go."

She didn't tell him anything else about what had occurred.

Something very strange had happened to Hisako in the bus on her way back from the show. She had picked out two ten-yen coins from her wallet to pay for her ticket, and was about to slip them into her hand, when she noticed that her palm had a bright red stain on it. Shifting her purse, she examined her other palm, and discovered that it was the same color. Trying to keep her balance in the jolting bus, she managed to bring one arm up between the bodies pressed tightly around her, hold her hand out, and scrutinize it under the lights that had just been turned on. It wasn't a wet stain—it was more like the powdery dye that rubs off cheap origami paper.

Hisako pulled out the program, which she had folded and pushed into her shopping bag. On the back cover—the outside now—was a black-and-white ad for a stereo system. The only spot of red was a small trademark. The front cover—now on the inside—was colorful, but designed in yellow, purple, and blue. Only the lining of the magician's cloak was red. No matter how much she folded or fingered the program, it wouldn't leave a stain. The glossy, good-quality paper couldn't have leaked any dye.

Pushing it back inside her bag, she pondered where the scarlet stain could have come from. After leaving the theater, she had boarded a train, and when she had changed lines, she had made two purchases of food at a department store near the station. After alighting from her local train, she had boarded a bus. All during that time, she had been taking money out of her purse, putting change back, and she hadn't noticed anything. The food purchases were wrapped in the usual pattern of white and lilac. What could it have been? She hadn't brushed or grasped anything at the theater, or afterwards. It wasn't as if she had gone up on stage after the performance of "The Beauty under the Electric Saw." Why then, were her palms, both of them, stained scarlet?

At home, the first thing Hisako did was pour an enzyme solution over her hands. It had no effect. Well, the stains clearly weren't an animal substance. When she tried soap, the bar immediately became pink, and both palms returned to their normal color.

A small incident, but it had caught Hisako off guard. She could not help thinking that it was an omen of something dreadful, some awful event soon to occur. And just as her palms had turned scarlet without her even noticing, this dreadful, awful disaster would happen because of some lack of attention, some lack of vigilance on her own behalf.

She had only visited Tsuneko that evening for diversion—Sumita was away on a trip—but it was nearly midnight when she got back to the house. She had intended to leave much earlier, but Tsuneko had asked her to stay longer, saying Noguchi wouldn't be home till late. Then, before she knew it, that was the time. Any number of opportunities arose when she could have taken her leave: she could have left after dinner; or when Noguchi came home at 8:30, having excused himself from a drinking spree; or when the children went to bed. But she'd simply sat back and continued talking, as if waiting for those opportunities to pass her by. Then she'd got caught up in their quarrel, and offered to go see the magic show. And she'd actually gone to see it. Why hadn't she known better? It was just as if she were asking to be accused. What if, for example, the house had been broken into while she'd been away? She'd been just as blithe toward Sumita: "I went to Tsuneko's one night. I stayed talking long after Noguchi came home. Then they had this fight. I said I'd go and see the show. Will you come too? 'Go by yourself,' you say? . . . Well, dear, I went! I went to see the magic show!" Sumita would have to think that she felt no compunction about enjoying herself while he was away.

Hisako's consternation on discovering her scarlet palms gradually began to develop into panic. Yes, she thought: unless she set about being extra careful about everything she did and said, some disaster would befall her. She told Sumita she had seen the show, but she had no desire to go into details, about the handsome Spaniard ascending the ladder with swords in his mouth; and she certainly wouldn't tell him about what had happened afterwards. The reason she didn't want to tell Tsuneko and Noguchi that she had gone was that she didn't want to make herself any more vulnerable than she already had.

One night, a week later, Hisako glanced at the newspaper Sumita had spread out on the tatami mats by the dinner table, and saw a handkerchief-sized advertisement for the magic show: "Final performances tonight and tomorrow only." She waited apprehensively for Sumita to say something about it. But he didn't seem to notice it, and simply turned the page. She relaxed and went on wiping the table.

The next moment, Sumita folded up the newspaper, and pushed it away.

"I wonder why women are such vigilant suspicious creatures?" he asked, wearily.

Hisako stopped wiping, and stared at him. He kept his eyes on the newspaper. Now what did he mean by that? Did he mean he didn't understand women, they were always up to some scheme or other? Was he speaking in general, or about her? It was quite inappropriate, she thought, if it were about her. And yet, it did seem as if he were suggesting something. . . . She was at a loss for a reply.

"Wouldn't you agree?" Sumita asked, giving her a glance. "Men aren't that way at all. Men just lay themselves wide open."

So he meant the complete opposite of what she thought. He meant why are women so distrustful of men.

"Do you think so?" Hisako said, carefully. She finished wiping the table, put the cloth in a corner of the tray stacked with dishes, and continued sitting there.

"Yes, I do," answered Sumita. "No matter how wicked a man may be, he'll lay himself wide open when it comes to women. That's why bandits are poisoned by their mistresses."

"But you also hear of women being poisoned by their husbands and sons."

"See what I mean? It's always so irritating to discuss things with you," Sumita complained. "With any woman, for that matter. Especially when it comes to discussing differences between the sexes: women all seem to get more stupid than usual. It's even worse than you discussing politics. I can't remember who said that women are no good at talking politics—but whoever it was, he was wrong: the thing women are really bad at is discussing differences between the sexes. Basically, they don't listen, precisely because they're suspicious."

Then he added: "I'm not just talking about the method of killing, you know!"

"I know that much," Hisako said.

"But you don't understand what I'm saying. What I mean is, men get murdered because they trust women—they're not watching for any false moves. When women get murdered, it's not because they're gullible like men, but because they're no match for men in terms of physical strength or resources. If men were half as suspicious as women, they wouldn't get killed. It would be impossible."

"Men get killed because they don't respect women enough."

"Wrong—they get killed because they trust women too much!" he replied. "Well, maybe they don't actually know that they trust them. I'd say their attitude is somewhere between trust and a lack of respect. But my point is, men aren't distrustful—they aren't always on the look-out. About his marriage, for example, a man will relax—he'll assume that something he's done wrong in the past is over—that it's all water under the bridge. But his wife won't forget. And she'll insist on reminding him. She won't rest easy unless he joins her, re-opening old wounds time and again—"

"What exactly are you talking about?" Hisako interrupted.

"She'll get furious when he forgets their anniversary—because she's suspicious."

"But for such supposedly suspicious creatures, look how easily women are deceived!" Hisako said.

"They're deceived precisely *because* they're suspicious!" Sumita retorted. "And when they're not being deceived, they're taking their men for fools!"

Throughout this exchange, Hisako kept trying to fathom why Sumita could possibly be bringing up this subject. With that small disturbing occurrence on the bus, she'd realized how inattentive she had become, and had resolved to really keep on the alert. Had he, perhaps, sensed something of her vigilance? She didn't think her manner had changed very much, but perhaps it had, and was annoying him. Or maybe he meant he liked her to amuse herself visiting while he was away. On the other hand, perhaps he was showing her how he wanted her to be from now on, and was trying to get her to reflect upon some past behavior. . . .

As Hisako weighed these alternatives, the one she least wanted to be correct was the last. But she kept returning to it, and only tearing her mind off it by telling herself that, surely, he wouldn't want to refer to *that*.

"Anyway," Sumita declared, "In my opinion, the worst thing about women is their suspicious nature."

Wishing to believe that these words referred to how he wanted her to behave from now on, Hisako said, ingratiatingly: "Is it all right, then, if I stop being suspicious?"

"What'll you do if I tell you it is? Will you stop? That wouldn't be like you."

Hisako fell silent. So he had meant what she feared. But his next words exceeded her worst expectations.

"You haven't been able to stop for the last three years. Every month I was amazed that you insisted on delivering the money yourself. Why do such a thing? Doesn't that prove your suspicious nature? Oh, I thanked you, of course. Two months ago, when you made the last payment, I thanked you. But your continuing to the very last disappointed me. I could understand why you'd do it at first. I'd wronged you; it was natural for you to feel wary. But after a year, why couldn't you have offered to mail her the rest? That really disappointed me—two months ago, your last visit, I realized you'd been to her place thirty-six times! That made me so angry, I considered divorce."

"Divorce!" Hisako jerked up her drooping head.

"Oh, I could divorce you now. If you can't stop being suspicious, what's the point?"

"I don't know what you—"

"What did you say when Tsuneko spoke to you about it?"

"What did I say?"

"I know she spoke to you. Three times, at my request. I couldn't tell you myself, so I asked her to tell you to stop going there. She told me you refused each time."

"You mean you actually decided on such an arrangement?"

"What do you mean, 'arrangement'?"

"Well, why couldn't you have just told me to my face. . . ."

"Do I *have* to put it into words?" Sumita muttered.

Those scarlet-stained hands flapped up before Hisako's eyes. She'd had a feeling something dreadful was going to happen—so, this was it. But had she really only become that to him? For three years, he had been watching her, and she had been unaware.

Sumita had broken up with Hisae three years ago—they'd been deeply involved. Ever since, Hisako had personally delivered a sum of money at Hisae's apartment every month, the day after Sumita's payday, for three years. The thirty-six installments added up to a tidy sum for the woman who had, after all, been her husband's mistress. But far from merely consenting, Hisako had pushed Sumita to agree to the terms—out of relief, of course, that Hisae had finally agreed to break with him. But she also had a certain memory of Hisae that affected her.

One night, the door bell rang, and Hisako went and asked who was there.

"It's me." It was Hisae's voice.

"He's not home!" Hisako replied, without opening the door. Twice before she'd treated Hisae in this manner, and both times Sumita had been home and had overheard her and come out, and a quarrel had ensued. That night, however, he really was away.

"Yes, I know," the voice said. "I'm sorry, but my child is ill, and if they don't operate—"

Hisako immediately unlocked the door.

"I'm sorry." Hisae's voice was shaking, and not from the cold: "My daughter's has a terrible ear infection—she's at the clinic. The doctor said her life may be in danger if we don't operate by ten tomorrow. I came because I need some money. . . ."

The next day, Hisako went to the bank as soon as it opened. As she'd promised, she withdrew money, and took it to the hospital. It was a single-doctor clinic, in Hisae's neighborhood. Hisae sat in a corner of the waiting room, dressed in a kimono. Seeing Hisako come in, she rose and bowed deeply; she wore no make-up, and her face was very pale. Hisako took the bank envelope out of her bag and handed it over. Hisae bowed again and slipped it into her sash.

"They've started," she said.

"Sit down," Hisako told her, and seated herself on the bench. "Can't you go inside?"

Just then, Hisae got up and pushing past people, ran to a nurse who appeared into the corridor.

"Is the operation over?" she begged.

"No, it's only just begun," the nurse replied, disappearing behind a door. Hisae returned, looking as if she were about to weep.

"How long will it last?" Hisako inquired. Half an hour, Hisae answered. Hisako looked at her wristwatch. If the operation had begun at ten, it had been eight minutes so far. Had that really seemed like half an hour to Hisae? Hisae was oblivious to anything she said after that. She sat frozen stiff, her shoulders hunched, her hands in her lap. She didn't bother to look at her watch, or to ask Hisako for the time. The same nurse came out and went back inside the door marked "Operating Room."

Hisako glanced at her watch several times. About three minutes remained when she looked up to see the door of the operating room swing open. The nurse leaned out and beckoned to Hisae.

"It's over."

"Well, I'll go now," Hisako said, rising. Hisae bowed hastily and hurried away—Hisako caught only a glimpse of her face, but she was shocked by what she saw. The night before, Hisae had looked much older and wearier than usual, and this morning she was even more pale and drawn. Sitting side by side, Hisako hadn't noticed but now she saw that Hisae's eyes were wild and staring, her lips parched—like a mad person's—all in the space of twenty minutes. She looked as drained and exhausted as somebody suffering from a serious illness.

What a terrifying thing to be a mother, thought Hisako, who had no such experience. From Hisae's desperate state it was obvious that her staring eyes could see nothing but her own child. The thought that the father of the little girl, hardly a year old, was her own husband, Sumita, disappeared from Hisako's mind.

It was curious, but after seeing Hisae in that state of terror, Hisako never once imagined her as a mother desperately hanging onto the father of her child. In fact, Hisako began to feel much less bitter about this baby she'd never laid eyes on. Perhaps because Sumita had been away the night Hisae came, she had experienced nothing like her usual reaction—the back of her head tensing at the thought that *they* had a baby. Somehow, she'd started to be able to think of the baby less as "their" child, and more as a child that each was responsible for individually.

Six months later, Sumita came home after two nights away. Sitting down at the dinner table, he announced: "The baby died." The little girl's health had apparently failed after the operation; she'd started to suffer periodic convulsions. The inflammation had flared up again, bringing on another attack, and she had died yesterday morning.

The first thing that came to mind was the memory of Hisae

in the waiting room—and then, fleetingly, Hisako felt as if a close friend, a widow, had lost her only child.

"Oh, how very sad for her," she said, sincerely. The next moment, she realized the baby was Sumita's, too. And she immediately started to wonder how this turn of events would affect her relationship with Sumita.

Less than a year later Hisae agreed to break with him, a decision which, surely, had to be related to their baby's death. A friend of Sumita's had negotiated matters for them. No doubt he'd been effective and persuasive, but Hisae had apparently remarked: "Well, I no longer have the baby. I'm under thirty. I can make a fresh start."

Hisako had been with Hisae in her terror and desperation; and she had experienced sincere, if only fleeting, sympathy on hearing that her baby had died. The idea that Hisae was breaking with Sumita because of the baby's death made Hisako feel she had to encourage her to stick to her resolution.

It wouldn't be true to say, though, that relief and sympathy were all that Hisako felt toward Hisae. With Sumita supporting two households, Hisako could only just make ends meet. Now, to pay Hisae a lump sum would mean either using up their emergency savings or taking out a loan. They decided instead that they would give Hisae as much as they could every month over a period of three years. Hisako was aware that she could transfer the money to Hisae's bank account: nevertheless, she had chosen to go personally deliver it.

Her reasons were complicated.

The main reason, of course, was her determination to look out for any dying embers of Sumita's and Hisae's relationship which could burst into flame. In short, she had, as he said, been suspicious. But even free of such worries she would still have wanted to go and deliver the money. Hisae had already inflicted financial strain on her. Though she was resigned to more strain for three more years, she was damned if she would let Hisae sit back, receiving money like a pension. Why should she use a bank transfer—or, for that matter, send a money order? What if the monthly receipts came to Sumita, or if Hisae started telephoning him at work to tell him the money had arrived? That would destroy the whole point: no, she would take it to Hisae herself. That way, she could make her see how bitter it was to have to give it to her.

The truth was, Hisako at one point had found herself spinning in such a whirlpool of emotion—jealousy, rage, bitterness, rancor, and disgust—that she'd often felt she no longer knew where her face was in relation to her head. She would be walking along a road, brooding about Hisae and Sumita, and a neighbor would call out a greeting. Thinking for an instant that she couldn't see the woman because her face was at the back of her head, Hisako would wheel around to return the greeting—but the woman would be right in front of her. If someone hailed her from behind, she would assume they were in front of her, she just couldn't see them—and she would spin around trying to get them in her line of vision.

The only times she could feel calm, all too briefly, was on the rare occasion of a casual visit at a friend's home with Sumita. Even then, she was never actually happy. Sumita would be unnaturally cheery; he'd stay away from her, and then rejoin her, making people laugh with comments he knew she would find irritating. She hated him at such times. She hated herself, too, for being unable to ignore him.

It was only during their most insignificant moments together, with nobody there to make them self-conscious, and too preoccupied to be aware of each other, that Hisako was able to feel some relief from her torment. A friend who'd left with them might remember something he'd forgotten and make them wait while he went to pick it up. The two of them might exchange comments like:

"What *is* he doing?"

"Who knows. Oh, there he is! What a slowpoke."

"He's always been like that."

"That's right. Old habits die hard."

Or they might be waiting for the train and catch sight of a sign flashing news on the opposite side of the platform.

"Who died? Did it say?"

"Wait a minute, the name will run by again."

It would suddenly dawn on Hisako that they were chatting like a happily married couple. As the thought struck her, she would carefully observe any other married couples nearby. For Hisako, young couples and old couples were easy, but with middle-aged people she found it impossible to tell how well they got along, even though this was their own age group. And perhaps this was why she thought they were conversing like a happily married couple. Or was it difficult to judge such couples' conversations, because she thought they must resemble their own?

But she had never actually been able to savor the illusion of being happily married with Sumita. It just felt utterly strange, that was all, and the feeling didn't develop into anything like hope: it just remained a cold quiet sense of strangeness. But at least the utter turmoil—the jealousy and rage, bitterness, rancor and disgust—was swept out of her mind for a little while. That, Hisako wanted to tell Hisae, is the very best I could do.

And Hisako had one more reason for delivering the money: to make a good impression on Sumita. She didn't want him thinking she was smug and self-satisfied now that she had her husband back—he'd hate that. No, she'd show him that she knew she couldn't afford to be smug, and that she cared about Hisae enough to look after her in her own way. Well, perhaps it was more truthful to say that if Hisae—who'd come to occupy so much room in their life—were suddenly to drop out of it, they would've been forced to wonder whether they actually had a relationship at all. Of course, none of this meant that she could refer to Hisae in casual conversation. But it was enough to be able to say to Sumita, once a month, "I went over and delivered it today."

And then there was finally the fact that she'd already delivered money once to Hisae—her trip to the clinic during the child's operation seemed to make paying in person less outrageous now.

Now that he mentioned it, Hisako did remember Tsuneko chiding her two or three times. Hadn't she gone far enough, Tsuneko had asked; why not stop delivering it in person; it was stupid. "Your husband must hate being reminded, even more than you," she'd commented. "And yet you still go, every month. It can't make him feel very good."

"I know," Hisako had replied. "I feel bad myself. I realize it's uncalled for. But I think it is necessary—for all three of us. It wouldn't be right if she automatically received the money every month like a pension—or if Sumita and I tried to pretend that nothing happened, that we have a relationship when we don't. No, we need reminding for a while longer. It's more natural." She'd given her a few more justifications, and then added, "Surely you don't think I would just creep meekly back, just because now he's got rid of her? I want to feel bad, and I'll make sure he does too. I don't care if it is over between them. I want to be mean to her. Every time I'm spiteful to her, I get closer to him."

"Spiteful how?" Tsuneko had asked.

"What? Oh," Hisako answered vaguely, "I have my little ways."

All the time she spent with Hisae, Hisako felt she was being spiteful. Sometimes, as she was signing the receipt, Hisako would rest her eyes on Hisae's profile and silently shower her with scorn.

Once, finding herself staring at Hisae's pink well-shaped earlobe, the image of Sumita came to mind: he drew Hisae to him and touched her earlobe. Hisako realized he was nibbling it. "Oh! Not like that!" Hisako pushed him away. "Bite it like this!" Placing between her teeth one of the strawberries from the dish Hisae had put before her, she imagined she was biting down on Hisae's ear. And she was disappointed by how easily the fruit yielded, which made her long for the earlobe all the more.

But Hisako hadn't ever actually acted spitefully to Hisae. And Sumita was wrong—she had, in fact, only delivered the money thirty-five times. She'd asked Sumita's friend to do it for her at the very beginning.

The first time she herself went to deliver it, she got everything accomplished standing in the corridor. To enter the room her own husband had been staying in till very recently was repugnant. Hisae hadn't seemed eager for her to enter; she didn't press her after her initial refusal. "Are you well?" Hisako had asked, and handed over the envelope. Hisae went back inside and brought out a receipt, which Hisako folded and put in her handbag. After remarking on how pleasantly quiet the area was, she had taken her leave.

Hisako didn't go inside on her second visit, either, but Hisae had thanked her as she left, and added, "Well, I'll see you next month, then." Her tone hadn't been patronizing—and, at that time, she couldn't have known Hisako's intentions. She'd simply meant to convey her gratitude at the regular payments, and her hope of being able to count on the same thing next month.

"Yes, see you," Hisako had answered, to reassure her.

There'd been a time when Hisae herself had showered Hisako with scorn: "Don't think, just because he's your husband, you can treat me like dirt!" She remembered Hisae yelling at her: "Ask him who he'd prefer to commit suicide with—me, or you!" But she seemed a nice woman at heart. Hisako had even come to feel a kind of intimacy during their monthly encounters. Sometimes, seeing the small Buddhist altar, its doors open, in a closet in the next room, she'd want to light a stick of incense to put inside. She wouldn't be saying a prayer for her husband's ex-mistress' child; it would be for Hisae's baby.

When Hisae took a job as an insurance saleswoman, she asked Hisako to take out a policy.

"Someone else will come to the house to collect your payments," Hisae had added, trying to encourage her.

"Well, we can barely make ends meet," Hisako replied. "And we also have to pay you. . . ." They both laughed, feeling foolish.

Nevertheless, on her way home from Hisae's lodgings, Hisako would be conscious of being exhausted by the day's task. Not wanting Hisae to think that she was avoiding the subject, and even welcoming the chance to needle her a little, she'd casually drop little facts—just small, inconsequential things—about her husband into the conversation. Sumita had had the flu, but he was better now; he was away on a trip. She would hungrily observe Hisae's response, trying to see whether Hisae in her heart was still gasping with love for him.

"Yes, I know," Hisae might reply. "So he said, last time he came. . . ." Hisako refrained from any outright lies about Sumita.

When Hisako had finished paying the settlement two months ago, she'd felt relief—matters had finally been brought to a close. True, she had chosen to do it; and she had enjoyed the challenge in a way. But it had placed a strain on her finances and taken an emotional toll. Yet with every trip she had felt sure that her relationship with Sumita was returning to normal. Perhaps it was after her third or fourth visit that he had remarked, "Considering how poorly I've taken care of you, you haven't aged much, have you?" The words made her shed hot tears. What a natural way to express his feelings! If he and she had just erased all memory of his affair, and pretended everything was all right—surely, he would never have said anything so tender. Yes, she thought, their relationship would recover, in time. And after about a year, when she reported having made a visit, Sumita had thanked her, joking, "I could do with a little pocket money myself." Hisako had been surprised at his easygoing manner, and loved him for it.

But now she'd learned that Sumita had been viewing her in a different light entirely. To think that everything—the way he had made her shed hot tears, and love his easygoing air—had been an illusion! He had told her her behavior disappointed him so much that he wanted a divorce. Why hadn't she realized what was happening? How could she have been so blind? Had he deceived her, or had she been too self-righteous to see?

"I think I understand your disappointment," Hisako told him. "But disappointed in what sense?"

"By your suspicious nature!" Sumita retorted. "I told you, didn't I?"

"All right. But I didn't go just because I was suspicious, you know. Didn't Tsuneko say anything else?"

"Yes, she did—I've never heard such nonsense. It's bad enough having a suspicious nature, but that's ridiculous."

"Are you angry because I wasn't able to forgive you and Hisae for three years after you split up?"

"Idiot!" Sumita shouted. "It's not just that you're unforgiving! It's because you continued for so long! Even if women are unforgiving and suspicious by nature, don't you think I would have noticed if you'd bothered to *pretend* you'd forgiven me— just once, in three years? Forget whether I would have been taken in. You didn't think to even *pretend*, not once! That's what disappoints me!

"I didn't even feel as if the money was going to her," he went on. "Forget *her*. I feel that *I've* been used. I earned all that money, just so you could take it away. It's so cruel, so damn cruel."

Hisako felt the blood leaving her face. Nausea blocked up her throat. For the moment it was all she could do to lie down on the tatami.

"Did you go and see the show?" Tsuneko asked, as soon as Hisako sat down.

"Oh, I meant to, but I missed it."

"It's on till tomorrow. I saw a poster. But tomorrow's Sunday, isn't it. It'll be crowded."

"Yes," Hisako said, pretending to be uninterested. "By the way, sorry I stayed so late last time I was over. I shouldn't have just sat on and on. . . ."

"That's all right."

"But I should have left much earlier. It was half past eleven by the time I got home. It was stupid of me."

"Did your husband come back from his trip a day early, or something?"

"No, but—"

"Well, that's all right then," Tsuneko said. "I won't be a minute—I'll just put the kettle on."

Hisako watched her back leave the room, and wondered what words would come out of her mouth when Tsuneko returned. Would she say, "Something awful's happened!" Would she tell her everything Sumita said, break down, and beg for her advice? Or would she accuse her: "Tsuneko, you've really let me down!"

For some time now, Hisako hadn't felt up to crossing swords with Tsuneko. She did not remember feeling this way when they were classmates, or when Tsuneko was Sumita's colleague, or when Tsuneko continued working even after her second child, able to call her mother over and make her do the housework—she hadn't even felt it when Tsuneko started to go out on dates with her husband. No, the feeling had first started when Tsuneko told her about educating her three daughters.

"Do you know the most important thing in educating girls?" Tsuneko had asked her. "Apparently, the only way to make sure girls grow up normal is for their mother to be a gossip. It's important for a daughter to hear her mother poking her nose into other people's business, and passing gossip on. It's the only way they'll learn what's logical common sense, or interesting—and you only tell them not to pass it on after giving them an earful. Children who grow up without mothers, or whose mothers are eccentric and unsociable, or proud, or know-it-all, or gullible, or feeble-minded, end up eccentric themselves. It's not that they inherit that eccentricity—they've just been deprived of vital information."

Hisako was sure that even if she'd had three daughters she would never have been so practical and clear-minded. In fact, she would probably have become even less so. Ever since that conversation, she felt Tsuneko outclassed her in every respect. And because of this, though she thought of Tsuneko as a source of support, she also began to find her repellent at times. She found her repellent now, as she remembered the magic show. Offering to go and watch it for them, to go and be the judge, she'd thought herself so kind, but now she was beginning to suspect that she'd been duped by Tsuneko right from the start.

The day she discovered her scarlet palms in the bus, overwhelmed by a sense of panic and foreboding, she had resolved to keep on the alert—and surely, some of her consternation had stemmed from realizing how false was the security of having completed Hisae's payments. And then last night, her forebodings proved correct, and Sumita had brought up divorce. She was certain all this had happened because she'd stupidly gone to the magic show. She had only gone to see it at Tsuneko's suggestion—that she had been so manipulated and deceived was what she found repellent. Well, at least she could deprive Tsuneko of the satisfaction of knowing she'd gone.

And Tsuneko still had not confessed that Sumita had asked her to warn Hisako. If he'd asked her to keep it a secret, Tsuneko still kept her pact with him, never admitting to Hisako what had really happened. Wasn't that a betrayal of their friendship?

Tsuneko returned with the cups of coffee.

"Tsuneko, you've—" Hisako stopped herself from saying, "—betrayed me!" and said, "—been put out, haven't you, by my coming by so early?"

"Not at all," Tsuneko replied. She placed a cup in front of Hisako and seated herself in the armchair. "It's Saturday. The children come home early. I've done everything I had to do. Is your husband well?"

"Yes."

"You seem a little gloomy," Tsuneko remarked, looking at her. "Is anything the matter?"

Hisako stirred her coffee and looking at the silver spoon and the cup's gold rim, she imagined she was watching the flimsy metal ladder and the swords swaying back and forth in mid-air. High up, Hisako was swaying between her options—"You betrayed me, didn't you!" and "Can you blame me for being gloomy? Oh, Tsuneko, can we talk?"

Instead she said: "Last night I realized something that made me a little sad."

"So something did happen."

"No, not really. I just had a sudden thought." Hisako strained her whole body to correct the angle between the swords balancing in her mouth. "You know the payments I've been making. For three years, I put my heart and soul into it, and now it's over, I feel a little empty."

"Relief, probably."

"Well, yes. . . . You told me, didn't you, that I should stop delivering it, that it was stupid."

"Yes."

"What did you mean?"

"Well, you gave me lots of reasons, and I knew what you meant. When I said stupid, though, I meant stupid to be giving money to a woman who had done you wrong, and even more so to deliver the money yourself. It was really the latter I wanted to stress."

"Did you ever think it would make Sumita angry?"

"Has he a right to feel one way or the other?"

"And your husband? What did he say?"

"Just how scary women are. . . ."

Hisako shut her mouth and clenched her teeth. She wished very much that a sword would pierce her throat so that she'd fall dead to the floor. She was shaking the ladder and leaning the sword in her mouth forward, longing for it to drop, but her tense body wouldn't let that happen. She gave up, and started the descent.

Hisako was suddenly curious to know what Sumita had said about her when he'd made his request. But now it would be difficult to find that out. It might have been different if she had started by remarking, "My husband says he asked you to tell me to give up doing such a silly thing—what did he say about me?" But Tsuneko would only get angry if she came out with the truth now, and she wasn't somebody to cross swords with.

"Oh?" Tsuneko might even say, "So you're jealous that he and I came to such an arrangement?"

Hisako was bothered, it was true, by their arrangement. Especially since Tsuneko hadn't told her the truth, then or now. Had he asked Tsuneko by telephone, or in a note? Since they were old colleagues, perhaps he'd invited her out for coffee. Last night, in the heat of the moment, he had said he often asked Tsuneko for such favors. Most likely he asked her this time because she was a mutual friend. But he would never have asked somebody he didn't trust and like. And Tsuneko was still faithfully keeping her pact with him. . . . Surely she wasn't doing this to spare Hisako's feelings. If that were the case, she would have shown more sympathy when Hisako told her about feeling guilty; she would also have tried much harder to persuade her originally. Wasn't Tsuneko looking a little tense and alert herself today? Wasn't she feeling guilty about keeping another secret from Hisako?

Hisako recalled Tsuneko and Noguchi's obstinate acrimonious quarrel the other evening. Perhaps neither was aware of it yet, but hadn't some kind of change, a change for the worse, come over their relationship? . . . And Sumita had said he was disappointed in her. She'd never thought that Sumita's relationship with Tsuneko amounted to much, but now her dreadful foreboding seemed to be homing in ever closer on its target. And once it did, who could tell what other tricks might be coming into play?

"You know," Tsuneko was saying, "My neighbor insists small eggs are more nutritious because younger hens lay them. Wouldn't you think bigger eggs were more wholesome? She seemed so sure, but . . ."

Pretending to listen to Tsuneko, Hisako started to detest herself—what a liar. She had been doing nothing but lie since her arrival. And the person in front of her went on deceiving her. Hisako wanted to start yelling, and smash the coffee cups and sugar bowl on the floor. She managed to contain herself, however, and say:

"Sorry to change the subject, but you know when couples are waiting on the platform for a train, chatting, the kind of conversation you drop as soon a train arrives? I think their conversation would be the same whether they were happily or unhappily married—don't you? It would be so nice if all one's conversations in life could be like that, with no worries about the harm one is doing to—"

On the spur of the moment, she tacked on a harmless explanation: "On my way here, I saw a middle-aged couple on the platform chatting—and all this occurred to me." Another lie.

It was Saturday, and Tsuneko's children would soon be back from school. Sumita had been quite cool to her this morning, so he wouldn't be in any hurry to get home. But if on an off-chance he did return, he wouldn't be able to get into the house, since she'd locked it up. And at any rate, she thought, she couldn't stand being here a second longer.

"Well, I should be going." Hisako stood up. "I don't want to overstay again." She lied one more time: "I was a little sad thinking over what I'd done. But I feel much better now that I've talked to you. Thank you so much."

Hisako's feelings were far from settled when she left Tsuneko's house.

Last night, when she started to feel sick, Sumita had showed little concern.

"Feeling bad?" he said, observing her coldly. "Well, go to bed if you're going to sleep," he said, probably thinking she was having one of her dizzy spells, and switched on the television. He'd left this morning without saying anything more to her.

With Sumita's departure, Hisako's anxiety had begun to mount. Suddenly between today and tomorrow there was a space of time which seemed terribly important. How should she behave toward Sumita, then? Rushing over to ask Tsuneko— the very person he had asked to deceive her—had resulted only in a deepening of her suspicion and disgust.

Emerging in the midday spring sunshine onto the street of shops, Hisako, who last night had hardly slept at all, felt dazed by the throngs of people, the traffic, the signs, and the merchandise laid out in front of the stores. She continued walking, however, determined to bear it. Suddenly, at the corner of her eye, she glimpsed an electric saw, dancing. It was nearly lunch time, and customers were crowding into a baker's, where a silver electric bread-slicer was speedily cutting through a loaf.

Hisako remembered the blonde girl being wheeled out on stage for "The Beauty under the Electric Saw"—in silence, peacefully asleep on the operating table. Hisako herself was utterly exhausted: she wanted to be wheeled out on a table too, unconscious, and at peace.

And just then, her whole body became so painfully heavy, she doubted whether she could keep moving. Nevertheless, she crossed the public square in front of the station. As she passed through the ticket barrier and along the passageway, she shuffled along so slowly, it must have amazed the people walking briskly toward her. When she started up the steps, everybody around her all at once started running. A train must have arrived. Continuing at the same slow pace, she could barely manage to bring one foot up after the other. She reached the deserted platform at last and headed toward a bench, sighing and gasping like an old person.

Her body was so heavy, heavy with all the lies that the four of them—Sumita, Hisae, Tsuneko and she herself—had packed inside her, she thought. How many lies, deceptions, and schemes had been concocted and carried out from the time Sumita had started his affair? All the intertwined tricks had been packed inside her belly. Her weighed-down appearance must have convinced Sumita that she was delivering the money to Hisae purely out of suspicion. Now she would never have a chance to explain her other motivations. She was too immobilized by all the deceit.

The electric saw began buzzing again, in front of her eyes. Yes, she thought, that would be the best way: it won't do any good to just tell you; that won't make you see how all your tricks are gathered, intertwined, and packed inside me. The only way to prove it will be to have you cut me open and look. Look, everybody. Here they are: all the deceit and tricks I was forced to hold inside. And while they look, I will be unconscious, anesthetized.

Hisako had no idea whether the greatest fault of women was their suspiciousness, as Sumita said; or if she herself had this fault; or if she could correct it. The only way to find out for sure was to lie down under the electric saw like the blonde girl on stage, get them to open her up, take a good look at all the lies and deceit, and cut them out.

But what if it was too late to excise the lies and deceit? Perhaps they were already becoming a part of her. In that case, Sumita must look soon, before she and the deceit became indistinguishable. Now was the time, wasn't it, to see how many lies and deceptions had been packed inside her, how they had all woven together, and started to become one?

And exactly what kind of magic had she witnessed in that

gruesome performance, anyway? Nothing strange or unbelievable—nothing involving deftness or skill. The audience had simply been shown a horrible spectacle, that was all. That was not "magic."

Hisako had heard stories of mountain priests slashing open their own arms and healing themselves in a burst of terrific energy, wiping the blood away with no trace of a wound. To injure somebody for a magic show was not a crime, providing she was an adult and you had her consent. But murder, now, that would be a crime. The performance had stopped short of showing the girl "coming back to life," which would have been where the real magic came in. Oh, but *murder* is a crime, ladies and gentlemen: we're not actually killing her—we'd never break the law. We're only cutting open her belly. We'd love to show her to you when she's recovered, but naturally that'll take time. You'll have to take it on faith that she will. . . .

And that had left it unclear who the real magician was supposed to be in that act. And even if they had gone so far as to "kill" her and show her coming back to life, it still wouldn't have been clear whether it was the surgeons in white coats, or the blonde girl herself who had brought about a recovery.

A train arrived. As Hisako rose from the bench and approached the edge of the platform, she was conscious that her stomach felt strangely heavy and weak. The car wasn't crowded, exactly, but all the seats were occupied. The doors closed, and the train set off. Taking hold of a strap, Hisako felt the wheels' vibration directly beneath her feet rise through her body, and blend with the heaviness in her stomach, gradually easing it. After she had been cut open by the electric saw, she wondered, would Sumita help her recover? Or would she have to do it herself? Would they do it together? Since neither possessed the powers of a mountain priest, recovery would take time. Perhaps Sumita would not put out a hand. Perhaps nothing would help and she would just lie there in a heap. It was Sumita's words that had made her yearn for the electric saw: remembering them, she felt apprehensive about what would happen after the curtain fell. Still, she couldn't help longing to hear that buzzing sound.

The train stopped, and the doors opened. Two college students, a couple, came inside. The girl leant up against the post at the end of a row of seats. The boy stood facing her. A window behind was wide open, so when the train set off, the roar and clatter of the wheels on the tracks rushed into the car. The boy started talking to the girl, shouting above the noise. Hisako, standing four seats away, couldn't catch the words. But he was talking, smiling, with a know-it-all expression, and the girl's head nodded from time to time. Very different from a middle-aged couple.

There were several stops before the train reached her station. Hisako resolved to watch and see if any middle-aged couples entered on the way—yes, she thought, she could try counting them. If the number were even, that meant she would recover from having her stomach cut open, but if it were odd. . . . On the other hand, perhaps she should try to refrain from making such frightening predictions.

Bone Meat (HONE NO NIKU, 1969)

TRANSLATED BY LUCY LOWER

IN WAS LAST FALL, BUT THE WOMAN COULD not seem to take it into her head to dispose of the belongings the man had left behind when he deserted her.

A day or two before, it had been raining. Four or five days later she noticed his umbrella and her own lying by the window. She had no recollection of putting the umbrellas there, so perhaps the man had done it. In her panic over being deserted, however, perhaps she had forgotten what she herself had done. She opened them, and found they had dried completely. The woman carefully adjusted the folds of each, wound around the strap, and hooked the metal ring over the button. But after standing her own umbrella in the umbrella rack inside the shoe cupboard, she wrapped the man's umbrella in paper, along with another of his she had found there, tied them up with a string, and put them away in the closet.

It was, perhaps, around the same time that she threw away the man's toothbrush. One morning, as she was about to pick up her own toothbrush, her eyes fell on his lying beside it. The bristles at the end of the transparent, light-blue handle were bent outward from hard use. Once, he had come home with an assortment of six toothbrushes for the two of them which he had bought on sale. She also recalled having bought them toothbrushes two or three times. Whether the toothbrush that remained was one of the six the man had bought, she didn't know. But as she picked it up she remembered his purchase and, seeking an excuse for discarding it in the painfully worn-out bristles, dropped it in the wastebasket. Next, she threw in three or four old blades from his safety razor. She also removed the blade still clamped in the razor, on which were hardened bits of soap mixed with the man's whiskers, and discarded it. But the razor she wrapped in his dry towel, together with several small boxes of unused blades, and put them away in his underwear drawer.

That drawer was the top one in the woman's wardrobe. Previously, the man's clothes had hung inside together with hers, but before leaving he had collected them quickly. However, the woman later noticed a faded gray lizard-skin belt which he no longer wore, and that too she put in his underwear drawer.

There were other things of his that ought to have been put away. Two or three of his shirts were probably at the laundry, and she intended to go pick them up and put them in the drawer too, though she hadn't done it yet. She couldn't imagine he had gone to get them. . . . Atop the wardrobe lay his four clothing boxes, a couple of which seemed full; she put them in the closet in place of her own.

The man's pillow stayed where it was for quite some time. Each night when the woman laid out the quilts, she first took the man's pillow out of the bedding closet, holding it by the opening of its oversized pillowcase, and put it back when she had finished taking out the quilts. And in the morning when she put the quilts away, she took it out once again. This continued for several weeks before it occurred to her to pack it away. She washed the case and set the pillow in the winter sun, choosing as bright a day as possible; then, replacing it in its cover and putting it into a nylon bag, she laid it on top of the man's clothing boxes in the closet.

The woman knew perfectly well that the man would not be back. How many times had she been unable to refrain from saying things like "I'd be better off without you!" and meaning them. And one day when she had again been unable to restrain herself, the man had replied "So it seems, doesn't it?" and left. The remorse she felt afterward had been painful. She acutely regretted having become accustomed to speaking in that way, and having said those words once again the day the man took her up on them. But what made it so painful, in retrospect, was that she had no right to regret, considering the man's attitude for some time past as well as his adroitness in taking advantage of her words. And the pain bereft her of the energy to pursue him.

The woman no longer wanted even to ask the man to come pick up his things. His reply was certain to be: "Do whatever you like with them." And, in fact, perhaps what he had left there he cared nothing about. As their relationship had begun to deepen and he stayed at her place for long intervals, he had little by little brought over personal things he needed. But even after he was virtually living with her, he didn't move out of his own lodgings, where he must have still had a dresser and desk, several boxes of clothing, ski equipment, and bedding. He had taken away the everyday clothing he had kept for convenience in her wardrobe; furthermore, it seemed that he was rising to a higher position at work. Surely he felt no attachment to the worn-out things he had left behind.

The woman, however, was at a complete loss as to how to dispose of them. Aside from putting them away, she simply could not decide what to do with the objects the man had left lying about. If she called him to come for them, it would be equally disagreeable whether he told her to throw them out or said: "Are they still there? Well, just send them over." Even if someone else would see to it, getting in touch with the man like that was itself distasteful. Yet it was also disagreeable to take it upon oneself to throw away someone else's belongings—still quite useful things—or to have them carted off by a junk dealer. Besides, she couldn't give these things, which the man had abandoned along with herself, to someone else.

She regretted she had not had him take all of his belongings when he left. She regretted it with all her heart.

The first hints that the man was beginning to think of a life in which she had no part appeared even before his work took a turn for the better. His decision to abandon her had been reflected in both his private and public aspects; even the clothing he wore was all newly made. She felt the sympathy of a fellow-sufferer for the old clothes that he took no more notice of, and yet felt scorned by the very things she tried to pity. And thus the woman found even more unbearable these troublesome leftover belongings.

She had several times considered taking the man's underwear, which filled the top drawer of the wardrobe, and his woolen clothes that lay mixed with her own in the tea chest on the lower shelf in the closet, and making a single bundle of them, but the mere thought of it made her feel weary and feverish. If one were to open them and look, there might also be just enough room to put the man's underwear and woolen clothing in his suitcase which was on the tea chest, or in the four clothing boxes that she had put in place of her own on top of her suitcase on the upper shelf. The man's rucksack and canvas shoes, also on the upper shelf, might well fit into one of these too. But she didn't feel like opening any of them. She always felt that the things the man had left weighed upon her.

She was terribly envious when she thought of the man's delight as he abandoned her and his belongings with the single comment "So it seems." She had decided that the best method of dealing with the perplexing problem of the man's belongings was herself to abandon them entirely, along with her own, and move to a new place. But she didn't have the money to move to a new place or to buy all the necessary things for it. Although the woman would have liked to abandon it all, she could not, and even her own belongings and the place itself became repugnant to her.

The woman could only trust that circumstances would arise

in which her lack of money presented no obstacle. She felt she would like to burn it all—the man's things, and her own, and the place. If she too were to burn up with them, she thought, so much the better. But she merely hoped for it, and made no plans. Strangely, for a woman who wanted even herself to be destroyed in the conflagration, she was inclined to be wary of fire. She always recalled one late winter night in her childhood, when there was a fire close by and she saw an old man from the burning building, with a padded jacket slipped on over his flannel nightshirt, being swept along in the crowd, barefoot on the asphalt where water streamed from the fire hoses.

Now she was even more careful. She was tortured by the fear that if she were to start a fire accidentally it would seem like arson. When she went out, especially, she felt she had to check for fire hazards two or three times, all the more so if she was in a hurry. Once, after she had locked the door and taken a few steps, she suddenly became uneasy. Unlocking the door and reentering, she checked the outlets and gas jets. She held an already wetted ashtray under the faucet in the kitchen and ran more water in it until the ashes floated. Reassured, she went out, but she hesitated as she was about to drop the key into her handbag. She couldn't help recalling an impression she had had just now. When she picked up the ashtray she had been reminded of how she had smoked half a pack of cigarettes the man had left behind. Ordinarily, the woman smoked only her own brand. When she ran out, even if the man had some, she found it unsatisfying to make do with a brand not her own, and she would take the trouble to go and buy some. However, the day the man left, or perhaps the next day, when her cigarettes ran out, she was so distressed that she did not want to go. Her eyes fell on the half-empty pack the man had left, and in her agitation she thought, Oh good—any brand, as long as there are cigarettes. All that the woman had disposed of among the things the man had left behind was the discarded toothbrush, the old razor blades, and the cigarettes. A moment before, when she had held the ashtray in her hands, she had the dreamlike feeling that everything would, happily, burn to ashes like the cigarettes. She felt then, suddenly, that when she had first locked the door she had already taken care of all possible fire hazards. Having gone out a second time, she found herself worrying that she might now have unthinkingly contributed to an outbreak of fire. And again she had to use her key.

Winter was almost over, and from time to time a springlike sun shone. The woman recalled how, last year about the same time on just such an afternoon, she and the man had gone out together. Where they had gone and with what purpose, she had forgotten, but she retained a vivid impression of the window of a shop where they had stopped to buy bread on the way home, and of various sorts of bread in steam-clouded cellophane wrappers.

As she waited for her bread, the woman looked again at the loaves heaped in the window and noticed a glass case next to them. In it were a number of whole chickens glowing in an electric rotisserie, roasting as they revolved. She took the bread and, glancing around at the man, moved toward them.

"Are you going to buy some?" the man said.

"I thought I might," She replied.

"Are the ones here good?"

"Hmm, I've never bought any from here before. . . ."

Inside the glass case each row of four chickens, richly glazed, rose, turned, and sank back down. As they rose again, with hardly a trace of the severed necks, they seemed to be lifting their wings high. The row of plump breasts rose, then began dropping out of sight, and the bones that peeped out from the fat legs as they rose made the chickens appear to be falling prostrate, palms up, withdrawing in shame.

The woman stood waiting for the man to speak and watched the movement of the chickens. The man, too, seemed to be watching them and said, finally: "Would you mind not buying any? Lately they're fattening chickens with female hormones. It seems a man shouldn't eat too much of it."

The woman wondered if he weren't thinking of American chickens. She had been present when one of his friends, home from the United States, had spoken about cooking for himself there. He said that he had often bought small fried shrimp that were sold cheaply at the market, and salted and ate them. He had often bought halves of roast chicken cheaply too. "They weren't so tasty, though. They're fattened with hormone injections," he had said, pantomiming an injection. The woman didn't remember for certain whether he had said simply "hormones" or "female hormones," nor did she know whether Japanese chickens were so treated or not, but she wondered if the man weren't misremembering that comment. She didn't say anything, though. She realized she could hardly claim they didn't often have roast chicken.

"I see. Well, shall we have oysters? On the half-shell?" Although that too they certainly had often enough.

"Yeah, that would be better," the man agreed this time.

They went into a department store. What with the heat from the steam that clouded the inside of the bread's cellophane wrapper, and the store's intemperate heating system, the woman breathed a sigh of relief when she stood before the cool abalone-filled glass water tank of the shellfish stall in the basement. Pointing to the oysters in the glass case next to it, where frost had crystallized on the horizontal bars, she asked for ten of them. The clerk picked out ten of the larger ones and put them in a short, wide oilpaper sack, and then on a rear table wrapped it up in two sheets of paper. As she took the parcel, the woman could feel the same bulk and weight as always.

She had become skilled at opening the oyster shells. In the beginning the man had opened them, and she had enjoyed watching him do it. But he relied on strength alone to break open the shells, always leaving their contents in a sorry state, so the woman learned from someone else and undertook the task herself. With the rounded side down and the hinge toward her, she held one firmly on the cutting board, tilted at an angle away from her. The brownish color and rippled surface merged so that it was hard to tell the seam from the shell. Searching for the point near the middle of the edge where the inside of the shell peeked through, or, if she couldn't find it, somewhere in that area, she inserted the knife forcefully, blade turned outward, taking care not to damage the oyster, then turned the blade sideways, slipped another small knife between the shells, and with the tip of that blade scraped downward, cutting the hinge. Then the top shell would loosen abruptly and she would catch a whiff of the seashore. But if the top shell had not been cut loose completely she once again turned the blade in the opposite direction and sawed upward. That usually did the trick.

That evening, too, the woman opened the oyster shells in this way and laid them on a plate of ice cubes. She added lemon wedges and carried it to the table.

"Go ahead and have some," the man said, taking one from the center of the large plate, dropping it with a clatter on the small plate before him, and trickling lemon juice over it.

"Mm," she replied, but did not reach for one.

"No, really," the man continued, lifting the edge of the oyster he was about to eat with his fruit fork.

"Mm," she again replied, but took pleasure in not reaching for one.

She watched the man's hand, clenched so tightly around the fruit fork that it appeared even more delicate, as he maneuvered it right and left, trying to cut loose the hinge muscle. He seemed to have done it neatly. As he lifted the oyster to his mouth, seaweed still clinging to its shell, he worked it slightly with his fork and the sound carried the smell, taste, and freshness of the seashore.

"Is it good?" the woman asked. The man nodded, laid aside the shell, and with the same hand took another from atop the ice on the large plate. He placed it on his small plate and the woman squeezed lemon juice over it.

When he had progressed to his third and laid the shell on the table, the woman transferred one of the shells he had discarded to her own plate.

"Have some of these," said the man, indicating the large plate.

At this, she took even greater pleasure in not doing so, and instead scraped with her fork at the bit of muscle left by the man. At last she got a tiny piece of white meat on the tip of her fork, and rubbed it against her lips. She liked to hold the morsel of meat pressed firmly to her lips and feel her tongue become instantly aroused with the desire to have its turn. The hinge muscle lay in a slight hollow of the shell, and she had still not taken quite all of the meat the man had left there. She again moved her fork toward it, urged on by lips and tongue that had already finished off the first piece. As her hand holding the fork responded violently to the impatience of the urging, she found herself struggling with the bit of meat. This made it that much more difficult to get loose; once loosened, more difficult to get hold of; and when at last she lifted it to her lips, her hand trembled. Holding both her fork and the empty shell aloft in her hands, she savored the eager rivalry of her lips and tongue for the meat.

The woman did not yet lay aside the shell. All that was left of the oyster was a brownish arc in low relief, where some flesh was still attached. She sliced at it with her fork and, bringing the shell to her mouth, tipped it up. The woman felt that all the parts of her mouth were contending for the taste, the smell, the freshness of the seashore. So it seemed, from the intensity of the rivalry in there. But it also felt to her as if all of these many parts stirred simultaneously with the pleasure of gratification. Before her, she could see nothing but the glistening inside of the shell, with its matchless white, pale purple and blue, and yellow. All the parts of her mouth reverberated at once with pleasure when she put that last brownish ridge of meat to her lips, because it seemed that this fresh glistening flowed in, too, with a rush.

"Ah, that's good," the woman sighed, at last putting down the shell.

"That's because you're only eating the best part," the man said.

"True. . . ." Nodding emphatically, she took the next shell that lay beside the man's plate.

"Shall I give you one?" the man suggested after a few minutes, speaking of the oysters on the bed of ice. "Or maybe I'd better not."

"Let me have just one," the woman said, holding her fork in one hand and a shell with a bit of meat attached in the other.

"For you, that'll be plenty." He pointed to the shell in her hand.

"Don't say that—please give me one," she said.

The man quickly picked one off the ice and laid it with a clack on the small plate in front of her.

"Try it and see," he said. The woman, with this departure from the usual order of things, felt somewhat at a loss. He went on: "They don't seem to be as good as usual. I was hungry, so at first I didn't realize it."

The woman put down the shell she was holding and, cutting loose the oyster the man had laid on her plate, she sucked it from its shell. In an instant the entire cold, slippery thing slid through her mouth that had leapt so at just the tiny morsel of meat.

"How is it?" the man asked.

"Well, I can't really tell," she replied. What she could tell was that it was not nearly so good as the taste of the hinge muscle scraped from the empty shell or the other bit of meat that had given her such ecstasy. And it seemed distinctly inferior to the flavor, the smell, the freshness of the seashore called up in her mind by the voluptuous sound the man made when he raised the shell to his lips and sucked out the oyster. Even the flavor evoked by that sound amounted to little more than imagining a long-past and much-faded sensation. For the woman, the whole raw oyster always tasted the same. She could by no means tell by tasting one whether tonight's oysters were as good as usual.

"They don't seem quite so good to me," the man said.

The woman noticed that it was unusually bright and sunny for a winter's day. "Are they diseased, I wonder?"

"No, you could tell right away. The taste is completely different."

The man took another from the large plate. He loosened the oyster, but did not squeeze lemon over it; picking it up in its shell, he raised it to his mouth with an air of examination.

"Maybe it's just me. They look all right, don't they?" he said. He laid one from the large plate onto the woman's plate and one on his own. There remained one more on the large plate. When she had finished hers, the woman ate that one too.

She gathered the empty shells on the large plate of melting ice and carried it to the drainboard. She washed the knife she had used in the preparation, put it in the dish drain, and picked up the cutting board from where she had left it. As she was rubbing it clean under running water at the faucet, something broad and sharp pricked her palm. She shut off the water and felt the board to see what it was, then took the board to the man.

"Look here." She took his wrist and placed the palm of his hand on the board. He withdrew it immediately.

"What happened? It's so rough," he said, touching it again lightly with his fingertips.

"This is where I opened the oysters. When I stick the knife in hard, the edges on the bottom are crushed and cut into it. It always happens." The woman spoke as though in a dream. It did happen every time, but for once, instead of smoothing it with pumice as usual, she couldn't resist bringing it to show him, because she felt dissatisfied that the scene they always played when they ate oysters on the half-shell had not been followed. The man took her hand and stroked it. She wished she might feel that on another part of her body.

"Do you think it's all right?" she asked.

"It's a cutting board. So it can't help getting bloody sometimes."

That evening, however, which ended without the usual fulfillment of the scene she associated with the taste, was the last time they ate oysters together. Before too many more days passed, spring was upon them and the raw-oyster season was over. The summer passed and autumn came, and by the time the air again began to turn cold, the man had already left.

This year as the days turned more and more springlike, the woman had grown very thin. The man's belongings, as always, remained with her. To him they were invisible, but they weighed upon her whenever she was at home. These troublesome belongings of his, and her own which for lack of money she could not abandon, and the place, became all the more unbearable to her, and she frequently saw herself being swept along the crowded late-night street flooded by the fire hoses, barefoot, with something thrown quickly over her nightgown.

It was about this time that the man's stored belongings, which weighed so on her conscious mind, gradually began to obtrude on her vision. It was as though the top drawer in the wardrobe had changed into some semitransparent material, so that the man's underwear within it shone white and what seemed to be his socks shone black. Little gauze-covered windows appeared here and there in the thick paper sliding doors of the closet, and the bulky shapes of his suitcase, the umbrella package, his clothing boxes, his rucksack, and his pillow showed through. From within one of the drawers he had used in the desk, too, a plastic box began to be visible.

The woman herself thought that she must be terribly weak. At meals, she must try to eat as much as possible. She must gain some weight. She must get stronger. If she didn't, perhaps the wardrobe drawer, the closet door, and the drawer in the desk would turn to glass. Perhaps too the man's suitcase and clothing boxes would become glass cases, and his rucksack and canvas shoes would become like the nylon pillow cover, or a cellophane bag. At this rate, she might very well find herself being swept along barefoot in the night in the crowded street flooded by water from the fire hoses, with only something slipped on over her nightgown. It might happen she thought, if she didn't eat a lot at mealtimes and recover from this weakness.

But when she tried to carry out her resolution, the woman realized that she ate even less. It had always been a peculiarity of hers that when she was excited—pleasantly or unpleasantly— she would become strangely hungry. She seemed to give way to the excitement and gorge herself whenever she had been aggravated into saying "I'd be better off without you!" and meaning it, and especially during her agitation after the man left her. But she had by now lost the energy and the momentum of the excitement, and her appetite no longer asserted itself even in that form. No matter what was set before her, after one or two bites she could not proceed.

Since girlhood, the woman had hardly been what could be described as plump. However, from about the time the man began gradually bringing in his personal belongings, she had started to gain a little weight.

Their tastes concurred, and they both liked dishes with bones or with shells. The woman was poor, and the man's prospects, up until about the time he abandoned her, had not looked good, so in order to serve such dishes often, they had to economize on their other meals. Even so, it was mostly the bones or shells which went to the woman. But although she seldom ate richly, she began to gain weight.

The woman recalled this odd phenomenon as not odd in the

least. The man would attack a boiled tuna tail avidly and set the plates rattling, and although the woman called what little was left a "bone-tail," the flavor that could be drawn from each hollow in it made her want to exclaim: "Are there such flavors in this world!" Likewise the sight of the scarlet-wrapped slender morsel of flesh bursting from the single lobster claw granted her made her want to sigh. All those varied bone and shell dishes began to give her the feeling that a sense of taste had been awakened throughout her body; that all her senses had become so concentrated in her sense of taste that it was difficult for her even to move. And when she awoke the next morning, she felt her body brimming with a new vitality. It would have been odd had she *not* gained weight.

Even after she had noticed a change in the man's behavior and had become critical of him (though not yet to the point of being unable to refrain from saying "I'd be better off without you!"), the two of them continued to enjoy these dishes with bones or shells. Whether because of that or because their relationship had not yet deteriorated too badly, she continued to gain weight.

The day the man had said that males probably shouldn't eat too much chicken, she had deferred to him, although afterward he still brought home roast chicken any number of times. In the intervals between roast chickens, the woman sometimes fixed boiled tuna tail as before, or bought the head of a coastal sea bream and boiled it. Because of the season, that night was the last time they had oysters on the half-shell, but during the summer they often ate abalone. The man liked the whole abalone, and seemed to enjoy begrudging the woman the least morsel. For her part, she took intense pleasure in savoring the meager flavors of the big shell itself.

The woman had never been critical of him when they had dishes with bones or shells, because at those times he never made her anxious or brought her troubles to mind. He coveted meat even more fiercely than before, and she even more wholeheartedly savored the tiny bits of bone meat. They were a single organism, a union of objectively different parts, immersed in a dream. Sometimes both would sigh simultaneously from the excess of flavor, and then laugh so much that they had to put down the food they were holding.

The woman, now grown thin, realized that she longed only for the taste of those dishes. It was not only herself and his belongings that the man had deserted, but that taste as well. However, her sense of taste did not yet seem to understand that it had been abandoned. When she ordered one of the old dishes with bones or shells and something else was brought out, she rejected it at once, saying "No, not that!" The woman began to wonder if this weren't how a mother, abandoned with a young child by her husband, must feel. And like the mother, she now took pity on the young child's unreasonableness, now scolded it, at times hugged the still uncomprehending child and cried; she even thought of killing the child and then committing suicide. Once, at her wit's end with the unreasonableness of her own sense of taste, she raptly imagined the man to be standing just beyond the grillwork partition devouring a chicken thigh, then tearing the stripped bones apart at the joint and throwing the pieces in to her, so that suddenly she felt she heard the sound as it hit the floor. If she could be sure that she would be able to share it, she thought, she wouldn't mind being swept along the crowded asphalt street barefoot where water streamed from the fire hoses, with only something slipped over her nightgown. Then, becoming aware of the semitransparent top drawer of the wardrobe, she stared at it, trembling. She lacked the courage to look around at the desk drawer, which of course must have become transparent, or at the little gauze-covered windows that must have appeared here and there in the thick paper doors.

"You going to burn this?" The voice seemed to belong to one of the children in front of the large cooperative trash incinerator.

"Yes, I am."

"Give it to me!"

"I can't do that, I have to burn it, Throw it in, please. I'll buy you an even fatter red pencil. That's right—that's the way."

"Are you going to burn the clothing box?"

"The box? Yes, I am."

"Shall we help you?"

"Well, thank you. But you mustn't open it. I don't want the contents to get scattered around. Just burn it that way."

"OK. Everything in here can burn, huh?"

"Yes. Can you burn these up for me? I have a lot to bring over here."

"Bring all you want."

"That's great."

"Shall we help you carry it over?"

"Would you mind?"

"Of course not."

The words echoed pleasantly in her ears. It was an exhilarating feeling. Tomorrow when she awoke, she would no longer be troubled by anxiety over the semitransparent drawer or all the little gauze-covered windows in the thick paper doors, or whether they might be getting even worse. It was months since the woman had felt calm, and so exhilarated; the thought put her completely at ease.

Just then, there was a knock at the door.

"Aren't you the one who used the incinerator today?"

The woman realized that she hadn't checked on how the schoolchildren who had helped her had left things, but she knew it was part of the dream, so it was all right. Trying to keep from awakening and interrupting her dream, she kept her eyes shut, the quilt pulled up around her head, as she rose and went to the door.

"Won't the people who use it later have a hard time? Leaving a mountain of bones that way. We're supposed to clear out what's left unburned. Why, there are oyster shells alone to fill a bucket."

To fill a bucket—what fraction of the oysters they had eaten together would that be? But there weren't very many from that last time, so when might these shells be from?

The siren of a fire engine wailed somewhere continuously. But what caused her dream to recede was less the siren than the words she had just heard in her dream. From the ashes of the man's belongings, that there should be so many bones and shells! "Is that so? Is that so?" she said nodding, and the siren, to which was added a furiously ringing bell, filled her ears. Was what she had been told in the dream perhaps prophetic? The bell stopped, and just then the siren arrived blaring under her window. But the woman, her eyes closed, nodding "Is that so? Is that so?" simply snuggled deeper into the quilt as it seemed to begin to smolder.